HAVE YOU SEEN THE
MOON
TONIGHT?
& OTHER RUMORS

JONATHAN LOUIS DUCKWORTH

JOURNALSTONE
YOUR LINK TO ARTIST TALENT

ISBN: 978-1-68510-104-6 (sc)
ISBN: 978-1-68510-105-3 (ebook)

First printing edition July 21, 2023
Published by JournalStone Publishing in the United States of America.
Cover Artwork and Design: Don Noble
Edited by Sean Leonard
Proofreading and Cover/Interior Layout by Scarlett R. Algee

JournalStone Publishing
3205 Sassafras Trail
Carbondale, Illinois 62901

JournalStone books may be ordered through booksellers or by contacting:
JournalStone | www.journalstone.com

CONTENTS

THE MAN WHO HAS IT
by GABINO IGLESIAS

I've read a lot of intros and written a few myself, so I know how they work. There are two ways I can tackle this. This first one is to more or less offer you a short review of this collection in which I briefly tell you about the tales you'll find in its pages. I don't want to do that because you already bought it and thus don't want a review. That, my friends, leaves us with the second option, which, in theory, is much harder: talking about Mr. Jonathan Louis Duckworth and his words.

As a reviewer and editor, I read a lot of short stories every year (no, seriously, a LOT). One of the reasons I don't mind the work is that short stories are a superb way of discovering new voices. Yes, short fiction is how I discovered Mr. Duckworth. If you've ever edited an anthology or magazine, you know there are short stories you know you're going to publish even before you're done reading them, and that's the kind of short fiction Mr. Duckworth—let's call him Jonathan from now on, yeah?—consistently delivers, and the collection you're holding is no different. I've published Jonathan in the past, and look forward to doing so again. Why? Because he brings it. He brings it every damn time, and that's a rare thing. In fact, the reason you're reading this intro is that I told him I wanted to write it a while ago. I said it because I knew this collection was inevitable. Writing is a war of attrition, and when talented writers keep at it and steadily deliver great stories, things like this book are bound to happen. Oh, that reminds me, kudos to JournalStone Publishing for putting this out. Y'all have great taste.

Back to the stories! I could tell you that the tales in *Have You Seen the Moon Tonight?* all have solid pacing or that the dialogue is always entertaining and does a great job of carrying the action forward or that the characters feel fleshed out and unique despite the length or a million other things about craft that Jonathan always nails. However, the elements that make Jonathan's work special go above and beyond mere craft elements. You see, the main thing about Jonathan's writing is that it feels crisp and unique. Yes, he's a scholar and a student of the game, but he's also a hell of a writer who knows that short fiction must punch you in the face in order to leave a mark or it'll quickly be forgotten. For readers, having so many great writers out there is a treat, but for writers, it means they must deliver the goods or they'll quickly slide into oblivion. Jonathan knows that, and he puts the work in to ensure his stories stand out and make you remember his name.

The second element that stands out in Jonathan's stories is that they're smart. I've been told in the past that saying fiction is smart sometimes acts like a deterrent because some readers feel like "smart" means a writer will make their brain do push-ups or that the prose will be unnecessarily dense or ridiculously convoluted. That's not what I'm talking about here. What I'm saying is that these wildly entertaining stories have substance. Jonathan can write a fun story that suddenly touches on the philosophy of escapism or tell you a tale that makes you laugh before dropping a ton of darkness on your soul or deliver melancholy while hiding a bit of strange love under a mermaid's scales. All of this and more lies ahead, so get excited.

There are no guarantees in the writing world, but I like to break the rules, so I'll give you some guarantees here. First, I guarantee you some of the stories you'll read will feel unexpected or will outright surprise you. Second, I guarantee you that this won't be the last time you'll see Jonathan Louis Duckworth on the cover of a book. Third, I guarantee you that, if you're a fan of good writing, you will, like me, think this at least once before the collection is over: "Damn, I wanna see what this guy can do with a whole novel." Lastly, I guarantee you that you'll be entertained by what follows. I told you before and I'll tell you again: Jonathan always delivers, and here's a whole collection that proves the man has IT. Welcome to his world. Buckle up and enjoy the ride.

Gabino Iglesias
Somewhere in the Caribbean, June of 2023

HAVE YOU SEEN THE
MOON
TONIGHT?
& OTHER RUMORS

DARKE'S LAST SHOW

My face still tingles from all the smiling when the car pulls up. Silver Honda Accord. Driver: Raul. 4.9 star rating, meaning some monster gave him a petty 4-star review once—there is no circle of Hell low enough. Raul's a handsome kid: maybe twenty, lots of hair product, a fade shaved onto the back of his head, a winning smile, and soft-spoken. I take a quick shine to him.

Traffic's light for a Thursday night in South Beach. It should take half an hour to get to where my friends will be expecting me, not that I'm in a rush. The car's body trembles from the bass of an impressive sound system; I feel each pleasant pulse in the roots of my molars.

"You mind turning it up, kid? I like this one."

Raul's surprised. "For real? No offense, but you seem a little old to be bumping Shorty BoomBoom."

If only he knew *how* old. "I try to keep up with the times."

The next song on the kid's playlist is a classic. Biggie's "Kick in the Door" with the Screamin' Jay Hawkins sax sample. It was Biggie who first made me a hip-hop fan back in the 90s. Maybe I saw some of myself in him, he who had many enemies and once wore a crown.

"Quit my job today," I say, unprompted. "More like got fired actually."

He sounds legitimately sympathetic. "Damn. Sorry, bro."

In my hands is the final check, $500, made out, as always, to cash. In the corner is Mr. Wentz's narrow, peaked signature. How long will it take for his club to start smelling ripe? In Miami? Three days, tops.

"No, it's a good thing. Shit job. I was depressed for a long time, a stranger to myself, Raul, but now I'm feeling better."

He keeps sneaking glances at me through the rearview. Finally he asks, "Hey, bossman, you look familiar. Were you on TV or something?"

"Did you ever see the Netflix special, *Occult Mastery with Devin Darke?*"

"Oh shit! No, yeah—you're the magic guy."

"Yeah. I'm the 'magic guy.' Used to be a lot more of us."

"A lot more of who?"

"Magic guys, like you say."

Like every old man, I start talking, and maybe it's because I'm a little drunk, or maybe because I'm past the point of holding back for the sake of the Farce. At first, I can't tell—and don't care either way—if Raul grasps what I'm saying, or if he's even listening. Maybe he's just polite, humoring me, dismissing me as just another one of the loquacious weirdos his job throws his way.

* * *

"Look, it started with Jesus. Don't get me wrong, Yeshua was a good guy. Big heart, and talent out the ass; one of the best warlocks to ever call on the Old Science. But he fucked up. He made the mistake of trying to help people, and you know how that ended for him. He also called attention to our kind, and that's when the Hunt started. A thousand years of slaughter, right up through the Middle Ages, witches and warlocks wasted like passenger pigeons. And maybe it's because we're scary, because of everything we can do. But regular people are scary too. How many species will have gone extinct while we're talking? How many nukes are just sitting in silos in the Dakotas waiting to be launched?

"There weren't even any of us left—not really—by the time Salem rolled around. Sure, some pretenders came up in the 1800s, guys like that lot in Germany who knew a few tricks, but that's amateur crap, open-mic-night sorcery by store-brand warlocks. And anyway, they're all gone. Now it's just me, and maybe a few others hidden so well not even I can find them.

"I'm rambling. All that doesn't matter. Here's what matters: I'm done hiding. Starting tonight, the Old Science of the Dark returns. Let angels weep, and all that.

"What? No, I'm not going to do another special. That production was hell. I got maybe two hours of sleep a night for six straight months working on that show. Bad as this last gig was, at least I only had to work a few hours a month at the O-Club.

"Yeah, that's the one—the one on Collins.

"No, it's not a skinbar, not exactly, more like *burlesque*.

"Well, sure there's 'titties,' but that's not really the point.

"Okay, fine, it's a skinbar, you happy? Anyway, I put on a show every Thursday night, an hour of magic, something to give the girls a break between shifts—and look, they deserve it, they work a lot harder than I ever have. Anyway, it was good money for a while, but Wentz—that's the club owner, or should I say the guy who kept the papers for the Russians who really owned it—he was a trip and a half. Greasy little guy in a white suit with his tacky combover and a scrunched-up, pug-looking face.

"I got there tonight thirty minutes late. I won't bullshit you, that was on me. I was drunk, and yeah, it was noticeable. And no, it wasn't the first time this had happened. I just stumbled in through the back entrance and Wentz was there, purple as a plum, eyes all wide and bloodshot and twitchy from whatever he'd been snorting.

"'You're done,' he said. 'Do your little show and then see me backstage for your last check.'

"I didn't say anything. Just stared at him. He was firing *me*? This little garden gnome was firing *Devin Darke*?

"'Well, what are you waiting for?' he asked. 'Listen, the crowd's losing their patience.'

"And they were. Beyond the curtains I could hear the grumbling and the booing while the DJ kept saying my name as if I'd just pop out on his command.

"Call it an epiphany, but as I stared at Wentz's angry pug-face, I got to thinking about what I used to be, and what I've been reduced to. I used to have a palace. Hell, I had a cult that built shrines in my honor from Rome to Transoxiana. And now there I was, living in a studio apartment in Brickell, working at some hole in the wall, inhaling body glitter, doing birthday party tricks for checks.

"I just started laughing at the absurdity of it all, and of course that got Wentz madder.

"'Don't worry,' I told him. 'I'll give those people a show they'll never forget.'

"So I dressed up in my duds, the cape and hat and everything because I'm old-school like that. I wobbled out through the curtains.

"'Let's hear it for my boy Devin Darke!' the DJ said a last time as I walked out into the light of the stage.

"The applause was tepid at best. But what could I expect? What sort of people are you going to find at the O-Club on a Thursday night? Winners.

Winners, every last one of them. I hadn't even introduced myself when the heckling started.

"'We came for tits, not for some Tim Burton-looking magic bitch,' this one guy yelled. He was this tall, Body-by-HGH guy. $500 jacket, $20 pants, tigers, snakes, and empty proverbs in languages he can't read tattooed onto his biceps; you know the type.

"'You, sir,' I said, beckoning to him with my finger. 'Why don't you come up and help me with my first trick?'

"Simple suggestion is barely even an exertion of power. I can do it like wrinkling my nose, and the targets go along like it's their own idea. This guy strutted up to the stage all grins and *hurhurhur* laughter because he thought he'd have an even better vantage to heckle me from: to my face.

"His guys were cheering him on. Finance Bros, by the looks of them. Like I said, winners.

"'Pick a card, sir,' I said, unfurling a fan of cards from my sleeve.

"He laughed ugly, got all wheezy. 'You serious? Card tricks? What is this, my sobrino's birthday party?'

"The crowd laughed, his friends loudest of all, but I laughed too. I was a little rusty at maniacal laughter, and the walls of the O-Club didn't quite have the acoustics of marble temple walls, but I shut them up with five awkward seconds of riotous cackling. A warlock always needs a malevolent cackle; or a sinister guffaw, as the case may be.

"'Once more, I ask you to pick a card,' I said.

"He picked his card.

"'Let the audience see it, but don't show it to me. Now put it back in the deck.'

"He slid the card back into the deck while cutting eyes at his pals—*This guy, right?*

"I shuffled them, taking care to drop at least one card, which brought some giggles from the crowd.

"'Is this your card?'

"'No,' he said. And the audience laughed because they'd seen the card—the Ace of Clubs—and this wasn't it. Two more tries were just as fruitless.

"'Bro, you ever done this before?' he asked.

"'Where could that card have gone?' I said, with bombastic, exaggerated aplomb. And while I was hamming it up and Finance Bro was laughing, no one noticed the squirming puddle of darkness that had gathered in the far back corner of the club, a living gloom insoluble to the neon lights—no one heard my whisper to it, nor heard its whisper to me, the bargain we struck.

"Finance Bro's laughter got more obnoxious, and the guy doubled over from it, holding his chest, grasping his ribs. And then the convulsions started. A rasp tore from his throat like he'd swallowed a chicken bone, and then he spat out a playing card, bent and damp and touched in one corner with a fleck of red. But it wasn't the right card.

"'What's ha—?' he choked out. I'm sure he was trying to ask, 'What's happening to me?' but he didn't get much out before he hacked up another card, this one spattered with more than a little blood. Another came, and then another. The guy fell to his knees. First in spurts of a few at a time, and then in a torrent, cards flew from his mouth, crumpled and messy and red.

"I knelt beside him to search the deepening slushpile for the Ace of Clubs. I gave a running commentary as I sifted through. 'Nope, nope, nope, not it— hey, what's a baseball card doing here?'

"Some in the audience were shouting for someone to call an ambulance, while the few who had their phones out weren't calling anyone, but instead recording videos of the scene—you know, the usual thing. Off to the side, a pair of the club's girls were watching, and though Marbella looked sick, the other— Sandy, I think her name is—looked ecstatic with schadenfreude. Maybe she knew the guy.

"And then there was Wentz, who had his phone out but was too shellshocked to dial an emergency number. And maybe he wouldn't have wanted cops there anyway.

"'Ahh, found it!' I said, at last holding up an Ace of Clubs so richly dyed in arterial crimson that you could barely tell its suit. 'Here, sir, is your card,' I said, waving the Ace of Clubs over the sightless eyes of the man who'd fallen into a heap of himself, sprawled over a slurry of bloody, crimped cards.

"One beat. Two beats. I dropped the card, turned my face to the audience so they could see my mask of shock, then thumped my heel on the stage. A trapdoor yawned open to swallow the corpse and the cards. A few in the audience were still recording on their phones, probably because the mediation of their screens was the only barrier between their minds and the impossible. The rest stared fish-eyed and open-mouthed. Backstage, the girls looked much the same. But Wentz? Wentz's expression was funny, a question scrunched into his forehead, like he was trying to recall if the stage had ever had a trapdoor.

"'Wow, what a volunteer,' I said. 'Let's hear it for him.' And just as I spoke the words, the club's back door flew open and in strutted Mr. Sun's-Out-Guns-Out, looking none the worse for having disgorged a deck of cards from his bowels. His shirt was clean—not even a drop of blood.

"One beat. Two beats. Then the applause. Drunken cheers and hoots, loudest of all from the guy's Finance Bro buddies. As the applause died down, off to the side Wentz stepped away from the brink of an aneurysm and slid his phone back into his pocket. I saw the Finance Bros asking their pal how it works, and he just shook his head and grinned, heckler turned coy accomplice of illusion's tremendous power to astound.

"For the next few acts I went vanilla. Real birthday party fare. Coin tricks, flowers up the sleeve, pablum to ease the crowd. It worked, and by the time I said I wanted to make some shadow puppets, the audience was starting to look bored and listless again, the latent spell of my first illusion fading.

"'Now, I'm not the best at these,' I said as preface, and held my hands in front of the stage light, the obnoxiously bright spotlight used whenever Larisha did her chorus line routine in the silver sequin leotard.

"I made birds. A sailboat. A wolf's head.

"'Next act,' someone shouted from the audience.

"'Next,' another said, and soon the rest of the audience took up the chant.

"They wanted the real stuff, the sublime, the terror of the illusion so solid it casts your life in uncertain, fictive aspersions.

"I made a bat. The bat flapped and fluttered. The bat divided to two bats, and while the first bat stayed where my hands moved, the other broke away, gliding over the curtains and across the stage, a little shadowy film, and broke into more bats. Soon bats were gliding everywhere, shadows moving freely, untethered. My hands had stopped moving and now lay slack at my sides. Shadow bats slipped over pant legs, on the ceiling, on the floor, across eyes. For one second, everyone covered their ears as the club exploded with a hurricane of flapping wings and squeaking, shrieking bats.

"And then it was quiet, and the shadows were gone. Another storm of applause. This time I took a bow, but only a short one. I'd save the big bow for the big finish, for the ovation. Through my peripherals I caught Wentz at war with himself. I could see the calculations in his eyes, what he was thinking—*Maybe I should keep him on; if Darke can do this every night, maybe I won't even need girls to bring the crowds.*

"When the applause tapered, I announced my next trick and asked for two volunteers to join me on stage, preferably a couple. As luck would have it, I found one.

"Yeah, a man and a woman, is that so strange?

"Well, yeah, I know it's a stripclub. But, you know, sometimes a couple wants to try something new, something to spice up the old Insert-Rod-into-Slot-B routine.

"They were in their late thirties. Both blond and blue eyed. Nice clothes. We'll call them Mr. and Mrs. X. Not sure where it came from, but I got a very specific vibe from those two, a They-Once-Doused-a-Bum-in-Gasoline-Set-Him-on Fire-and-Fucked-While-He-Burned vibe, but underneath that was a They're-the-Only-Ones-Who-Don't-Know-They're-Already-Dead vibe. Two walking corpses locked in a loveless, childless purgatory of cohabitation and occasional bodily collision. But what do I know? It's not like I can peer into their souls and see their miasmic inner corruption or anything.

"Anyway, they were *so* excited when I told them I wanted to saw them up. Wentz was stumped again when I brought out the equipment from the other side of the stage: a saw and two people-sized boxes on carts. He *knew* he didn't have anything like that back there.

"The trick went off perfectly. I assured the audience that everything was perfectly fine as they all heard the wet resistance of flesh against the steel sawblade and the dry rasp of bone and gristle giving under the saw's persistent chew. They were screaming too. You'd think I was *killing* them the way Mr. and Mrs. X shrieked, crying for help until their heads were free of their necks.

"I made a slapstick show of chasing after Mr. X's head while it rolled around, painting sanguineous ellipticals onto the stage while someone—I think one of the Finance Bros—yelled about how it was the most obvious rubber prop he'd ever seen.

"I'll admit it, that hurt me. I didn't think it looked rubber at all.

"When I opened the panels to the boxes, the audience saw all the parts: the unspooled intestine, the grinning ribs, the blushing organs. Groans, gasps, a few laughs. I unfurled my cape, much more voluminous than it looked, and covered the carnage. When I lifted the shroud, Mr. and Mrs. X lay side by side, smiling and holding hands, looking at each other like the old spark was back. And who says there aren't miracles these days?

"The applause was disappointing. The noise was loud, but the air was stale; none of the tense, ecstatic crackle of the earlier ovations. Like they'd been expecting every beat. It happens sometimes, with the more well-traveled tricks.

"The last polite claps were tapering off when the club doors opened and a cop—off-duty but still in uniform—shuffled in. I don't like cops, but then, who does? Their uniforms might change over the centuries, but they're always the same crooked, cruel bastards who used to hack off kids' hands in marketplaces.

"My eyes found his across the distance of the club, and he came my way, toward the stage.

"'Officer, welcome to the show,' I said. 'You're just in time for my grand finale.'

"A few minutes later, the cop was with me on the stage, watching with everyone else as I rolled out a dolly bearing a glass case of water big enough for a man to drown in. I explained how it worked, not that it needed any explanation. This was another old one; Houdini pioneered it, after all. And yet escapology never gets old, because it's so elemental. It's not man vs water or man vs shackles or even man vs his own bursting lungs. It's man vs time. The water represents time, finality, our struggle against the inevitable. And that's the power of the escape, the greatest illusion of all: that there *is* a way out. Eventually time always wins, whether you're inside or outside the glass.

"I told the cop that I was trusting him to hold the hammer that would shatter the glass and free me if I failed at picking the locks. I had the cop use his own handcuffs to cuff my hands behind my back, and then he helped me immerse myself in the water, secured the top of the tank, and set a timer. He stood by the tank, tired but smiling, a hammer in one hand and a timer in the other.

"Everyone in the audience watched me as the clock ticked down. And I did nothing. I didn't thrash, didn't contort myself out of the cuffs or reveal a pick in my hair to jimmy the lock. I just waited. I crossed my legs into the lotus position and waited. Did they notice the lack of bubbles? When, I wonder, did they first realize the water was draining from the tank? As the water ebbed lower and lower in the tank, the cop began to tremble. He didn't make a sound; he couldn't make any sound more than a helpless gurgle.

"People in the audience were shouting, having a meltdown.

"I winked one eye open to see what they were screaming about, and it appeared that the cop was swelling. Not just his gut, his *everything.* His fingers were like sausages, his face was stretched to obscene and gruesome proportions, his eyes bulged from their sockets. The hammer and timer dropped from his now-useless, ballooned hands. His belt snapped, his shirt and pants tore at the seams.

"The water was almost all drained from the tank, and I waited in my lotus pose. When I opened my eyes, the cop burst. Not, as you might expect, in a shower of red gore chunky with gray offal and bits of white bone. Rather, as a wave of water. Just ordinary water. It washed over the stage, splattered over the rim, splashed the people sitting at the tables up front.

"And they cheered. They cheered like they were at the Seaquarium getting blessed by an orca's spray of brine.

"I stood up in the tank, the cuffs sliding off my wrists, and pushed open the front panel of the glass case. I stood before them and twirled under the stage lights so they could all see my clothes were dry. I waved my hand, and for a blink, every light in the club died. Not just the stage lights or the blacklights on the ceiling, I mean everything—cell phone screens, emergency exit signs, everything.

"When the lights returned, the glass case and its assembly were gone, and in its place stood the cop, looking bewildered but in perfect health.

"I took a bow. The deep bow that cues a standing ovation.

"The people were still clapping when I walked backstage, wended the corner, and found Wentz waiting for me in his office. His lips were pinched and white as he slouched over his desk to write my check. When he slipped it to me, his words were crisp and hushed. 'How did you do that?'

"I said he'd have to be more specific.

"'All of it,' he said. 'Any of it. You've never...' He trailed off. I don't think he really wanted to know, but he had to ask just the same.

"I winked. 'Magicians. Secrets. Never tell.'"

* * *

"So be honest," I say. "How much of that did you actually hear?"

Raul doesn't answer straight away, but when he does speak, I'm pleased to find that listening isn't a completely dead art.

"How'd you do it though?" Raul asks. "If the Wentz dude didn't have all that stuff, how'd you have it? Did you sneak it in before the show?"

"A logical assumption," I say. "But remember, I got there thirty minutes late, not three hours early."

"So then how'd you do it?"

"Way I see it, kid, you've got two interpretations. One, I'm full of shit and none of this happened. Two, I'm magic. Which do you believe?"

"I think you're full of shit." He sounds sure enough. "But it'd be cool to catch a show of yours sometime."

"You're a good kid, Raul."

We're almost at the destination. He's checking his GPS again. I can tell he wants to ask me what I'm going to get up to in the parking lot of a shuttered Toys "R" Us, but he's either too polite or too smart to pose the question. Raul pulls off the road and turns into the lot. Though the store is dead and unlit, the lot lights are still shedding their wan cones of fluorescence on the cracked blacktop. The wind tumbles soda cans and plastic bags through the islands of light and the surrounding straits of darkness.

"Is here good?" he asks. For the first time, he sounds nervous. The conveyer belt of bright cars on 167th Street aren't even a football field away, and this kid's making a face like he's about to get mugged.

"Here's perfect," I say. "Here, something for your trouble."

Tipping through the app only stuffs money into the oligarchs' pockets, so I prefer to tip my drivers directly, just as I have since the days of palanquins and chariots.

Raul takes the check, stares at it, and tries to offer it back. "Bro, I can't take this."

"Sure you can. It's made out to cash."

"No, I mean—"

"I know what you meant. Take it—I don't have use for it. Not anymore."

I'm stepping out of the car when something occurs to me. "Hey, Raul. You got any more rides after this?"

"No doubt, bro, it's about to be peak hours."

"Raul, listen to me, don't pick anyone else up tonight. As a matter of fact, go straight home, and when you get there, lock your doors and windows—don't forget the windows—and don't leave until after sunrise. Don't unlock your door, no matter who you think you hear begging or threatening you to open up, whether it's friends, family, cops, a woman saying she's having a baby, or anything else. Stay inside."

It's the same warning I gave to the girls before leaving the O-Club.

I walk away. The car's engine idles for a few seconds like Raul's still thinking about it, but then the brakes squeak as the car rolls away.

Now alone, I skirt around the edge of the derelict Toys "R" Us. There's more power here than any cemetery, this graveyard of consumer capitalism and children's unfulfilled desires. Around the backlot of the store, where workers would have once off-loaded deliveries and crushed boxes, a single sickly bulb burns from a crooked post, and in that umbrella of jaundiced light, my *friends* are loitering.

A big, tatted-up Finance Bro in designer shades, a skeevy looking blond couple, and a cop all stand waiting for me. To the uninitiated eye, they would look entirely normal, but a closer inspection of the shadows they cast in the parking lot light, and the odd, warbling way they shift as oil swirls do on the surface of water, would tell of their unseen inner dimensions. Vast, anarchic possibilities straining against the limitations of the three-dimensional meat-puppet semblances that contain them, semblances patterned in the shape of the living sacrifices I offered to entice them into this world. If he survives the night, greedy little Mr. Wentz might discover the moldering carrion under his stage, the last gift Devin Darke left for his tawdry little house of flesh. The show's over; now it's the world's turn to hide from me.

I address them, these eager children of the Nameless come for their mischief. "Friends, you may unmask now. The night's so brief, and we've so much town to paint red."

THE BRINE'S EMBRACE

Both versions of Buddy Towne start wondering if there's too many boats darkening the shallows. Usually, Reeta would have shown by now. The largest and loudest of the fishermen, Howie Thurgood, belches and tosses his empty beer can into the surf. It washes right back, almost like the sea spits it out. "Some night we have," Howie says, clapping Buddy on his back. "Shame this woman of yours ain't showing."

Both possible versions of Buddy feel like an idiot, even more than usual. He's always the butt of every joke, the cautionary tale to every young boy in Apalachicola of how not to be a man or a fisherman, and now it'll be worse. *Come meet my gal*, he said. *Come out to St. George Island when the tide's low and the moon's bright*. But Reeta's not here, and the men—ten of them come in on three outrigger boats—are drinking and giggling and whispering about what might drive a man to make love to a manatee, and Buddy's clenching his fists, feeling like a rube.

The beam from the lighthouse swings overhead like bright fishing wire casting for something in the dark of the Gulf of Mexico, while the wind-tossed sea oats susurrate on the dunes. The men are starting to get bored, already a few have climbed back in their boats. They'd already have left if it weren't such a pleasant night. The oldest of the men, Ellis Briggs, pushes a frosty beer into Buddy's hand and then punctures it with his can opener.

"Loneliness can be a mean thing," Old Briggs says, not so softly that the other men don't hear his unexpected kindness to the social leper, but soft enough they can pretend they didn't. One possible Buddy—call him Buddy One—slaps the can out of Briggs' hand and the old man just shakes his head. The other, Buddy Two, accepts the beer and receives a pat on the shoulder. In both versions, Briggs leaves his unopened beers and the can opener for Buddy on the sand—fine as sugar and cold and pale as snow—and then climbs into his boat, hauls up the anchor, and putters away. The other men are soon gone, leaving their empties to keep Buddy company.

* * *

At some point in the past, someone—maybe it's his father, or one of the guys in his squad in Korea (these things always mash together)—tells Buddy that men don't need to be pretty, they need to be useful. This is said as a kindness, because Buddy is awkward and funny-looking, but he still needs to feel beautiful, and Reeta lets him feel that way. Reeta is everything he's ever wanted in a woman. She's not just beautiful, she's kind, smart, and curious about everything. But most important of all, she's *compatible*. In their first encounters, after Buddy overcomes his apprehension of wading into the waters and Reeta her fears of getting beached, Buddy is stunned by Reeta's vigor and enthusiasm, as well as how smooth and silky her scales are, soft as polyester. But the Buddies experience different first times. While Buddy Two enjoys a storybook fuck, Buddy One cuts himself on the sharp armored ridges that protect Reeta's gills. He thinks he might bleed out on the sand, but Reeta's cold black tongue wraps around his wrist, and the enzymes of her saliva coagulate the wound. Her amber eyes dilate with pleasure and then close as she tastes his inner sea.

* * *

The last of the boats is a little firefly twinkle on the western horizon when Buddy—on his third beer now—sees the shimmer start. Bright green and full of froth, like the water's boiling, coming toward land.

"Now she comes," he mutters. Buddy One says it loudly, Buddy Two says it under his breath.

But even as low and bitter as he feels, he can't help but gawk when she breaches the water. He's seen it a dozen times, but Reeta's emergence is never less than spectacular. First the eyes—amber and bright, further to the sides of the skull than a human's eyes—glimmer like brass foil. Then there's the cascade of brine as she shakes her head and the water drips from the berries and flosses of her wig—the wig of red algae she shaped to look like Rita Hayworth's famous mane. He calls her Reeta for this reason, but also because her true name is not something a human voice could pronounce unless they were drowning. Moonlight glimmers off the fine golden scales of her shoulders and throat and her mirrorlike silver stomach, while shadows puddle on the undersides of the round, firm mounds on her chest she's said are egg pouches. Reeta rises to her navel, the pair of strong, finned limbs halfway between legs and tails still submerged in the low water. Pink slits where a human's ribs would be—her gills—vent open and spray gasps of vapor, and her throat croaks as she opens her mouth with its thin lips and crystalline teeth like little green emeralds.

"Why didn't you come?" he asks. "You made me look like a fool."

"You have no right to be angry, Buddy Towne," Reeta says. "I told you not to tell your people of me. You broke my trust."

Buddy's anger melts against these words, and he goes cold despite the balmy evening at the thought of her leaving him. *Stupid, stupid man, Buddy.*

"Please don't," Buddy says. "I'm sorry. I won't do it again. Those men won't be a danger—they think I'm a rube, a crazy fool."

But Reeta is already withdrawing into the waves. He'll not touch her tonight, won't feel her scales against his skin. Buddy's running into the water, but she's gone.

She doesn't show the next night. Nor the night after. He starts to feel like he did before he found her, those dark times he'd walk the deserted beaches of St. George Island under the lighthouse's blind eye and imagine opening the estuaries of his body to the ocean.

* * *

Once on his lonely nocturnal walks, in the time before he meets Reeta, Buddy One meets the old keeper of the St. George Island lighthouse. He's a short bald guy with a wild white beard streaked with yellow tobacco stains, and he wears a heavy oilcoat even though it's a balmy, clear night. The old salt, who's out fishing, finds Buddy looking out at the ocean with haunted eyes and approaches him and says, *The ocean gonna take what's offered, son, and what's offered it ain't like to give back.* Buddy Two never meets this man, and comes to believe the lighthouse is a derelict pulsar, a bright tombstone on the shore.

* * *

Four days after his stupid mistake, four agonizing days and three painful, fruitless waits at the beach later, Reeta finally shows again. Each of the no-show nights, Buddy plays his guitar on the sand with the spume and foam lapping at his toes. He plays and sings the songs of Elvis, Tennessee Ernie Ford, Chuck Berry, and Hank Williams, but more than any of the rest he plays the songs of his hero, Buddy Holly. He doesn't just like Buddy Holly because they share the same name—though unlike Holly, Buddy was given the name at birth—but because Buddy Holly is like him, a gangly, goofy-looking guy who no one would ever accuse of being handsome. Sometimes when he's vain, Buddy dreams of making it on *American Bandstand* and playing some of the songs he's wrote himself but won't ever perform, not even for Reeta.

That fourth night, Reeta comes with her show of light and froth. Buddy plays his favorite song, Holly's "Not Fade Away," for her, and she listens with her head just an inch under water, because her earholes hear better submerged.

When he's finished, Buddy puts his guitar down and Reeta drags herself out of the water, fine white sand dusting her limbs and belly like sugar. Buddy One puts his hand around her narrow waist and nibbles on her throat the way she likes. She tastes just a little like the fermented seaweed he remembers floating in the broths the locals cooked when he was at the army hospital in Okinawa. Buddy Two hauls her all the way onto the beach and she coils her impossibly strong tail-legs around him as he rests his head against the pillowy swell of her bust. Both Buddies cry just a little, because forgiveness is a potent opiate. Buddy One lets her lead, lets her use her lower appendages to position him. Reeta is like almost every species of fish: ectothermic, cold-blooded. It's always a surprise when Buddy is inside her and she is colder than the balmy waters of the Gulf that lap against his hips. Buddy Two is more assertive, and flips her over onto her belly so he can admire the thin gold sheet of protein-silk projecting from the keel of her spine, a dorsal fin rigid and bladelike in the water but slack and soft as muslin to the dry air.

Reeta tells him to slide his fingers into her gills, and Buddy Two's never cut himself there, so he doesn't hesitate. It's clear it causes her pain to have his fingers jammed into such sensitive fissures, but the way Reeta quivers and thrashes her tailfeet speaks to a greater pleasure. After the passion is spent, both Buddies slump and pant, feet in the surf and heads in the sand.

Reeta holds Buddy and shudders as the protective moisture around her scales begins to dry. Soon she'll have to return to the water, but for the moment she squeezes Buddy tightly. She's much stronger than him—that would bother some men, but Buddy likes the feeling of safety her strength offers.

"I'm sorry I did not come the other nights," Reeta says. "I was angry with you still."

"That's okay. You're here is what matters."

She closes her eyes. She has a humanlike face, but there is just enough ocean in it that he never forgets she's not a human woman. Her eyes are too round, too far apart, her lips too narrow and rigid, and there are two vertical slits for nostrils and a shallow ridge of cartilage where a nose would be.

Buddy plays with the tangled weave of her kelp wig. A thought occurs to him. Buddy One lets it lie, but Buddy Two works up the nerve to ask. What's she look like under her wig?

Reeta is clearly nervous, but she removes her wig, and Buddy finally sees what she's been hiding from him. Three short, translucent fins run along the dome of her skull, spider-webbed by luminous veins aglow with a soft green like the color the water turns when she approaches the shore.

"You don't need to bother with the wig anymore," Buddy says.

Reeta lets out a hiss of vapor. "But I like the wig. I like being Rita Hayworth."

Maybe there's a deformity in her fins, something she's ashamed of. Buddy doesn't press, because he doesn't know what a mermaid's scalp is supposed to look like and he doesn't want to embarrass her.

Reeta secures the wig again and then rests her head on Buddy's chest. "Would you ever want to see my world? To meet my people?"

"Golly, it'd be some kind of outing," Buddy says, thinking she's joking.

"I'm serious. What if you could live with me in the water?"

"Well, it's not possible."

"But would you?"

Buddy thinks about what living in the ocean with Reeta would be like. He can't begin to imagine such a life, even if it were possible, but he knows how little he'd miss the life he has. "I'd make a go of it."

She ripples with excitement. "That makes me happy. Give me a few days to make arrangements."

"Huh? What arrangements?"

"I can make you like me," she says.

"How?"

"With magic."

* * *

Before she ever reveals herself to him, Reeta observes Buddy out on his daily fishing trips. The first hint he has a guardian angel in the water comes when he loses his daddy's gold watch and it's thrown back onto the deck of his boat.

"Why don't your people ever wash ashore?" he asks her once, early in their courtship.

"The ocean doesn't give up its dead," she answers.

Her kind don't speak the way humans speak; she learned to imitate human speech by squeezing gasses through the valves of her throat, gasses produced by a form of indigestion. She always eats fatty fish and underripe kelp before meeting him so that she'll be able to "talk." It touches Buddy that she'd make herself uncomfortable for his sake. Her voice is a raspy croak; it reminds him of a jazz singer he once heard.

"How come you never get caught in ocean trawler nets?" he asks. "Those nets catch everything."

"We have knives. We are a people of science and tools, just as you are."

Buddy wonders if Reeta is like him, an outcast. Maybe she's considered ugly, even hideous, and that's why she's a fool for him. Maybe she was thinking of beaching herself and letting the sun dry her out before she found Buddy.

* * *

The next time Buddy sees her, almost a week has passed again. Each night in the interim he takes his boat from Apalachicola to St. George Island and anchors near the lighthouse and camps by the shore and waits, and each night when she doesn't show up, he plays his guitar and sings Buddy Holly songs to nobody. He keeps thinking about the last thing she told him. It can't be true— there's no such thing as magic, even in a world where fishpeople exist. Buddy Two wants to believe though, while Buddy One laughs at the idea so that it won't hurt him when it doesn't happen.

* * *

She lives to learn. She teaches herself to speak English before ever meeting Buddy, learning it from eavesdropping on fishermen and tourists. She studies the glamorous wives and mistresses of the millionaires, congressmen, sportsmen, and movie stars who come to the Gulf to fish, get drunk, and fool around at sea far from the flashbulbs of Hollywood, New York, and

Washington D.C., and she learns to love as human women do from watching their deckside escapades. The rest of what she knows about humans she learns from discarded magazines and trinkets from shipwrecks, or from what Buddy teaches her.

One day he builds a fire for her on the shore, and she loves the colors it makes but loves less the way it dries the scales of her face when she leans in for a closer look. Fire is a nice place to visit, but Reeta wouldn't want to live there. Still, she collects the shards of glass shaped in the sand from the heat, and the next time Buddy sees her, she's created a necklace from the pieces.

Once he brings her whiskey. She doesn't drink it from the bottle, and instead has him pour it into the water. The brown liquor dissolves in the ocean, and Reeta breathes it in through her gills. She says it's like a kind of venom, and wonders why any intelligent creatures would knowingly poison themselves. When they kiss, Reeta funnels a concentrated stream of whiskey into Buddy's mouth, and he's quickly drunk. The stars blur and the ocean tides become radio static in his ears. Reeta coils around him and they look up at a dazzling show of light that's labored a thousand years to reach their eyes.

* * *

At last she returns after a week of lonely nights.

"It's all prepared," Reeta says, slithering serpentine through the foam and onto the shore.

Buddy can't help himself, and throws himself onto her, kissing her cold lips and shuddering when her tongue eels into his mouth and the anodynic enzymes numb his own tongue and gums. When she pulls away, she says that she's made the arrangements, and whenever he's ready he can come with her.

"Come with you and then what?" Buddy asks.

"Come with me and stay with me."

"In the water?"

"Of course in the water."

Both versions of Buddy are full of worries, both are disbelieving. Both want to believe. Both have been hurt too much—by parents, by laughter, by shrapnel and sepsis and shellshock—to believe in magic. Buddy One wants to laugh it off; Buddy Two wonders if it will hurt, whatever it is Reeta will do to let him live with her.

"Could I ever go back?" both Buddies ask their respective Reetas.

Reeta's amber-backed eyes glitter with kindness, and she asks him what he'd have to go back to.

When neither Buddy can answer, Reeta's tails coil around him. She tears open his shirt, shredding the cotton as if it's wet paper, then rips open his blue jeans with the same ease. Both Buddies let her strip every scrap of cloth away until he's as naked as her. Between Buddy One and Buddy Two is only a minor divergence: Buddy Two goes slack while Buddy One wraps his arms around her.

Reeta slides onto Buddy and tacks him into her cove while her twin tailfeet constrict his legs so tightly his ankles start to ache and his calves throb from the pressure. And then they're in the water. Not bobbing on the edge of the surf like all the times before; this time they're drifting out into the darker depths of the Gulf.

"Let it come," Reeta hisses into his ear, and then she unclasps from him, slides away, and leaves him to bob and kick in the water.

His toes can't reach the sea bottom, and all the pleasure he felt a moment ago alchemizes to fear as he realizes he can't see the shore, can't see anything but water in every direction, water and the impossible brightness of the moon melting like a luminous slick of oil on the surface. Humans invented clothes to feel like they control the world, nakedness only reminds them of the truth that they don't, and it's this nakedness that puts the thrash and rattle into Buddy's mammalian heart.

"Reeta!" Buddy One calls out, while Buddy Two can't say anything because he's coughing on some seawater he swallowed when he gasped from surprise at being released.

And then there's Reeta, beautiful and luminescent under the moonlight and from the emerald glow of the veins under her skin. There's something in her hand, something that shimmers under the water, and Buddy catches only a glimpse before she slashes it at him, twice, one incision on each side of his throat, deep wounds that break the arteries open, exposing the ocean inside Buddy's veins to the greater ocean outside his skin.

Buddy One looks at Reeta, his love, with wide-eyed shock as his warmth leaks out in brushstrokes unseen in the darkened, turbid surf.

Buddy One dies quick, and mostly without pain. And Reeta breathes the coppery taste of his life through her gills, then takes his pale corpse and holds it close to her in one final embrace. Poor Buddy, who could never be with her, who was despised by his own kind. Poor Buddy, who believed in magic, when she told him very early on that her people were a people of science. And it is science—the cold science that must kill a thing to preserve it—that will immortalize him. A body—any body—that perishes in the sea is quickly gone, made a nothing by the frenzied feeding of the ocean's bewildering web of life, the plankton and fish and so on. Whale carcasses never reach the ocean floor, they are bare skeletons by the time they sink to the mesopelagic zone, and these bones become forests of calcium in the nighted trenches. But Reeta will not let this happen to Buddy. She takes Buddy to her lair in the benthic zone, where she has the apparatuses ready to preserve her beloved. A transparent membrane of hard plastic insulates Buddy from the predation of microorganisms and an injection of a powerful preservative distilled from the brainmatter of a deep-water octopus will maintain his internal structure for decades, if not centuries.

Reeta secures this dead man, already forgotten by the surface world that disdained him, into an impenetrable cask of glass in a shrine where she will always care for him, and when she is old, long after she has spawned her final clutch of young, she will tell her progeny of the love she shared with this sad creature of the dry world. Here he will remain, in a place where he is loved. So ends Buddy One.

Buddy Two is also bleeding. Buddy Two is also thrashing with his arms, kicking his feet as the iron rills leak from his wounds. But then the pain stops, and Buddy is dragged under water, and he gasps again, but instead of an invasion of water, he feels invigorated, a rush of breathable air filtered from the water that courses into the newly made gills shaped from the incisions in his throat.

There is Reeta, smiling at him through the water that he suddenly sees in perfect clarity, his eyes now changed to be like hers, capable of seeing through fathoms of murk, to perceive the ocean's secrets with the aid of only a thread of starlight. Reeta touches Buddy with her shell knife again, dragging the blade across his sternum, making a seam in the skin. Split, the skin peels away, sloughing off cleanly to open Buddy's new scales to the moonlight.

Buddy watches his old skin float to the surface like a rumpled pink towel, then drift away toward the sand of the dry world he's left behind. Electroreceptive ampullae awaken all through his face and feel out the life in the water, Buddy now aware of the crackling energy in even the tiniest plankton. Reeta calls to him through the brine in the electric language of their kind, and Buddy swims after her into the beckoning depths.

ONE OF THOSE NICE GUYS

Karl is finishing his chili when he notices the girl—ninety pounds of skin, bones, and dirty-blonde split ends in a grimy pink crop-top—trying to talk up the pair of bikers at the diner's counter.

"We ain't interested," one of the bikers says.

"Dumb skank must think we're congressmen or something," the other guffaws.

They laugh; meanwhile the girl watches them mutely for a few seconds before turning away and shuffling down the counter to an empty stool. She's barefoot, her pink shirt piled and grease-stained, her denim cutoffs faded almost white. Underneath the hem of her crop-top, her ribs show like piano keys. This is a little truck stop in the long stretch of nothing—the Llano Estacado—that comes after Lubbock, TX. She had to have hitchhiked here.

She's sixteen, maybe seventeen. The age Zadie would be now.

The waitress, a stocky woman built like a beetle, approaches her. "Babydoll, you need me to call somebody for you?"

The stare the girl turns on the waitress is so strange and impassive that the older woman—twice her size, easy—flinches back. "No," the girl says. She's got a scratchy voice, a smoker's voice.

The waitress doesn't press the issue, and seems relieved when the girl turns from her.

But now the girl is looking at Karl, and Karl's eyes meet hers. Before he can even think of looking away, the girl is walking on her bare feet toward his booth.

"Hi," she says, sitting down across from him.

"Hi," he says back. He reaches for his coffee mug, and even though it's empty he still tries for a sip, just so he's doing something.

"I need a ride."

She needs more than a ride. She needs shoes, a shower, a good meal. Well, he can give her one of those things.

"You hungry, kid?" Karl asks.

She smiles. For how dirty her face and hair are, her teeth are like brushed porcelain. "Sure, mister, I could eat," she says. The way she trills the *mister* makes Karl's skin crawl.

Karl orders her the same bowl of chili he just had, and a small cup of coffee. As they wait for the order, the girl just stares at Karl, not quite smiling, not quite making any expression really. If he had to put an adjective to what her face is doing, it'd be *patient.*

One of the bikers points to Karl, and the two of them start sniggering. "You like your jailbait lean, huh, buddy?"

Karl doesn't say anything. He just fixes the biker a withering stare. For maybe half a second the two jokers eye him, size him up, but Karl's a big guy, and since he hasn't said anything they don't need to get their own back. They turn from him, back to their own business, whatever that may be.

"What's jailbait, mister?"

She asks it so innocently. How do you answer a question like that?

"What's your name, kid?"

"You can call me Liz."

You on any milk cartons, Liz?

"Short for Elizabeth?"

"No."

Silence. There's that patient look again. For the first time since noticing her, Karl starts to feel a glimmer of trepidation. Maybe it's the optics of a trucker sitting in a booth with a scrawny blonde teen whose name might as well be Amber. Maybe it's how quiet she is.

Or maybe it's that her baby-blue eyes don't reflect any light.

When the waitress arrives with the chili and cola for Liz and the coffee for Karl, Karl's relieved.

Liz doesn't even touch the soda, but she sniffs the chili and her nose wrinkles like she's sniffed pure vinegar. Without even a glance at her silverware, Liz reaches with her fingers into the steaming chili and plucks out a cube of chuck dripping in chili sauce. She brings it to her lips and pushes it past her teeth, her fingers and thumb disappearing behind her lips before emerging again. She swallows; no chewing. She repeats this with two more pieces before pushing the bowl away.

Skinny as she is, Karl would have figured she'd be hungrier. Unless she's on the crystal—the sunken eyes, the slightly jaundiced skin, the avian slenderness of her frame would all hint toward her being a junkie. Or she's sick with something.

"Too spicy?" he offers.

"Too tough," she says, crossing her arms over her chest. "And it's been dead too long. So how about that ride, mister?"

"Where are your people, Liz?"

"All around, if you know where to look. Now how about that ride?"

He should tell her no. Instead he asks, "Where are you headed?"

"Anyplace you're headed is fine."

A runaway for sure. Maybe he'll drop her off at the highway patrol station in Plains near the New Mexico state line. Not that he trusts highway cops to do right by a lost girl. Perverts, most of them.

He pays his check and then uses the toilet. She's waiting for him when he gets out—that is, she's standing right outside the bathroom door. When he leaves the diner, she follows him closely, never allowing more than a foot between them.

"You must be one of those nice guys I've heard about," Liz says.

He's got his misgivings, but what can he do? Leaving her in the diner would be worse than whatever risk he might take by giving her a lift.

He'll take her to the next town before he gets onto 380. To Brownfield. That's less than a half hour's drive, and then she'll be someone else's problem. But even that bothers him; a person shouldn't be thought of that way—as a problem. She's someone's daughter, or at least she was at some point.

She climbs into the passenger seat and buckles up. She looks tiny, like a bug in the seat's leather cushions. After pulling out from the diner and onto the road, the next few minutes are quiet, just the steady grumble of Karl's rig. It should be peaceful, except Liz is watching him.

"How about some music?" Karl suggests, and then puts in a CD before Liz can say anything.

Through the speakers, the soothing warmth of Vivaldi's "Spring" begins to play, for only a few seconds before Liz jabs the eject button and pulls out the CD.

"Not a Vivaldi fan?" Karl asks, forcing a smile.

"It's unbearable," Liz says. "Just like every sound up here."

Karl decides not to ask; decides to let sleeping dogs lie and accept the uncomfortable silence. Brownfield can't come soon enough.

A few minutes pass, with Liz's watchful eyes never straying from Karl. Is it wariness? No, it's not that. Whatever Liz's deal is, she's definitely not afraid of him.

"So, uhh, where are you from?"

"Someplace you've never heard of."

"Small town?"

She doesn't answer. When Karl glances over at her, he notices something that makes his guts twist. Her throat has started swelling, two huge lumps on either side just below her jaw. It's a painful sight, recalling the hospital visits when Zadie was fighting her losing fight, back when Karl had a full head of hair, back when he and Mia still had every reason to be together. Those last days were the worst. He still keeps the last crayon drawing Zadie made for him in the glovebox—Zadie as a monarch butterfly. On the reverse side of the drawing, in yellow crayon—so hard to read, in more ways than one—are Zadie's mathematical musings: *Daddy told me 100 butterflies together weigh 1 ounce, and there's 16 ounces in a pound, and I'm 42 pounds, so I weigh the same as 67,200 butterflies! That's a lot of butterfly!*

Just thinking about it, Karl feels close to tears, but he doesn't cry. He can't bear to look at Liz right now. As bad as it was for Zadie, at least she had parents who held her hands till the end. What does this poor kid have? He wants to ask what's killing her, but he knows that's the last conversation a sick kid wants to have, so he decides to let silence be silence.

But Liz starts talking. "I love the fields of dry grass here. And the cracked earth warmed by a full day's gift. This used to be beautiful, before the roads, before the electric wires that make their horrible hissing that drowns out the beautiful deep music. Once I could hear that deep music from the cracks in the world, but not anymore. Now your wires run everywhere."

Karl looks at her. The swollen nodes in her throat have grown to the size of plums. Her eyes are more sunken than ever, her lips pale, almost translucent. For the first time he notices what looks like a scar running along her cheek from the corner of her lip—a hair-thin line.

"There's still beauty," she says. She's looking out the window at a skeletal row of cottonwoods and the big, star-dusted sky above them. "There's still so much beauty up here, but the music is gone. Even down below it's gone. To find the music, I'd need to go deeper than anything living ever has, deeper even than the great worms who thresh the crust and slumber in the lungs of the earth."

Again, Karl feels himself on the verge of tears. Even though he doesn't understand what she's saying, there's something in her voice—a haunted longing for what can't be. It hurts him because it plucks a chord inside him whose tone he knows too well.

"Why haven't you stopped the truck yet, mister?" Liz's voice is sharp and scratchy again, the wistfulness gone.

Before he can answer, Liz's hand settles on his thigh. He almost starts out of surprise, but manages to keep his hands steady on the wheel.

"Hey, kid, you mind taking your hand off me?"

"Usually, by this point, they pull off to the side," Liz says.

He looks at her now. This kid who's flashing her strange perfect teeth at him, who's got her little hand on his jeans. He looks at her and all the pity he's been feeling turns to something else, something he can't quite reckon.

"Usually, they'd have at least touched me by now. Brushed my wrist, pushed my hair away from my eyes, something like that."

Karl feels sick. He shakes his head as if to shake off whatever revolting images his imagination might conjure from her words. "Kid, I don't know what kind of fucked-up bastards have picked you up before, but I'm not—"

"You don't seem to want me," Liz says, her head tilting one way then the other. "Not even a little. But you're not telling me anything either, so you must want to fuck me. It's always one way or the other with you truckers. Except when it's both."

"What are you talking about?"

He tries to push her hand away, but despite her wrist being twig-thin, she manages to keep a hold of him—hell, her grip tightens, and he feels her fingertips pressing into the muscle and fat of his thigh.

"Some of them, they cry to me. They pick me up because they need someone to talk to about how shitty their lives are. It's pathetic. You people have no idea how much your tears *reek*. And self-pity ruins your flavor, like if you cured meat with alum."

"Kid—"

Her fingers dig deeper, and Karl almost drives the rig off the shoulder. The truck judders and rattles and bounces, but he manages to get it back onto the lane.

"And then there's the ones who think they're heroes for picking up a little lost girl. They always leave me with the cops, who want to call my parents, and it's always an absolute fucking mess to get myself out of those revolting stations with their noisy ceiling lights and all the smells. So I kill those ones as soon as I figure them out."

Karl's heart jackhammers against his ribcage. His lungs are burning, his gut feels knotted. He wants to be somewhere else—anywhere else.

"But then most of them just want to fuck me. I like those ones. They're simple, easy. They do most of my work for me. They take the truck off the road, drive it somewhere dark where no one will interrupt us. Sometimes they want me to suck their cock, and that's always fun. Hilarious, really, when they find out their mistake." She laughs, and there's a wet sloshing sound in her throat from where the nodes have expanded. She almost looks like a frog, a bubble in her throat as big as an orange.

"I don't, I don't want to—"

"I know you don't," Liz says. "I knew from the start. But you didn't start crying either, and I don't think you consider yourself as some kind of white knight. So what is it? Why'd you pick me up?"

"I—"

"Let me guess, you pitied me because I remind you of someone. Is that it?"

Karl, his eyes still on the road—the strobing white lines are the only thing grounding him now, the only thing keeping him from shaking apart entirely—watches Liz through his peripherals. She doesn't look like Zadie. Not even a little bit. And in terms of personality, there's nothing in this strange, hellish teen that could ever recall his sweet baby girl.

She digs her fingers into him again, and this time he knows she's broken not only the fabric of his jeans but also through his skin. "Tell me what it is."

"You looked like—" he starts, but then whimpers from the pain.

Liz relaxes her grip. "Yes?"

"You looked like someone who hadn't been treated nice in a long time."

Liz lifts her hand from his jeans. He doesn't look down, but he feels fresh blood pooling from where her sharp nails dug in. "You're lying," she says. "What do you want from me? Everyone wants something—it's what gives you people your flavor."

He takes his eyes from the road, from the soothing, hypnotic lines illuminated by his headlights, and looks at her. There's anger, hunger, and emotions he can't begin to guess at.

"I don't want anything," he says. "I just want to get to the next truck stop, that's all. I swear on my daughter's soul."

Liz's expression cycles through a progression of moods. First shock, then anger again, then a flat look of frustration. And then she looks away, as if she can't stand the sight of him. "Pull over." He hesitates, and Liz clamps her hand—her claw—on his knee. "I said pull over."

His arms are flabby, his legs are two soggy noodles held together only by his jeans. Somehow, he manages to turn the wheel and pump the brakes. The rig rumbles off the asphalt and onto the uneven terrain of the Llano Estacado. Once the truck grinds to a halt, the headlights illuminate a swath of tall grass and scrub brush.

Karl expects Liz to order him out of the car, but instead she flings her door open and almost tumbles headfirst out onto the ground. She shambles, then stumbles, falling into the path of the headlights. The engine is still on, a voice in Karl's head reminds him. She's in the path of the truck; he could run her over.

But Karl just watches. Watches as the bulge in her throat swells to obscene dimensions, and then watches her fall onto her hands and knees and heave and retch, and then—

It's bright and yellow, almost a neon color, the jet that sprays from her mouth. It sizzles and fizzes as it strikes the earth and the grass and the greasewood shrubs, first withering and then blackening what it touches, the stalks and branches shriveling and then dissolving entirely.

The way Liz buckles and almost falls on her face invokes a powerful instinct in Karl, and before he knows what he's doing, he's gotten out of the truck and limps toward her.

He gets halfway to her before she throws her head up and hisses, and Karl recoils, most of the way expecting to be sprayed with the same liquid that melted the greasewood shrub, but there's nothing but a blast of rotten meat breath, and for an instant, the skin breaks along its seams, and Karl glimpses the face beneath her face, the leathery dark scales and rows of teeth beneath her soft veneer. But it's gone, and then there's the same tired, sickly girl he first saw at the diner looking up at him.

"Get back in your truck and get out of here," Liz growls. "Only a fool picks up strangers."

He does just what she says. He drives away, and it's only ten minutes later, after he's blasted past a weigh-in station and has the strobing lights of a highway patrolman on his tail, that he realizes he's been pushing his rig past 95 miles per hour.

Karl never picks up a stranger again. But he does watch them. He knows what to look for. Once near Tacoma it's another barefoot girl like Liz he notices at a gas station, watching him and the other truckers filling up. Once in Arizona it's a college-aged guy in a Sun Devils shirt who stinks of skunky weed and who claims his car broke down, but Karl spots the narrow seam around the corners of his lips. And once in a diner in Altoona, Pennsylvania—and this is the one that really keeps him up some nights—he sees a pair of highway patrolmen eating raw hamburger with their fingers, carefully stowing pinches of meat past their false teeth to the true mouths beneath.

THE FOLLOWER'S REVEL

Postcard – "Arrival in the Adirondacks"
Postmarked: November 9th, 1912.
From: Thomas Kampel, Roughneck Junction, Adirondack Park, NY.
To: Dorothea Kampel, 635 Park Ave, #23, New York, NY.

Obverse: A charcoal sketch of the platform of Roughneck Junction, with the slope of Roughneck Mountain in the far background and the shore of Drane Lake beneath it. The trees on the mountainside, rendered as jagged, hatched black slashes, taper into a fine dust further up the slope, while billowing clouds roll over the lake. Other mountains and hills cup the lake's shores like hands holding out a gift. The sketch is consistent with other artwork attributed to the pioneering documentarian filmmaker Thomas Kampel (1885-1912).

Reverse: In a tidy but sharply slanted hand, Thomas Kampel writes to his wife, Dorothea Kampel (1890–1969). The message reads:

Beloved Dora,

How to describe the smell of spruce, the brisk mountain air that floats down to needle my lungs, the sun on the lake, the crunch of clean snow underfoot, the splendid *emptiness* of it all? There is not a house or cabin visible any way you might look, for even the logger camps & miner towns are hidden behind a concealing timber wall of surpassing beauty. What want for a restaurant or ragtime club have these woods? What want for the bray & grumble of motorcars have these mountains? I have scarcely been here an hour & not yet met my patron, nor made the acquaintance of the likely & rugged men who'll be my picture's *dramatis personae*, & yet I'm already giddy with the promise of this unspoiled country & its denizens.

When my work is done, lets we return to these mountains, together, for the romance & splendor such climes might offer us!

Please write back to me post-haste, transmit my regards to your mother, & tell me how little Caroline is adjusting to her new bedroom.

Ever your smitten schoolboy, confidant, & devoted servant,

—Thomas

Reel #1 – "Loggers at Work"

Format: 35mm celluloid

Length: 17:29

Description: The film begins with a shot of a pair of sleeping loggers in their shared bunk within the bunkhouse. At 00:25, the first of the loggers stirs from the top bunk and rises from under his covers, followed soon after by the other. From 00:38 to 01:59, the film follows the loggers at their breakfast, with intermittent shots of the cooks at work on their Bussey & McLeod cast-iron ranges, preparing the meal, including fried donuts and baked beans. After some shots of the wilderness, from 2:45 to 13:27 the film details the day-to-day work of the Adirondack loggers working for the Drane Timber Co.: felling trees, chopping them into logs, loading them onto ox-driven sleds and a treaded steam hauler, and then launching logs onto the water where Drane Lake flows into the Hudson River, whereafter log drivers ("river pigs") guide the logs' progress with peavey sticks. Intermingled with the shots of work are scenes of recreation and relaxation, such as a scene starting at 07:15, where a white-haired logger in his bunkhouse whittles a many-segmented insect from a tree branch, or a scene of two loggers locking arms and dancing at 08:22. At 09:42, while following the work of the pair of engineers who maintain the Lombard steam log hauler, the camera drifts from their work and captures a flicker of movement further out into the forest. A close inspection of the frame at 09:47 shows an obscure, lanky, roughly human shape moving through the woods. The figure seems to turn to regard the camera, and as it turns the branching antlers radiating from its head become apparent. At 12:17, while a team of loggers sit around a campfire and eat an afternoon meal of beans and cornbread and pie, one logger in the background appears to be shaving his head with a rip saw, holding the sawblade with both hands and scraping at his scalp. None of the other loggers seem to remark this, and indeed, several others walk directly past him unbothered. From 13:27 to the end, the film focuses on the snowy wilderness, with occasional appearances by loggers, such as at 15:29, when once more loggers are shown loading timber onto an ox sled.

At 15:36, a logger bends down to lift the end of a wayward log. He wears a plaid jacket, against which the dark shape of a foot-long serpentine creature shows starkly. A closer inspection of the frames between 15:36 and 15:41 reveals the "snake" has numerous small limbs and a pair of long head-feelers as well as sizeable mandibles. The logger evinces no concern even after noticing the creature's presence on his sleeve. From 17:15 to 17:22, the film tracks the slow descent of the sun over Drane Lake, while small pancakes of ice drift across the surface. The final shot is of the bunkhouses at night, with slender whiskers of smoke rising from the chimneys.

Postcard – "Dinner at Drane Castle"
Postmarked: November 11th, 1912.
From: Thomas Kampel, Roughneck Junction, Adirondack Park, NY.
To: Dorothea Kampel, 635 Park Ave, #23, New York, NY.
Obverse: A charcoal sketch in the same style as the previous postcard. This sketch is split-paneled, with the left half showing an exterior rendering of Drane Castle, home of industrialist Henry Prospero Drane (1839–1919), while the right half is an interior scene from the perspective of the unseen observer, Kampel. The exterior scene of Drane Castle makes use of the charcoal medium's facility for contrast with the dark granite façade of Drane Castle athwart the snowy slope of Roughneck Mountain. The composition exaggerates the height and prominence of Drane Castle's three Gothic Revival-style parapets and depicts a large waxing crescent moon sitting just above the tallest of said towers. The interior scene depicts a banquet table, set with a generous assortment of food and drink including a half-carved roast boar on a platter and champagne in an ice bucket. Two individuals are depicted, one turned toward the observer and engaged in conversation, the other, sitting to the side of the first, turned away and in profile. The first person, likely 20th century mystic William "BW" Wallace Riser (???? –1920), is a gentleman of middle age with shoulder-length black hair, prominent eyebrows, and a thick handlebar mustache, dressed in a robe with alchemical symbols (for fire and earth) on the sleeves. The second gentleman, Henry P. Drane, is elderly, white-haired, and full-bearded, wearing half-moon spectacles and a three-piece suit with a single-breasted waistcoat.

Reverse: Kampel writes:

Beloved Dora,

I have enjoyed the most stimulating & electric of evenings with my host, Mr. Drane, & his esteemed friend, the estimable & incomparable Mr. Riser, a magnetic orator & astute scholar of many obscure disciplines. Listening to him talk, I perceived I was in the presence of a mind so capacious it contained my own with ample room to spare. & Mr. D was scintillating in his own right, describing the painstaking process by which he & his workmen transformed an uninhabitable mountainside into a foundation for this latter-day Xanadu. He's a powerfully religious man, & tells me he sees God everywhere, even in human suffering. Now, lest you think I wasn't being myself, I talked my share of ears off too! Both men seem eager to learn about my trade. D perceives the potential for film as a tool of recruitment. Even though he pays a fair wage—(you wouldn't believe how well-fed these miners & loggers are; sheiks & maharajas would gain from picking up an axe!)— he's always short on workers for his mines & logging camps. He hopes my film can convince more men to leave the city for an honest wage & the thrill of this alpine splendor!

& you? Are you well? I hope to hear from you soon. D tells me the post is usually slow to arrive this near to winter, but I'll positively *die* if I have to wait another day to read your reply!

Ever your chatterbox, nomad, & co-conspirator,

—Thomas

Reel #2 – "Into the Mines"
Format: 35mm celluloid
Length: 21:38
Description: The film begins with a shot of twin columns of miners, one column entering the Prospero Mine, the other exiting as one shift replaces the other. Notably, the departing column, many of the men mustachioed, show exuberant smiles as they pass the camera. At 00:47, a closeup shows a sizeable chunk of magnetite (iron ore) in the gloved hands of a miner, while another miner holds a handful of small crystals, most likely garnets. From 00:59 to 06:52, the film shows life in the company town, a cluster of log cabins built in a clearing at the base of Roughneck Mountain. Many scenes show the presence of wives and children among the workers, as well as the workings of a

schoolhouse where miners' children learn grammar and mathematics. At 04:19, a chalkboard is shown, with the alchemical symbols for fire, earth, and iron (identical to the "male" symbol ♂) drawn alongside a basic multiplication table. Another unidentified symbol appears beneath the alchemical figures: a centipede, beside which the word "FATHER" is drawn. Beneath this symbol, a pair of antlers appear, beside which is the word "FOLLOWER." Other scenes in this section show the medical care miners receive with camp doctors and a recreational hall where miners listen to music on phonographs. From the 7th minute to 19:02, the film then shows the daily work of the miners in the shafts, detailing their methods and equipment, which ranges from simple pickaxes to dynamite to carbide lamps and gasoline-powered pumps. Starting at 08:35 till 10:42, the film showcases a very innovative (for 1912) technique of filming from the front of a mine cart as it descends into the tunnels, giving a first-person perspective. At 11:01, miners begin slipping sticks of dynamite into pre-drilled holes in preparation for blasting. At 11:21, the rock is blasted, and after the smoke clears a viscous, black substance seeps up from the blasting site and subsequently many of the miners will be shown coated in the same liquid. From 13:01 to 13:59, a scene shows miners loading ore into carts. From 13:52, rat-sized insects resembling centipedes can be seen swarming over the miners, who continue working without interruption. After more scenes in the mines, 17:45 to 17:53 depicts teams of miners outside of the mine struggling in concert with oxen and a Lombard steam hauler to drag chains and ropes paying into the mineshaft, as if trying to haul something immense up to the surface. Whether they are successful or not isn't shown. The final three minutes, from 19:02 to 21:38, is a continuous static shot of the mouth of the Prospero Mine, an almost perfect circle cut into the mountainside.

Postcard – "The Chapel in the Woods"
Postmarked: November 22nd, 1912.
From: Thomas Kampel, Roughneck Junction, Adirondack Park, NY.
To: Dorothea Kampel, 635 Park Ave, #23, New York, NY.
Obverse: A charcoal sketch of a wooden structure surrounded by snow-laden pines and spruces and hemlocks. The structure depicted is rustic and simple, with certain design elements borrowed from early modern European cottages such as an A-frame hay-thatched roof with eaves that nearly reach the snowy ground. There are footsteps in the snow leading toward the chapel's

circular wooden door. Two sets of human feet, and between them hoofprints closely resembling moose prints (two thick teardrops with a pair of dots underneath). The hoofprints fall in pairs, like the human tracks beside them. A thick billow of black smoke rises from the chapel's chimney, and in lieu of a cross a set of moose antlers decorates the gable, while centipedes have been etched into the door.

Reverse: The writing is sloppier than in prior postcards, with many words illegible or crossed out. Unlike the previous postcards, the message is written in pencil rather than pen.

The message reads:

> Beloved Dora,
>
> There are beautiful songs here, some [sung?] by human voices such to drown ~~us~~ me and others of a music no mortal [throat?] could shape. I have come out here ten times now, in between my work, my important work, and listened until my face ~~was~~ became [entirely?] windburnt. I have not received your correspondence, but I trust we ~~shall~~ will see each other soon, & to [hold?] your warm hand in mine will be better medicine than what the camp ~~quack~~ doctor has prescribed me. The world is bigger & older than we think, & the wars we [humans?] wage are schoolyard scuffles compared to the TRUE war. I want to help fight that war, but I'm afraid I may not be strong enough. If the Follower accepts me, then all will be well. ~~& if not~~ Give my best to the neighbors, & keep Caroline SAFE. I have much to teach both of you when my ~~duty~~ work is finished & I return to the city's lights. I am positively sick of all the LOVE I feel. Sick of love for you, & I ache for our reunion. All is well, [illegible]—I am a guest here.
>
> He who [advocates?] on behalf of your soul,
>
> —Thomas

Reel #3 – "Expiation"

Format: 35mm celluloid

Length: 12:12

Description: The reel begins with a long, brooding shot of a crackling bonfire built from thick logs and a tall pile of branches. In the background, a structure built with an A-frame roof of thatched hay hovers like a rumor in the shadows beyond the fire's reach. At 00:39, two figures walk into frame and come to stand between the camera and the bonfire. Both wear robes embroidered with alchemical symbols. The figure to the left is recognizable by his hair and mustache as BW Riser. The figure to the right towers over Riser despite its hunched posture, and its robes conceal its shape, but there is the suggestion of some rigid, wide structure underneath its hood. The scene then changes, and now the shadows of the flickering bonfire roll as dark, oily waves over the assembled faces of three separate columns of people. Most are men, but within the ranks of all three columns are a smattering of women and even a few young children. The rightward column, comprising a dozen men and two women all standing upright, are dressed in robes like Riser's. The middle column, some twenty men, five women, and three children, are all kneeling. They are dressed in common cold-weather clothes, but even in the low lighting and poor film quality their discomfort is evident as gusts of snow blow through their ranks. The final, leftward column is thirteen strong—nine men and four women, no children. These people lay prostrate in the snow, their naked backs heaving and writhing in the cold, their hands stretched out in front of them, trussed with rope bindings. Each column is inspected, given several seconds of screentime before the camera cuts briefly back to Riser and the hooded giant. From 01:48 to 06:23, the camera observes ritualistic dances and pantomimes performed by the robed members of the rightward column as they circle the bonfire. Several of these performers shed their robes, revealing themselves naked underneath, while one of the disrobed men wears a costume that dimly resembles certain feathered regalia of various tribal societies, only in place of feathers rigid, carved spines of wood radiate from his body, approximating the form of insectile legs. Another performer, also stripped down, wears moose antlers, and at 02:27 the antlered performer begins walking on his hands and knees in the snow, until the centipede performer embraces him. The pair then rise together, link arms, and dance with abandon. From 04:29 to 06:23, the robed men, both stripped and clothed, fall to the ground and writhe and wriggle on the frozen earth like worms. At 06:24, the camera fixates on some large burrows in the earth in an indeterminate location from which naked men wriggle out, crawling on their bellies over the snow. At 07:09, the camera fixes on the chapel, showing an immensely magnified full moon presiding over the bonfire revel. At 07:24, the camera focuses on Riser with a medium, chest-high closeup shot. Riser holds a heavy woodcutting axe (single beveled broadaxe) over his head, and begins to speak.

At 07:52, a large, bearded man in logger's clothes—a head taller than Riser but still dwarfed by the hooded giant—comes and accepts the broadaxe from Riser. After the axeman takes a few practice swings on a nearby stump, he then proceeds to the leftward column. Many of the prostrate have stopped moving, but some still try to squirm away. From 08:16 to 10:36, the camera watches with the unflinching nerve of glass and celluloid as the axeman moves up and down the column, carrying out a rote process with mechanical certainty and efficiency: a boot on the spinal column, pressing the victim into the dirt, followed by a powerful downward stroke, hewing heads from necks as easily as loggers hew the bark from timber. Some of the heads roll away from the bodies, some settle in place where they fall. The camera keeps filming, the glass eye panning steadily to match the axeman's progress, the cameraman's hand turning the crank ever faithfully. The scene breaks from slaughter only once, from 09:52 to 10:09, to show some of the beheaded carcasses being carried by the plainclothes initiates to the human burrows, and dumping them at the tunnel mouths, whereupon eager pale hands rise and grope like worms and find their prizes, dragging them into the dark. At 10:36, the camera fixes on Riser once more, then shifts focus to the other figure, the forgotten giant, who now sheds its cloth cocoon, revealing its hidden form. At 10:52, the Follower stands revealed: ancient, impossibly tall and lanky, dark and hirsute, wrong-faced, antlered, a thing fallen into the taxonymic cracks between primate and cloven-hoofed beast, warped but powerful. Standing to its full height, the creature seems impossible, its human legs too skinny to support its broad moose antlers. The Follower somehow shambles forth on its toothpick limbs and awkward hoofed feet, and now its belly, a vessel engorged and visibly squirming with a living manifest, juts out from its skeletal frame. From 11:09 to 12:01, the camera dares to stray closer to the Follower, to see from close as it kneels before the middle column of initiates. The Follower opens its broad, cervine jaw and lets its tongue dangle limp as its mouth becomes a chute for the squirming passengers of its body, and the initiates open their own mouths to receive, one by one, the gift. Centipedes travel from one mouth to another. Some initiates manage to accept the gift without falling, others convulse and fall to their sides and writhe and wriggle in the snow and dirt. The final image, from 12:02 to 12:12, is of Riser, shot such that the engorged moon crowns his head. A shadow falls over the brilliant moon, the jagged, many-legged silhouette of a centipede.

Postcard – "My Window at Dawn"

Postmarked: December 1ˢᵗ, 1912.

From: Thomas Kampel, Roughneck Junction, Adirondack Park, NY.

To: Dorothea Kampel, 635 Park Ave, #23, New York, NY.

Obverse: A pencil sketch of a simple box-frame window. The sketch's style is much less elaborate than the other postcard images, with much less detailed shading work.

Reverse: The writing is more restrained and lucid than the prior postcard's message, with no strikethroughs or illegible words. The message reads:

> Beloved Dora,
>
> I'm happy to report I'll soon be home. Mr. Drane and Mr. Riser are satisfied with my work & have given their blessings for me to return to the city. Today is my final morning here on the mountain, & soon I'll be on a train to sinch shut the frayed threading that ties us two together. Please don't take to heart any silliness I might have stained my last postcard with. The truth is, darling, I've been feeling *positively* something other than myself lately. It's been days since I've seen the sun. But the fog is beautiful in its own way too. If this postcard reaches you before I do, & if I fail to turn up, please don't look for me, & don't worry—all that will mean is that I've found somewhere safe. Give my love to Caroline.
>
> Your ever devoted husband,
>
> Thomas

SOMEPLACES IT'S TURNIPS

Dad always talks to you in salvos when he's upset. "You don't want to see the potato?" he asks you. "Every man in town wants to see the potato. They pay top dollar to see the potato. Hell, breadline men would give teeth for a glimpse of the potato. So why don't you want to see it? What's wrong with you?"

You wish you could tell him. You wish you wanted the things you should want, what normal teenage boys want. Dad walks beside you, his arm draped around your shoulder, like he fears you'll lose your nerve.

He's been talking for half an hour now, since you left the house. "Someplaces it's turnips," he says, shaking his head. "Can you imagine? Turnips."

You tell him you're glad you don't live in a turnip town.

"Damn right," he says. "We didn't fight all those wars and heap all those corpses on foreign beaches just so we could pay money to see *turnip shows*."

The potato barn with its red corrugated roof stands in a cornfield at the edge of town. Plowfurrows from when crops still grew here wrinkle the brown earth. Already a crowd has gathered outside the barn's doors, some twenty men, though it's not even sundown and it's the second week of the potato show. For a hopeful second you wonder if the old man will be discouraged by the crowd and give up. No such luck. Dad has two tickets he bought yesterday morning. The men waiting outside grumble about the foreigners camping in the woods, the promised government supplies that still haven't arrived, how the nights keep getting longer. But at least we have the potato show. Yeah, at least.

Cold wind blasts the feeling from your fingers.

Inside the barn, the air is warm and stale with old men's breath, cigar smoke, and the sweetly stink of mildewed alfalfa.

"This'll make you a man," Dad says. "Squeeze the sissy right out of you."

You almost hope he's right. It'd be simpler that way.

When it's your turn, Big Jim Hoskins is waiting to take your tickets, a patriot's smile on his face. Big Jim lost a hand in the last war, but he won't tell anyone what it was that bit it off. He takes your tickets in his hand, then with his hooked prosthesis peels back the cloth partition. You and Dad pass through the curtain—stitched from old horseblankets—and you see the girl before you notice the potato.

Darlene, or maybe her name is Charlene. Marlene? You don't know her well and you've certainly never seen her naked or with her hair down, but you're sure it's the girl from your math class who once lent you her protractor, and somehow that recognition needles you more than anything. Sweating under the glare of kerosene lamps, she looks like a dewy peach. Is she as happy as her blissful, virginal smile and the rolled-back whites of her eyes tell? You wonder if she's in pain.

It must hurt her, the way the potato feeds on her. Gorged to the size of a toddler, the potato she cradles is a dull garnet color, tumescent with starch and blood, bearded in splotches of caked soil, and rosetted with white carbuncle sprouts. With pallid, barbed flagella, the spud has latched to the girl, drinking her drop by drip by drop through tiny pricks in her skin.

You know what's needed of you; you don't even wait for Dad to say it to agree with him.

"It's beautiful," you hear yourself say.

Dad's arm wraps around your shoulders, gentleness and warmth in the gesture now that he's found his son again.

PAPER WINGS IN THE HOUSE OF LIGHT

Day whatever. Month six of the end of the world, which, like the ending of a bad musical, dragged on and on. Clive was going back to the city he'd once called home, taking the scenic route through the forests. In the earlier days—month one and two—when the ghouls were fresh and limber, going off-road had been unthinkable. But it was different now; the ghouls were slowing down and thinning out, and the last couple weeks he'd gone entire days without seeing one. There were fewer people too—thankfully—and fewer cars on the roads, but much like the symptoms of Headrot, once you spotted a car it was probably too late for you.

So here he was, taking the slow way through the forest, batting vines and gropy branches with his crowbar, when something flashed in his peripherals through the green, the glister of sunlight on glass. A mirrored surface could mean a lot of things, most of them bad.

"Could be a car, Clive. Maybe with supplies still inside."

"Sure, Clive. And maybe there's a cute little ghoul baby still strapped into the car seat waiting to rip off a piece of you."

These days he was always arguing with himself; sometimes he won, sometimes he lost. This time, Clive convinced Also-Clive to gamble and follow the overgrown footpath toward the glimmer of light. Through the tangle of vines and brambles, he emerged into a clearing, and there he saw the source of the shimmer: a house with a roof of solar panels. The dying sun coruscated off the panels, while behind the house's dark eyes little lights shone. *Electricity.*

The house was alone in the woods, with only a small paved road that led into an arbor of oaks. It was bigger than any house he or any of his friends—the old, long-dead ones, not the end of the world friends he'd made more recently and who were now also dead—had ever lived in, but still not what you'd call a mansion. Two stories, probably four bedrooms, a three-car garage, a flower garden out front now overgrown with weeds. The façade of the house was also swallowed by kudzu, a beautiful thing as nature's revisions of man's work tended to be.

He spent most of the remaining daylight scouting out the place. The last time he'd seen an electrified home had been back in month four, when he was traveling with Anthony and Jenn. It was a house like this, out in the country, untouched by the urban hordes or opportunistic survivors, kept by seemingly kind people. He was the only one to escape the Cult of the Thorn-God. Anthony ended up as a bowl of soup, and as for Jenn, well, maybe she was cooking up a cauldron of soup right now in her God's name.

"Best not to think of it, Clive."

"You're right—task at hand, task at hand."

If the place was guarded, he couldn't see any signs of it. He knew what to look for: tripwires, noisemakers, mirrors, a slightly ruffled patch of grass under which a man sits in a hole in the dirt waiting for someone to walk by, etcetera. All he found was a patch of turned earth with a shovel staked into it—a makeshift grave.

With daylight fading, he made his move and crept across the lawn, moving from cover to cover, before reaching the side of the house. He contemplated smashing a window, wondering whether the house would have a working security alarm, but then, in a flourish of random inspiration or madness or whatever Also-Clive might have called it, he walked to the front door and tried the handle. As he took the handle, he read a name engraved over the mailslot: *S. Roache.*

The door opened, a gasp of dust shook loose as he stepped inside, like it hadn't budged in weeks. He stood in the anteroom for a few minutes, listening for footsteps, chattering teeth, the rasp of a shotgun getting racked, anything. But nothing stirred. The house's interior was clean, orderly. In the anteroom there was a couch and some chairs and a neat stack of women's magazines on a coffee table. In the old days it would have been plush but not opulent, but by the standards of month six it was a palace. He gravitated like a moth toward a reading lamp situated next to an armchair and experimentally, cautiously, pressed the button.

When a weak but steady pale gleam washed over him, his mouth parted as if he might drink that heatless light. He turned it off and then moved on to the next room, his crowbar at the ready. He still had The Professor's 9mm tucked into the seat of his jeans, but only with the one bullet left, and it was earmarked for a special purpose.

The hallway led to several rooms, and Clive checked each one of them, then Also-Clive checked them again because he didn't trust Clive to spot a mole on his own asscheek. Living room, linen closet, spare room, and finally, kitchen.

In the kitchen, he set down his crowbar on the granite-topped island and explored its compartments. Glasses, bowls, and utensils lay forgotten in the yawning dishwasher's racks, clean but covered in a fine layer of dust. The fridge was, unsurprisingly, filled with rotten perishables and cottonball mold fluffs of various hues, but he'd seen and smelt worse.

The pantry was sparse, not in a raided-by-scavengers way but in a forgot-to-go-to-the-store-this-week way. The cupboards, on the other hand, guarded a wealth of non-perishables. Beans (canned and dried), spam, peas, fruit salad, condensed milk, rice, flour, salt, sugar. Again, Clive and Also-Clive listened, agreeing this was too good to be true, but neither of them could hear a thing.

He was searching the drawers for a can opener when the glimmer of a lightbulb on the serpentine neck of the sink faucet caught his eye.

"No way, Clive," he whispered to himself. "It's been months since the waterlines stopped flowing."

But still, Also-Clive had to try. The tap turned in his hand and that first gurgle spurted out, followed by a steady glut of clean water. Maybe the house had its own well, with a pump powered by the solar energy. He splashed his face and worked at the layers of sediment the days and weeks had caked into his skin, then he gargled and spat, then he massaged the fresh, cool water into his scalp. If someone—human or ghoul—had walked in on him in that moment, he'd have been a dead man, but he'd have died happy, his tears mingling with the tap water.

Once the initial rush of euphoria wore off, he took a glass from the dishwasher and filled it to the brim. The water was cold like the bowels of the earth it gushed from, and pure and clean-tasting, not grimy like the boiled rainwater of his canteen. How long had it been since he'd drunk from a glass? Month two, maybe day fifty (he still counted days back then) it was, when they raided a podunk roadside bar and got sick from whiskey and tequila giving The Professor a proper wake, only a few days after The Professor infected himself with the vial of ghoul slime he'd believed was the key to curing Headrot. Clive believed the vial breaking and the crud getting in The Professor's eyes was an accident, but Also-Clive thought The Professor broke it intentionally, a poetic way of conceding defeat to his implacable protozoic foe. Whatever the case,

Clive and his friends got stupid drunk, and ended up blasting a Hank Williams Jr. cassette from a boombox they'd found behind the bar until every ghoul within a country mile was laying siege to the place.

"Why are you still alive, Clive?" he muttered.

"Dumb luck, Clive," Also-Clive answered, almost too quickly.

He found a can opener and opened some corned beef hash, which a quick sniff confirmed as edible. Looking at the gas range, he contemplated frying it up in a pan, but hunger won out over refinement, and instead he stuffed tepid fingerfuls of grease and meat past his lips, shuddering from scalp to toenail with each salty morsel of vacuum-sealed civilization.

At a certain point, maybe halfway through the can, he started crying again. Ugly-crying, Jenn had called it. Well, lately he got ugly two or three times a day.

Midway through a heaving sob, he blinked his eyes and saw something move past his face. A graceful flutter of two large wings the yellow of old paper, now orbiting the overhead light fixture.

Neither Clive nor Also-Clive had ever seen a butterfly so large, as wide as his hand. It darned the air, its lanceolate wings opening and closing like the pages of a book. The smell of a library drifted down to Clive's nose, and again he shuddered, ambushed by a stream of good-old-days memories. With a sudden dip, the butterfly swooped away, out of the kitchen, and it was then Clive heard the unmistakable grunt of a chair leg dragging on floorboards somewhere upstairs.

Upstairs—neither of the Clives had thought to even scope out the upstairs, so distracted by the promise of food and water.

Footsteps, slow and deliberate, stressed the floorboards overhead and sent micro-tremors through the bones of the house. These tremors vibrated on the tips of the raised hairs on Clive's arm as he reached for his crowbar, remembering what world he lived in as if awoken from a dream.

Muffled by distance and the mediation of the floors, ceilings, and interstices, there now came music. Gentle brass instruments and the mellow purr of a famous old-time jazz singer whose name he couldn't remember. The music spread its tendrils through the house.

Clive and Also-Clive conferred in the privacy of their skull—maybe it was a good sign, that whoever it was didn't know he was there. It would be easier to sneak up on them with the music muffling his footsteps. Or maybe it was a trap, just to lure him there, to make him complacent.

With the sure, soft step of an apex predator, he ascended the staircase. Another butterfly, paler than the first, floated past his ear, tickling him. There were other butterflies when he got to the top of the staircase, where he followed the thread of music down the hallway to a door left partway open, through which a sliver of rosy light escaped.

Taking a deep breath, Clive listened. Aside from the music, he heard steady breathing, the creak of a chair, and what sounded like humming. It sounded like a woman.

One hand on the grip of The Professor's gun, the other white-knuckled around the crowbar, he shouldered the door open. The door was his ally, and opened smoothly, without creak or whine. The music played on from an antique record player with warm, soothing sibilance pouring into the silences between notes.

The room was an office, or a study—he never really knew the difference—with wood-paneled walls, a casement window, and a gorgeous desk of immense length, carved from tropical wood, at which the room's sole occupant was seated. A profusion of frizzy gray hair spilled out from the hunched head, while bony elbows, wrinkled and spotted, rested on the edge of the desk. The old woman hummed along to the music, while Clive crept closer, raising his crowbar in preparation for a strike. People and ghouls weren't too different—if you could do it quietly, the best defense against them was to kill on sight.

A butterfly alighted on the teeth of his upraised crowbar. Its wings folded shut, and it became so thin, so two-dimensional it almost disappeared. The butterfly perched there only for the space between two breaths, and then rose to cavort with two of its kindred, but in that instant, the woman in her chair lifted her head and turned around.

"Simon?" she said.

What had been a fragile eggshell skull sheathed in an old scalp and tufted with hair had grown a face, and the face had spoken, and now Clive was eye to eye with a person. Holding the crowbar high, caught in the act, he felt something he hadn't felt in weeks, months maybe.

It's called embarrassment, Clive.

Thanks, Also-Clive.

She had a plain, round face, leathery and worn. She had dark eyelids shot through by squiggly gray veins and thin, chapped lips.

"Simon? What do you have there?"

Was Simon her husband, her son? Was he out gathering supplies, would he be back any moment? Simon...S. *S. Roache*, the name on the mail slot, the man of the house. Clive lowered the crowbar as a butterfly flitted past his nose. He didn't speak.

The thick lenses of the woman's tortoiseshell-framed eyeglasses magnified her dark irises with their cataracts like two drops of bluish milk. She may not have seen him, but she knew he was there, and if he ran away now that she couldn't describe him to anyone would make little difference—to say a strange man had been in the house would be enough. Go on, crack her gourd, Clive. Easy for you to say where you are, Also-Clive. He'd killed people, of course— who hadn't? But never like this. Always they were trying to kill him, or running away, or pleading while reaching for the knife behind their back, or still asleep. Never staring through him with a vacant little smile.

The woman sniffed the air, and he could see in the tension of her muscles how she was trying not to make a face at his smell. "I'm sorry, I thought you were my husband. Who are you?" She had a bit of an accent; hard to place.

Also-Clive screamed to stay silent, but—maybe it was the way the old lady spoke to him, dredging up a vestigial politeness in him—Clive spoke up. "My name's Clive."

"Clive. I don't know a Clive, I don't think. Are you a friend of Simon's?"

"Yeah, that's right."

He took a small step forward, experimentally. She didn't react. From where he stood, he could see past the woman's head to what was on her desk. A few sheets of paper, one of which she'd been scribbling on, a pen, a glass of water freckled with tiny bubbles, and a small brass bell.

"If you're looking for Simon, he went down into the basement a while ago to fetch me some preserves. Maybe you'll find him there."

"Oh, that's all right," Clive said. "I can wait for him."

So, Simon was in the basement?

"Has Carla taken care of you?" Mrs. Roache asked.

"Who?"

"Carla, our—well, she's the maid, but I like to think of her as part of the family."

"No, Mrs. Roache. I haven't seen her."

"I'm very sorry, she's usually better," Mrs. Roache said, and groped around for the little bell. Clive told himself to strike, but his arms stayed slack at his sides, and he watched her lift the bell and tinkle it a few times. It wasn't even louder than the music, and his gut unclenched. No one would hear it. No one who wouldn't have heard him in the kitchen. "Carla?" Mrs. Roache called, pronouncing the name with a slight trill.

"Let's not bother her, I don't need anything," Clive said.

There was something else on the desk he hadn't noticed until now. A plain white pill bottle, unmarked, its cap unscrewed and missing. He recognized it straight away—lethenum. It was at the start of month two, when the government started including lethenum in their airdrops to survivor colonies, back when there were still airdrops. 48 mg of oblivion per caplet, perfect for soothing those irreparably broken by the collapse of society into unending serenity. Clive himself never took it, but then he'd always been straight edge.

"I'd take care of you, Mister Clive, but I'm writing a letter."

Clive's nerves relaxed some. So did Also-Clive's. No one with even an ounce of their wits left would be writing a letter now. Butterflies circled like his thoughts over his head. Here was an old woman, nearly blind and senile, or else so scorched by the lethenum she'd taken she could barely remember her own name. She wouldn't tell anyone about him—if there was even anyone to tell.

Maybe he could afford to relax. "Why don't I go downstairs and fix us both some tea, Mrs. Roache? Something to go with the preserves Simon's fetching."

"Oh, you don't have to."

"It's no trouble at all."

"You're a dear."

She returned to writing her letter.

Clive caught his breath once he was out of the study. Butterflies followed him out into the hallway. Part of him was wishing he'd bashed her skull open and saved himself from the entanglements of human society. Most of him was simply confused. Also-Clive had nothing. For the first time in weeks, he felt unthreatened, and there was something incredibly threatening in that.

"Keep your eyes open, Clive."

"Always do, Clive."

He started down the hallway. Maybe he'd make a pot of coffee or tea after all. Why not? Maybe this could be his home. Near the staircase landing, Clive stopped to study a row of framed photographs, portraits. Most of them featured the same man, a hefty bald guy with a satisfied face and a pink complexion. He looked familiar, and after a moment the memory came to him of a local politician named Roache, someone in the city government. Clive remembered participating in a protest once a few years ago where Roache was the man of the hour in the worst way.

Roache was probably dead now, or else flopping through a cornfield chattering his teeth. In some of the photos there was a woman with him, young enough to be his daughter, with a head of bright red hair and a practiced, demure smile. In one photo, she was in a white wedding gown, Mr. Roache standing opposite her.

Absent from any of these photos was Mrs. Roache. A butterfly alighted on the shimmering glass of the photograph and unfolded its wings. The irregular black markings scrawled across these yellow insects became clearer on this specimen, and it seemed to Clive the patterns were words of cramped cursive. On this butterfly, six inches across, he made out the words *Dearest Simon*, and then it fluttered away.

Down in the kitchen, where everything was perfect and quiet, he found a tin of loose tea and started boiling water in the kettle on the stove. He set his crowbar down and watched the steam begin to form in the spout, first a rumor of pale vapor, then a whisker, then a white plume. One butterfly flew too close and its wings crumpled, dampened, now divested of all lift. He watched the butterfly flop and spasm and then settle into its final shape, a spiral of damp yellow paper. His throat turned dry and he swallowed. Watching it die hurt more than he'd hurt in months. When he unfolded the paper to see what the markings said, all he found was a smear of running ink.

He poured the water into two prepared cups and smiled to watch the fine white foam form on the surface of the brewing tea. He'd missed these little comforts. As he steeped in nostalgia, a pair of butterflies frolicking with each other collided with him, nicking his skin with the sharp edges of their wings.

Over his head, more butterflies followed. He tracked them to where they rounded the corner. Curious, he took up his crowbar and followed. The butterflies were moving like a flock of birds, homing in on something. Their trail ended at a nondescript door. The butterflies slipped through the crack and disappeared into whatever the door concealed. From the feel of the cold air rising through the door, he reckoned it led to a basement.

"Well, you're smarter than this, Clive."

"Are we though?"

He tried the knob. Locked.

"Well, that's it, Clive. No point going further."

He put his ear to the door and listened. Nothing, but silence wasn't always a guarantee of safety. Clive told himself and Also-Clive he was interested in what Mr. Roache might have kept in his basement. Guns, hopefully. Or camping gear, something useful.

But if he was honest with himself, he just loved a good mystery, and what was a crowbar for if you didn't use it to pry?

The door and its lock gave up easily, but not without a powerful racket that echoed into the darkened cavern of the basement. He waited in the light, face to face with the black below, crowbar ready to cave skulls and crumple kneecaps. But nothing stirred. He descended the first step and groped around until he found a string-pull light-switch.

He pulled the string, a lightbulb crackled, sputtered, and fizzled out, and the dark remained illimitable. Good thing he had a flashlight. Not much of one—one of those little travel-sized things people used to keep in their glove compartments—but enough for his purposes. The light it made was weak and flickered, but it was enough to shine the steps beneath his feet. His shoes echoed off the concrete steps as he slowly made his way into the cold space. A ripe smell of mildew hit him after a few steps, and with it a sour, metallic undercurrent of old, stale blood. But of course, everything had been too clean so far. No house, no matter how remote or self-sufficient, could be untouched by the end of the world.

Butterflies flitted like sere dreams through the cone of his flashlight. Soon he reached the bottom of the stairs. There he stood, sweeping his flashlight through the dense gloom full of butterflies and billowing dust. Here, where the merest murmur became an exclamation, the butterfly wings susurrated like turning pages in a classroom during quiet study time.

His flashlight flickered off, flickered on, and then off again. He shook it back to life. The beam found something in the far corner of the basement, an unmistakable human shape. The sight of this made him jump a little, and as he did, his ankle caught on something—a length of chain—and he stumbled. As he stumbled and the chains jangled, clothed limbs rustled in the dark.

Clive, you idiot. This was how it happened. Just one little mistake, one moment of recklessness was all it ever took.

He kicked and thrashed and struggled to his feet, not knowing where the ghoul might come at him from but knowing he had to move fast.

Nothing happened. A drum thumped in his chest and he held out his crowbar, but there was no sound now but his own heartbeat and the flap of butterfly wings.

He traced the length of the chain on the floor with his light to the corner, where the body had startled him. What had been a man sat up straight against the wall had now slumped over, still and moving. Another smaller shape lay next to it—red hair glittering like copper wire.

Even under the uncertain illumination of his flashlight, it was obvious they were dead. The thing was, there was "dead," and there was dead-dead. His heart still in his throat, he approached with caution. The closer he got, the more detail resolved from the gloom. No question, these were ghouls. All the signs were there. The fingertips were gone, gnawed off. One of the first things a ghoul does is eat its own fingers. The patches of skin he could see were dry and taut, the frames wizened to scarecrow-like thinness. There was no smell of rot, only old blood smell. Ghouls, whether they're moving-around-dead or dead-dead, don't decompose. No scavenger will touch them, not a crow, not a rat, not even bacteria. They mummify, almost like one of those bog bodies he once read about. When he got within a body's length, he made out the trickles of crusted slime—a dark gray grease—on the ex-woman's face, running from the shriveled eyes and the earholes and nostrils. The Professor once explained Headrot worked by melting the prefrontal cortex, and those trickles of slime were the "deliquesced remnants of the brain extruded through the head's orifices."

He came to within four feet, three, and stopped. These ghouls weren't moving, but he knew they could play possum, some primitive ambush-predator mechanism retained by the undissolved portions of the brain.

A touch would put it to the test. He prodded the woman with the crowbar, tapping what had been her sternum. Like brittle ice in late autumn, or the fragile daub of a wasp's nest, a bone in the woman's chest snapped against the pressure. That was all.

He turned his attention to the man and hooked the crowbar under the man's slumped head, catching the chin and tilting it up. A shriveled bald head looked up at him and then, with a dry crackle, broke off and rolled free of its scaffolding. The rest of the body slid further down with the same rustle of old clothes that had startled him before.

He exhaled. Good. Dead-dead.

He swept the rest of the basement for anything useful or dangerous. He found a camping lantern in the opposite corner and turned it on, bathing the basement in obnoxious white light. The space looked so much smaller lit up, maybe twenty feet by twenty feet—the size of his studio apartment in the before times. There were useful supplies here, like he'd hoped. Canned foods, batteries, a new portable radio, a raincoat, gardening tools, seed packets, a can of lighter fluid, and a lot of other things. As he stuffed his backpack with whatever he could fit, the butterflies continued to flutter, accreting around the lantern, as cheerfully oblivious to everything as the woman who'd made them.

But she wasn't oblivious when she put the ghouls down here. Reconstructing the tragedy, Clive had to sit down, and Also-Clive sat with him.

An old woman, sheltering with her estranged husband and his young lover. Who had brought the virus in? Maybe it was the maid, the unseen Carla, probably the occupant of the grave outside. She turned first, infected the husband or his mistress, maybe both. Did they chain themselves up, or did Mrs. Roache do it? The infected, even before they turn, are agitated, difficult to reason with as the dread emperor of all fevers cooks their brains into neuron slurry. And yet, if nothing else the world's end has taught him not to underestimate anything human. Did that sweet old woman chain an uninfected person alongside their infected lover while they slowly turned?

The less you think about it, the better, Clive.

But what about the butterflies? Clive formed a theory for that too. Before he got infected, The Professor said something once, about how reality was less a thing people discovered and more something they *created*. Maybe that was true. And maybe there just weren't enough people left in the world to keep the old reality stitched together.

Think that's it, Clive?

How the fuck should I know, Clive?

Maybe it was a flicker of sentimentality, but he put Mr. Roache's head back on its neck, and then to keep it from falling off again buttressed the head against the mistress', leaving them huddled together. He threw a blanket over them, and wondered if they'd been happy before it all happened, if Carla really had been "one of the family" to them, and when it was the estranged Mrs. Roache returned to the house, and how long she kept her wits after corralling her husband and his young mistress in the basement. Was it a kindness to chain them together, or vengeance? It didn't matter anymore. With no one to remember, the truth was whatever he chose to believe.

The cups of tea were cold and oversteeped. He carried them up anyway.

"Mrs. Roache, I'm back," he said as he stepped into the study.

She was at her desk. "Oh." She shuddered when set down the tray with the tea. "I'm sorry, who are you again?"

"A friend of Simon."

"Of course. Very sorry. I'm so forgetful."

As she spoke, she carefully folded a letter and then slid it into the waiting pouch of a yellowed envelope. Clive and Also-Clive held their collective breath as the envelope twisted and reshaped itself, unnoticed by the woman who sat mere inches away. Barely perceptible limbs, like hairs made of ink, wriggled from the crease of the envelope flap, and then from the edge, shimmering with a translucent sheen of ichor, a fresh wing unfurled, then another, and the envelope with its letter inside shuddered into the air, at first square and unwieldy, then, fully shaped, took flight and joined the others circling overhead.

"Has Simon come up yet?"

"I wouldn't wait for him; he'll be down a while. By the way, why do you write letters to him?"

She smiled, something coquettish in the way her lips twisted. "Oh, it's silly, I admit, but we've always written love letters to each other, going back to when he courted me. It's a way to stay young, you know. The world gets older and older, we have to stay young."

The youngest of the butterflies was paler than the rest. Unthinking, he reached for it, and as soon as his finger brushed the lower lobe of its wing, it collapsed and fell as a tattered crumple. He gasped, but then covered his mouth so his breath wouldn't dampen the fragile paper wings.

"We should find Carla," the wife said. "It's so late, and I don't think there's any dinner ready."

"Don't worry. I'll fix myself something on the way out," he said.

"You're not staying?"

"No. I've imposed too much already."

In the kitchen, he found a notepad of lined paper, the kind people used for writing grocery lists or passive-aggressive messages to their spouses. There was a pen next to it. He wrote a short note.

My Dearest Wife,
I'm sorry we left you alone.
—Love, Simon.

He stood over it for a few minutes, both he and Also-Clive waiting for it to unfold its wings and take flight. But nothing happened.

Of course not, Clive. This isn't yours, neither the comfort nor the tragedy.

He left out the front door. Outside, the world buzzed and chittered and rustled with life, untouched and unbothered by the cell phone towers' silence or the skies bereft of airliner contrails. A phoenix world where anything was possible now, like a pointillistic flower grown from a grave. He followed the same path he'd taken back to the woods, and when he'd come to the familiar trees, Clive looked behind him and saw the leaves and moss had filled his footsteps, and the branches and vines had closed, walling off any glimmer of the house of light.

HARVESTMAN

I.   *Then.*

When I woke up, I knew from the sound of grunting chair legs and the rasp of a broom on the floorboards that it was a cleaning day. It was 1975. I was eight years old, living with Mom and Dad and Grandpa at the farmhouse in the middle of the Blackland Prairie. It was an innocent day in late October, cold was in the air and gold was in the leaves of the cottonwoods growing alongside the Brazos, the ones I could see from my bedroom window.

After breakfast, Mom gave me a choice: help her dust the house, or sort through a box of old photos. I chose the chore that would make me sneeze less. All of the photos in the box were black and white, though some had a buttery tinge to them. Most were from when Grandpa was a young man with a full head of hair and Grandma was still around, some with him in his Marine Corps uniform, but some were from earlier, when he was my age. Looking at those old portraits, I wondered how the smiling, gap-toothed kid with the bowl cut was the same person as the old shoe polish-smelling, question mark-shaped fossil who sometimes woke me in the middle of the night, pacing on the creaky floorboards outside my bedroom. I was too young to recognize that Grandpa was an alcoholic, and had been for most of his life. That he'd grown up in the Great Depression, what Mom called "the spare times." Or that the last time he'd voted in a presidential election, in '68, he'd cast his ballot for George McGovern and segregation. Eight-year-olds don't know these things, much less what they portend.

In all the photos in the box, there was at least one person in frame: Grandpa, or one or both of his parents, or my grandmother, or other dead relatives I never heard about—all portraits, no landscapes. All except one, a snapshot of the field behind the farmhouse, but instead of the open prairie behind the house, a carnival of whimsical tents with high, peaked parapets sat on the shore of the Brazos. It was this photo I was holding when Grandpa walked into the family room. I looked up to see his bloodshot eyes studying me. Mom wasn't in the room anymore—she was dusting the piano in the anteroom now.

"What do you see?" Grandpa asked. His voice was soft, barely more than a whisper, but there was the low, gristly warning of dogsnarl under the words.

I'd always been frightened of him. Even the occasional heat lightning bursts of his kindness were frightening, like the time he bought me a pecan pie and made me eat the whole thing until I puked, and I had to tell Mom and Dad it was my idea to overeat. But his anger was something else, something worse, and I felt it hovering like a thunderhead.

"What do you see?" he asked again, leaning closer. I smelt the fire of whiskey on his breath.

When I told him I saw a carnival, one of his eyes twitched and he grabbed me by my suspenders. "No you don't," he said. "You *can't*. No one can."

But I did see it; I could even almost hear the merry piping of the calliope when I looked at the faded image of the striped tents rising above the prairie.

He shook me just once, enough to get me to yelp, and his grip on me immediately relaxed, and in came Mom asking if everything was okay.

How suddenly Grandpa was smiling. "Oh, just looking at old pictures."

When Mom asked why I looked so scared, Grandpa said he was telling me a war story, which of course Mom didn't like. A smart trick on the old man's part: admitting to a little peccadillo to hide the greater offense.

"He's too young for that stuff," she said.

I didn't say anything. Just like with the pie, I was afraid to make it worse.

As soon as Mom left the room, Grandpa's smile withered. He wasn't as mad as before, but the twitch in his eye was back.

"Can you really see it?" he asked.

I didn't answer at first. He looked like he was about to shake me again, so I found my voice. Yes. Yes, I could see it.

He sat down next to me on the sofa, looking like he'd been punched in the gut. He tapped on the picture. "Can you see a man here? Or something that looks like a man?"

At first I didn't see anything, but then from out of the dark mouth of one of the carnival tent's entrances, a pale, slight figure resolved itself. To this day I'm still not sure if *he'd* materialized or if I just hadn't noticed him before.

"That's Daddy Longlegs," Grandpa said. "Stay away from him. Don't let him get you."

I barely heard what Grandpa was saying; I was watching his twitchy eye and the startled blue veins in his crusty hands.

That night, after dinner, I hunkered in my bedroom, cowering under my sheets while Grandpa and Dad shouted at each other and Mom threatened to call the sheriff—a hollow threat, everyone knew.

It started up when Grandpa told them that they ought to move out of the farm and take their son to live a proper life in a town, or even a city. Dad was the first to raise his voice, but Grandpa was louder. Dad said he grew up here, that this was his house as much as it was Grandpa's, while Mom said Grandpa just wanted to drink himself dead on his lonesome. Grandpa said the farm wasn't right for a little boy to grow up, that he didn't want me to turn out like himself or like Dad. What does it take for a crusty old Texan to say something like that? To admit he's lived wrong, raised his boy wrong. There was something beautiful and unnatural in those words, though I didn't notice it in the moment. When you're afraid of someone, it's easy to miss these things.

It was at this point in the dustup that Dad got worked up enough to start smashing Grandpa's liquor bottles, and that's when the scuffle started. I drew the covers over my head and tried not to listen to them grappling with each other and knocking over chairs.

All of a sudden, I heard the music of the calliope from outside.

It was soft at first. So quiet I thought it was my imagination. But it got louder, loud enough that I could barely hear the fight downstairs anymore, and I was glad for that. The merry piping of a steam organ somewhere distant called me out from under the covers, and when I moved to my window, the panes glowed with the pale splendor of limelight projected from a traveling carnival that had sprung up in the empty hand of the prairie. The striped tents and the colorful ribbons flapping from poles and the giggle of the calliope called me to the window's edge, and soon my hands and my nose were pressed flat to the cold glass. A banner hung over the largest of the tents, and on this banner, golden letters announced that Daddy Longlegs' Traveling Carnival was here, and all were welcome.

His voice found me before I saw him. It was a kindly voice, a gentle voice I wasn't used to hearing from anyone male. This is prairie country; all the men I'd ever known either spoke in a reluctant grumble, a doglike growl, or not at all.

At first I couldn't understand the words, only their pleasant, soothing tone. But by and by distinct words reached me: *Nice little boys...shouldn't fear...such games...such fun...*

When Daddy Longlegs first darkled into view, he looked very small. The spiral-patterned stovepipe barker's hat he wore looked bigger than him. But as he approached the house, his legs lengthened and his body gained depth and roundness, until he appeared as a merrily rotund man on stilts, except his legs were more supple than any wooden frame could be. His clothes were old and dusty, made of dark velvet and studded with large brass buttons of greenish tinge. That his clothes were so old and tattered made me trust he was real—only illusions were perfect, and even little boys know that.

He strode all the way to the house until he was standing outside my window—this upstairs window—staring at me through the glass.

His face was flat and pale and friendly. It looked like a normal face, except the smile was a little wider than it should be.

"Has he hurt you?" Daddy Longlegs asked. "The mean old man?" His lips didn't move when he talked, and the voice came through the window without any muffling, as if he were talking directly into my ear, or even closer than that.

He didn't sound like anyone from Texas, like anyone who'd ever hurt me or made me afraid. He sounded like how I imagined a storybook prince would sound.

I told him no.

"Well, you'd better not give him a chance. Quick, come with me."

Come where, I asked.

"To the carnival, of course."

But how would I get there? Mom and Dad and Grandpa wouldn't let me go, not at this hour.

He tapped on the glass. His fingers were very long. "Open the window and I'll take you along."

The more I looked at his face, the more it seemed less a face of flesh and skin and more a thin layer of off-white paper painted with a semblance of human features. The smile hadn't changed, and although there were shadows around the topography of his creased lips as flesh would cast on flesh, his eyes were without depth, like two little painted commas. His ears were a different color than the rest of his face—little shriveled greendark things like prunes hanging off the sides of his head. I remembered Grandpa once telling me about an unfortunate soldier who'd gotten his face burnt off on Iwo Jima and had to wear a mask to make it seem like there was still something there, and with a ripple of pity I wondered if Daddy Longlegs was the same way. A smell wafted into my bedroom—the warm, sugary aroma of cotton candy.

I was about to open the window when I remembered I'd need shoes and a coat if was going to go to the carnival.

"Fine, fine," Daddy Longlegs said. His face didn't change even as his voice flickered with impatience.

I got my shoes and put on a coat, all the while Daddy Longlegs kept tap-tapping the glass like he was getting short with me, but when I looked, he was still smiling sweet as a chess pie. Downstairs, the shouting had stopped.

I came to the window and struggled with the locks, stiff and rusted, and it was as I'd managed to turn the first one that angry footsteps started thumping up the staircase.

"Hurry," Daddy Longlegs whispered, and as if overhearing him, the footsteps on the stairs became more rapid—a sprint.

I got the second latch open and dragged the window up an inch, and just as I did, Daddy Longlegs leaned forward and his face *shifted*.

His skin—or rather the thin, papery smile masking his true skin—rippled, and while I didn't see his real face, I got a brief glimpse of its inhuman contours, and my heart squirmed and I tried to slam the window shut but Daddy Longlegs already had a finger under the jamb and that one finger was stronger than every ounce of me.

My bedroom door flung open. Grandpa, with a cut lip and a blackened eye, howled and threw himself at the window and together we slammed it shut. Daddy Longlegs, still smiling even as he let out a wrathful sound like the violence of a thousand droning carrion flies, recoiled from the window.

"Get out, get out!" Grandpa shouted, before letting rip a long screed of curses.

Daddy Longlegs receded and then vanished, but the tip of his finger—severed by the window—continued to squirm and twitch. When Mom and Dad barged in, they didn't notice the fingertip, not when Grandpa was lying on the floorboards, gripping his arm and pale as paper.

Grandpa had suffered the first of an eventual trio of heart attacks.

II. *Later.*

Grandpa died in 1980. For half a decade neither of us spoke of what had happened that night in '75 or even breathed a whisper of Daddy Longlegs, as if talking about him might bring him back, until a few nights after Grandpa's second heart attack in the summer of '79, when—as I was visiting him in the hospital—he confided to me that he'd begun to hear the calliope again, for the first time since he was a child. And then, about a week or so before the last and fatal attack, Grandpa whispered to me from his hospital bed that he'd seen Daddy Longlegs in a dream, waiting for him at the end of a long gallery of mirrors. In this dream, Grandpa was walking toward Daddy Longlegs willingly, and the closer he got, past each successive mirror the layers of his years were stripped away until a baby innocent and tender as a caterpillar crawled into Daddy Longlegs' hands to be drawn back into the fog of what comes before and after.

From time to time, I heard the music too. Until I left home. I quit the country for good—too quiet. I lived in cities, big, bustling cities where there was never enough quiet to hear the subterranean piping of a steam organ. I kept the finger in a cigar box, and I took it wherever I moved. Why I kept it I couldn't say, just like I didn't know why Grandpa had never thrown out the photograph. Maybe we couldn't. Maybe these little trinkets were all we had to remind ourselves we weren't crazy.

To anyone else I'd show the finger to, it didn't look like a fingertip, but rather like the husk of a dead insect, remarkable only for its unusual shape and size. Once during my college days, I showed it to a professor, an arachnologist, and he declared it to be an unusual specimen of the arachnid order *Opiliones*, colloquially referred to as "daddy longlegs" or "harvestmen." He asked me if I'd let him keep it for further study, but I said no, perhaps out of some misplaced sentimental attachment, or perhaps because as long as I'd had it, I'd been safe, and if I lost it, well, who knew?

It was also during my college years that I researched the myths of the Harvestman. A figure of murk and terror, a lurer and cajoler of children who cropped up in various guises across different folklores. El Coco in Spain, Babau in Italy, the Ijiraq of Inuit myth. There was the Hungarian legend of Az Arató—probably derived from older Central Asian myths—a lonely, kindly seeming spirit who preyed on children of hardship, steppe orphans with empty stomachs. He'd lure them from their camps or villages and take them to his *kurgan*, where he'd feed them rich foods and play them music whilst cobwebs slithered from the bone-strewn floor of his lair and cocooned them. Though the legends changed depending on cultures, one variable remained constant: the Harvestman offered children whatever they didn't have.

During a German seminar reading of Goethe's poem, *"Der Erlkönig,"* I walked out of the classroom and didn't come back until I'd managed to get my breathing under control. Reading that poem, I was certain Goethe had met Daddy Longlegs too.

I rented apartments near bars, beside train tracks, in ratty neighborhoods where there was always commotion. My girlfriends, and then eventually my wife, got accustomed to me waking them in the middle of the night with yelps and screams. My wife learned how to cradle me back to sleep. In therapy, I tearfully confessed to my therapist that my grandfather abused me. It wasn't a complete lie.

I settled down. I had children of my own, and when I showed them the old photograph, all they saw was an empty prairie.

III.   *Now.*

A week ago, I turned fifty-three. It doesn't feel that old. I don't feel that old. And yet, my oldest daughter has just given birth to a baby girl, my first grandchild. I should be happy.

But I've heard the calliope again. In the suburbs where I've settled down, it's quiet at night. I have nightmares—or maybe that's too strong of a word; I'm not scared of them, and I wake feeling calm—of a long passageway lined with mirrors, and at the end of that passage a paper face smiles at me. Each successive time I dream it up, the distance between me and him shrinks. Dad died of the same flaw as Grandpa, and the heart I inherited from them is a flawed clock that runs too fast. And yet, while that congenital defect seems constant, the other family curse seems to skip a generation.

I've had time to think about it. I've come to believe that it isn't that Daddy Longlegs or the Harvestman or *Der Erlkönig* (or whatever name I might give him) *wants* me. I'm already his, like Grandpa was, a Something briefly borrowed from the Nothing beneath his coat, and certain to return to that Nothing.

The first time I cradle my granddaughter—little Samantha—in my hands, I allow myself to cry, the way Dad and Grandpa never would.

Little Samantha, I hope some of the joy and innocent goodness I see in you is from me.

Little Samantha, I hope I'm wrong about everything, and that you'll live untroubled and die untroubled too.

Little Samantha, I hope I'll live long enough to see you grow, and that you'll never have cause to fear me. I hope I'll live long enough to protect you from what your mother can't know or see, from the Harvestman who waits in his phantom carnival, at the end of the passage of mirrors, deep in his bone-strewn *kurgan*, in his gray, foggy forest, in a place of autumnal chill, limelight glow, and calliope giggle where the inevitable lurks liquid and shifting behind a painted paper smile.

CONCERNING A POND IN MASSACHUSETTS

One – Old Letters in the Stones

I went out into the woods to live my life deliberately, and to learn what the woods had to teach me. No action since, no matter how minor or awful, have I taken without purpose and careful consideration. Some who learn of my prudent and regrettable work will believe my solitude drove me to madness. But if I am now mad, it is rather because I am *not alone*—that none of us truly are.

On the matter of solitude, I find it wholesome to be alone for the greater part of the time. The mass of men lead lives of quiet desperation, and in secluding myself I sought to, if only for a time, escape that desperation. How could I have known, when I planed the boards and raised the frame of my humble cabin, what I would discover lurking under Walden Pond and its surrounding woods?

This is not the first gathering of my writings. A larger, milder account of comparatively halcyon ordeals I have burned. I burned those pages, the work of many months, because a crooked house raised upon a faulty foundation cannot stand and must be cleared to make way for a proper structure. With these pages I hope to house a more clear-eyed accounting of the difficult, indigestible truths I've uncovered in what I had long thought merely a splendid pond sheltered by uncultivated land. Unfortunately, as I have learned, there is no such thing as *uncultivated* land here in Massachusetts, nor, I doubt, anywhere in the world. This earth we inhabit is but a point of space, and we are not the first to have found it.

My journey into more complete consciousness of men's tenuous position on this earth began with an innocuous discovery while hoeing my bean-field on a fair afternoon early in my second summer in the woods. How fondly in kinder times I wrote of my rewarding exertions in the bean-field, tending to the rows, contending with my arch-nemesis the woodchuck (*Marmota monax*), and working myself into a splendid thoughtlessness. In that pasture of tilled earth clothed by the broad leaves of the beans, I had found arrow-heads and other traces of the Indians who once lived in these woods, but on the day in question I found something else, artifacts of an even older nation. My hoeing dislodged four stones of more or less equal shape and heft, simple chips of shale that fit snugly in the cup of my palm. Each stone etched with a different glyph. It was unquestionable that intent and intelligence chiseled these shapes, but what manner of man, if indeed men, shaped them, I could not and cannot say. I first took them for cuneiform, but they matched no alphabet I could recognize. Although the Indians of latter days possess no written language, I could not rule out that an older, long-extinguished tribe might have made the stones and sown them in what would become my bean-field.

As I no longer possess the stones, I cannot show them to any living soul, nor can I render their likeness from memory to paper. My one attempt to draw sketches of the symbols, that I might send them to my learned friend and mentor, Waldo, ended in a conflagration. The ink had not yet dried on the page when the paper caught blaze and burned to ash. I nearly lost my writing desk to the incident. Being a rational man, my mind proffered explanations for why the paper burned. A loose cinder from my hearth, or from the stack of the locomotive that passes twice a day through the woods, or from the smoking pipe of an itinerant town fellow. These were all more acceptable than to believe the symbols themselves possessed some supernatural protection against their replication, and I clung to this self-inveiglement as lichens cling to stone.

And yet, I did not attempt again to copy down the stones, which soon disappeared from my desk, crumbled to dust. This was only the first of my encounters with the impossible, and one more sublime than terrible.

Two – What I Found in the Bean-Field

Later in the summer, on an August day when my beans were nearly ripened for picking and trading, and at such a remove in weeks from the discovery of the stones that I had nearly regained my former serenity, I was hoeing the rows when my hoe encountered a certain meaty resistance. Scraping away the dirt around the point of contact, the blade unearthed a pale, spongy root the girth of a child's wrist. I scraped and dug with hoe and shovel around the root, which seemed to plump a great depth into the soil. Having surrendered the whole of that afternoon to this pursuit, I worked till dusk excavating the thing. The more of it I uncovered, the more that its powerful stench, like bad meat and shoe polish, increased in potency. It was soon evident what I'd found was no tree root.

The first appendage I'd found and sliced into was a leg. A skinny leg that ended in a crude semblance of a foot tipped in little tuber toes. Another leg I uncovered, and these legs led down, deeper into the dirt, till I excavated a flabby, sallow trunk that led to two withered arm-like projections, tipped in deltas of fibrous black wires where hands might be on the human form. As much as I was disgusted by the smell and shape of this fungal effigy, I could not stop myself from digging further, until at last I found the head.

It was an evil-looking thing. I do not use that word often, nor ever lightly, but I could not call it anything else, could not help but loathe what I had found. I call it a fungal effigy, for the flesh resembled the texture of mushrooms, and because its shape was akin to a crude likeness of human form, like a straw king burned in Revolutionary times, or like a lumpen man a child shapes from clay. It had eyes and ears and a nose, or at least the rudiments of them, like lumps left unchiseled by the sculptor. The mouth, however, was different. The flesh around the curvature of the lip blackened and became dry, even abrasive, and these lips, bent in what I can only describe as a mischievous smile, sheathed rows of teeth like darning needles, and these were made from a material harder than the surrounding flesh.

The light was failing, and the darker the world's aspect became, the greater the loathing and dread incurred by the effigy's presence. And yet greater still was my curiosity, my wonder at finding such a strange specimen, which I would have assumed dead were it not for the remarkable sight of the wound my hoe had inflicted mending before my eyes. It was alive, but dormant, or perhaps, like the mushrooms it resembled in texture, inert by design.

Thunder grumbled as storm clouds descended upon Lincoln and the surrounding woods, including my little plot. I cannot account now why I lifted the strange thing and carried it to my wood-pile. Perhaps I feared it would be washed away by the storm, disappear as the stones had. Whatever the case, while the effigy was practically weightless, its flaccid, spongy amorphousness troubled me, its limbs and head flailed and flopped against my chest and arms, and its stench leached into the fibers of my clothing and onto my hands.

I changed my clothes and left the soiled garments out for the storm to cleanse. I went to sleep, and though it hardly seems possible now, dreamed through the thunder, untroubled.

The next day I went to check on my discovery, half-expecting to find it gone like fairy gold, but I found it exactly where I'd left it, in the same boneless slump over the wood-pile. When I lifted it to inspect for any damages, I discovered that the pale flesh of the thing had grafted itself onto the wood, leaving bits of white mold on its grain and bark.

Why this minor revelation moved me to decisive action, I've long since forgotten. I do not recall being overly frightened or disturbed. Rather, it seems to me it was an unconscious, or half-conscious, act of prudence to carry the effigy and bury it into the soil, not in my bean-field where I'd found it, but deeper in the woods, away from my cabin, where the leaves would cover the traces of its tomb.

Three – The Loon

Fall came with its brisk winds and alchemy of changing colors. With the advent of the season also came new diversions and visitors to the woods and the pond. The loon (*Colymbus glacialis*) made the woods ring with his wild laughter in the mornings before my waking. Men make a sport of hunting the bird, with gigs and spy-glasses, on foot and in boats, ten men to one loon. Through great cunning the loon tends to make a game of this uneven contest.

One October afternoon, I was paddling my boat on the pond when a loon raced past me, betraying himself with his wild laugh. I gave chase, and he dived into the water, and when he surfaced I'd closed the distance to a few rods, but then he dived again, and on surfacing was a full ten rods distant. Unwilling to give up so easily, I endeavored to overtake him, and the loon seemed to bait me, laughing every so often. Each time he surfaced, he'd twist his neck to search for an opportune place to reemerge, and it became a game within itself to guess where he might next appear. Once, as if to taunt me, he emerged from the other side of my boat, having swam directly underneath me. As I paddled after him, I gave no thought to how the bird seemed to be leading me toward the pond's center.

I noticed, almost unconsciously, a gathering murk at the center of the pond, which my boat glided toward. The pond is many colors dependent on season and perspective. From childhood I had always regarded it as a safe and wholesome place, and in such fall afternoons as this one I had often found it pleasant to sit on a stump by the shore and watch the dimples on the glassy surface made by skaters and leaping fish. A pond is the earth's most expressive feature; the earth's eye, looking into which the beholder measures the depth of his own nature. On that day, in that moment as I chased a bird over a patch of water I'd traversed many times, the eye looked into me.

As I said, the pond is many colors, blue sometimes, various shades of green, and yellow near the shore. I had never seen the pond turn black, as it did that afternoon. At its greatest depth the pond is one-hundred-seven feet deep at the center, remarkable for such a compact body of water, but hardly a chasm of deep horrors. And yet here was a circle of black surrounding my boat, corresponding exactly with where the sun should have reflected. The sun shone white above, the water darkened below in answer, and between them was myself and my boat.

I write this now in full possession of my faculties, so it may seem as if I was aware, but I was no more awake and present to the moment as one who sleeps. I was a passenger in my own body, not even properly an observer. Quite how long my boat sat in the center of the black circle I do not know, but it must have been quite a span, as when I was called forth from my stupor by a human voice, the sun had begun to slant into the trees, where before it had been high in the sky.

It was my neighbor, the humble woodcutter, who, engaged in his work, had hurt himself and shouted a coarse oath I cannot print here. Without realizing it, he had saved me from a fate I can only guess at, for when I awoke back in myself, I was standing as if ready to step into the beckoning water, the boat wobbling under me. For his unwitting kindness, I have given poor recompense, and these days you will no more hear the woodcutter's axe ring against the pines and oaks.

Awake, and alone with the pond, I paddled back to shore. Other days I would see the loon again, but would never let him bait me. I do not believe there are evil places, nor that evil is something native to soil or water, but I do believe that people, and things like people, can impress their will onto a place, and that what I had nearly plunged into was the remains of an ancient will, one manifested long before I ever saw Walden, before any Indian ever saw it, before human feet ever touched the earth. If I believed once that Heaven is beneath our feet as well as over our heads, I now know Hell is in the same measure ubiquitous.

Four – What I Dreamed

For all I have since done, I have had my reasons. As I have written, I came to the woods to live life deliberately, and no action I took was without purpose. I fear that someone must have heard the Field child screaming before I caught up with him, and though I have burned everything, I cannot help but think that something escaped my notice. My thoughts have left no track, I cannot find the path again.

Where was my account when last I wrote?

It was fall, the boat, the loon, the black circle in the water.

As fall edged closer to winter and nights lengthened and turned colder, I found myself burning more wood in the hearth. By this point, I had not harmed anyone, and could still inveigle myself into believing my world was fundamentally safe and wholesome.

I made fires each night, and often with wood harvested freshly from the forest. But one night in November, during one of the first frosts, I found myself so tired from the day's exertions that I took my fuel from my wood-pile, and built a cheerful blaze in my hearth. So many nights my fire is my companion and house-keeper, and unlike with a stove, you can always see a face in a fire. On this evening, as I sat by the crackling flames, I noticed strange whispers of pale smoke rising, as well as a queer, simmering whine as if sap were bubbling out. But it was not sap, rather small specks of pale meat stuck to the wood, burning off now. When I smelled the awful odor of carrion and polish, I remembered at once the effigy and how it had grafted itself to my wood-pile. I poured ashes over the fire, and went to sleep in a cold bed.

I dreamed of terrible things, fueled by the odors of the burnt fungus. It is through these dreams that the nature of the effigy and its race were revealed to me. In a vision I glimpsed an unfinished Earth, one barely cooled from the heat of its celestial forge, and on this red orb a wandering seed from the outer dark found purchase. In this time before life as we understand it awoke, there was only one creature that mastered the world, a race and an individual all at once. Its corruption was all-encompassing, a pandemonium where species and habitat were indistinguishable, for not an inch of the world did it not colonize with its pallid flesh. In this first vision I had glimpsed the distant past. Hidden to me were the intervening epochs between the pandemonium and advent of more wholesome and diverse life, and what part the letters in the stones I had found played in the end of the fungi's empire, whether they were carved by the fungus or by the unknown foes who vanquished it, I do not know. In my next vision, I glimpsed the recent past, and saw how fragments of the fungus, tiny spores buried deep in the hidden lungs of the world, had survived the reckoning of the greater whole. These remnants slowly rose through the deep stone and pith of the world toward the soil, and once in the soil began to shape themselves into seeds of conquest. Over decades and centuries these seeds reached toward the surface, and learned what had taken root in the absence of their forebearer; namely, man. These were the effigies, of which I had found but one, but whose tally was beyond reckoning. These seeds perceived the forms of the young race and sardonically changed their shapes in mockery of us, the innocent race who superseded them, and who they would in turn subsume.

In the last vision, I learned of their plan, what they would make of us. It was in the nature of the effigies, of the fungus, to dominate and eclipse whatever it touched. As it had spread onto my wood, the fungus could also spread through crops. Anticipating the human drive to cultivate and grow food, the fungus seeded itself under fertile land, where it could corrupt the corn and fruit of human fields. My own beans, too, were the target of this plot, so many little Trojan horses for the conquest of human bodies. I saw more than I ever wished to see, and unlike most dreams, which are of the same evanescent character as dew, what I saw burned itself into my memory.

Once ingested, the fungus would work itself into the bodies, and grow, and wait until it was ready to emerge and burst free from its host with obscene violence, though by that time the body would already have been thoroughly eaten from the inside, in essence, a walking dead: pale profusions and squirming wires reaching out of every orifice and from wounds where the skin had stretched to bursting. This is not of my imagination—such profane grotesquery I have never been equal to conjuring, and it makes me ill now to write of it.

When I awoke, it was as if waking not from the sleep of an evening but from a lifetime of slumber, as if for the first time ever. I have not met the man who was quite awake, until I looked upon my own face reflected in the pond that morning. I knew, as terrible and heavy as the burden was, that *only I understood* the danger facing the race of man and all other animal and plant life.

I have said before that nothing I did was without careful consideration, and in saying that I have told a lie, for in my initial response to the crisis I acted rashly, and without consideration for how I might best combat the fungus. Were I thinking soundly, I would have dug up the effigy I had buried and shown it to men in the village, to men of learning and sense. Instead, in a fit of terror and fury I hurried to the forest where I'd buried the thing, dug it up, and then with my shovel hacked its hateful shape to a dozen little parcels of squirming fungus. These pieces I burned in an open fire, and in so doing I denied myself any chance of enlisting the aid of others in my war against the fungus. (A tired mind traces sinister geometries, and I wonder now if that rashness that seized me was not in fact the fungus exacting some influence upon me.)

With the help of others, with greater communal awareness, perhaps the other effigies seeded throughout this and other countries might have been located and extirpated. Instead, possessing only my own means and without any proof of what I knew, I could only save those around me from the fate that awaited them. All those who had eaten the beans of my field, which I had not eaten (for I am a Pythagorean where beans are concerned), had to be saved. My tools were the simple tools that man has had since his earliest days: an axe, and fire. I started with the woodcutter, and then moved on the poor Irishman, John Field, and his innocent brood. It was after I burned Field and his wife and children that some men from town came knocking. They did not understand. How could they? They only saw a madman in need of jailing.

Five – A Letter to a Friend

To Ralph Waldo Emerson,

Earlier today, you visited me, and for the second time in our acquaintance found me imprisoned, only this time for a graver matter than unpaid taxes. You were looking for your old handyman and student, but seemed quite disappointed by the man you found instead. I do not blame you for not believing me. My great regret was that I could not have enlisted your aid in this endeavor. The word of one so respected as yourself would have done much to credit my cause, and together we might have given men a chance of combating the fungus. As it is, I hold little hope for this world. You told me that they had found the woodcutter's belt buckle in the ashes of my hearth, and it seems this was the detail I had overlooked, the proof of my guilt in the recent disappearances. There is a certain humor in it—I have written in the past that our life is frittered away by detail.

Understand I did not kill anyone out of cruelty or wanton malignance. I have only done it because I perceived them infected, and saw that death by axe was far cleaner and easier than what the fungus would have made of them, how it would have gnawed at them from within, as worms do an apple, until it was only their hollowed husks the fungus sprang from.

If I am lucky, I will be locked away for the remainder of my natural life, or else paid headfirst through whatever waits beyond the loop of the hangman's noose. In either case, the fungus will have its way. Whether it takes ten years or a thousand, time is but a stream it goes a-fishing in. Still, we must resist while we have breath. If you read this, Waldo, please believe me. And do what you can to find and destroy as many of the effigies as is possible. There is so much beauty and goodness that wants for protection, and I can do nothing for it now.

The sun is but a morning star, this world I love but a point in space, a leaf adrift on strange tides.

—Henry David Thoreau
December 2nd, 1846

HAVE YOU SEEN THE MOON TONIGHT?

Ruben sits on his bed, refreshing his email app, as if any employer is going to respond to an application at 8 PM on a Saturday. Until last month, he was a contractor, sheetrock and carpentry mostly. There are pedophiles and Neo-Nazis still working construction sites across Miami, but trying to organize a union gets him blackballed. 32 years old and already functionally retired. Ruben hops onto Twitter to rail against the injustice of living in a "Right to Work" state, where he notices the top trend of the evening: *"Have you seen the Moon tonight?"* 52.3k tweets.

It's all over his timeline. Friends and acquaintances are tweeting the same thing, no hashtag, no context: *Have you seen the Moon tonight? So pretty so bright.* It's not just friends—a few celebrities and athletes are tweeting it too. Some kind of movement? Or does it have to do with the supermoon he saw articles about a few days ago? Through his bedroom window the moonlight shines through the blinds.

His phone buzzes with a notification, and his gut clenches when he sees who's just texted him. *Blonde Stacy*—his ex-girlfriend.

Just as he's wondering why she'd text him after a year of silence, a preview of the message flashes across the screen: "Have you seen the Moon tonight?"

Another buzz. The same message, this time from Rodney, one of the guys from his last job. Then another, this time Kevon from high school, then his cousin Violetta. Soon he loses track as a flood of such texts bombards his phone, which rattles and buzzes like a ball of Japanese honeybees in his hand.

Then a text comes in from his friend Fat Carlos. "we still hittin the beach tomorrow?"

An injection of reassuring normality. Ruben replies, "No doubt."

Outside of his room, the lock to the front door turns, and the door opens. It's his girlfriend. Vikki's heels click across the tile.

"Ruben, you there?" she calls.

A moment later, Ruben is up and in the living room. Vikki got her hair done today at the salon (afro puffs, a nice chic new look for her), which would usually mean she was planning something nice. However, he also notices she has a cigarette in her lips and is fumbling through her purse for her lighter. Smoking is always a bad sign with her. A last resort when all healthier coping mechanisms have failed.

"What's up?"

"This asshole," she says. *Cursing*, another bad sign. "Some crazy asshole was just standing in the expressway, hands up, looking at the sky. Almost ran him over."

She lights up and takes a drag. Between her full face of makeup, the heels, and the pencil skirt, Ruben figures it was a performance review day, but it's best to wait a bit before asking how it went. He likes watching her smoke, even though it only happens on bad days.

"You hungry?" he asks, as if he's got anything ready for her.

"Thirsty," she says. She clicks over to the fridge to take out a bottle of pinot.

Ruben's phone buzzes again. More of the same.

"You been getting those texts too?" Vikki asks.

"Yeah. It's weird."

"Creepy," she says. "Like it's some huge inside joke that no one's bothering to explain."

While Vikki drinks her wine, Ruben gets a pizza out of the freezer and preheats the oven. As he's waiting, he checks Twitter again. His timeline has now become a warzone between two trends: *Have you seen the Moon tonight?* and *#dontlookatthemoon.*

Ruben glances out the window. Clouds have rolled in to muffle the moonlight, while a light breeze nudges the palm trees in the neighbor's yard. A quiet evening.

Vikki's phone starts ringing. "It's Auntie Nicole," she says, and then answers. Ruben is thinking about how to broach the subject of moving out of Miami to someplace where he can work. Not a pleasant conversation, but one that needs to be had. Not yet though, wait for her to drink a few more glasses. Luckily, if her aunt's calling, that seems guaranteed.

But this is a different call than the usual *When you gonna get married, child?* He knows it as soon as Vikki tosses the rest of her wine into the sink. She ends the call saying, "We'll be there soon."

"What's up?" Ruben asks. He's already twisting the oven dial to off.

"Someone tried to break into her house," she says. "Smashed the window up."

"Jesus," Ruben says. "I'll get my tool belt."

His phone buzzes some more; he turns it off.

They take his truck. Auntie Nicole lives five minutes away, on the edge of Opa-locka in a mostly Jamaican neighborhood. He's driven this route so many times he doesn't even need to pay attention or think about it. His mind wanders, imagining where he might be able to find work. Orlando maybe? Or go back to New Jersey? Plenty of other Boricuas there who could hook him up with jobs, and Vikki can get work anywhere. Assuming she'd be willing to leave. Every so often he wonders what someone like her with a galaxy-brain is doing slumming with a sheetrock guy like him. Must be for his sense of humor, or maybe it's the way he handles his tools...

"Baby, look out!"

Ruben swerves hard just in time to avoid plowing into a man standing in the middle of the street. Instead, his trunk dings a nearby mailbox, bending but not upending it from where it's staked. He slams the brakes and rubbernecks to see the man staring at them. An older white guy wearing a bathrobe, curly gray hair, and a gold chain around his neck. Usually when you almost hit someone, they're furious, but this guy's just smiling wide and pointing with one finger up at the sky. His eyes—there's something wrong with them. They're too bright, too shiny, as if silver shavings float in the vitreous fluid reflecting the moonlight.

Vikki's hand squeezes his wrist. "He's fine, let's keep going."

With just one last glance at the smiling man, Ruben drives onward. On the way they pass more people standing in the street, while others are skipping along the sidewalks.

"They're high on something," Vikki says.

"Maybe just high on life."

"Freebasing life, more like it."

"Maybe we should we call them Moonheads."

"The moon doesn't do that to people. It's got to be something else."

While stopped at a stop sign, his attention flickers to a bright silver-white gush on the hood of a car parked on the curb. Something in the color is wrong, and he feels the first pinch of a migraine starting before he looks away.

Soon they arrive at Auntie Nicole's little pink house.

Auntie Nicole is one of those old school Jamaicans, so old-fashioned she believes—or forces herself to believe—that her precious niece and the man she lives with sleep in separate beds and won't push them together until they get married. When they started dating, Auntie Nicole distrusted Ruben, because a clean-shaven young man was always trouble. Was that a Jamaican thing or an old person thing? He still doesn't know.

As Ruben steps inside the darkened house, the familiar scents of Pine-Sol, cooking oil, and ginger root greet him. "Mrs. Lewis?"

"Auntie?"

"Oh, you're here," Auntie Nicole says. She shuffles out of the kitchen, brandishing a long carving knife.

"Why are all the lights out?" Vikki asks.

Auntie Nicole is a dark little woman with stark white hair. She wears large square glasses with thick lenses that make her face look tiny and telescope her eyes, exaggerating every emotion. Right now, they display her fear and bewilderment. "I turned them off so they wouldn't bother me anymore."

"Who's 'they'?" Vikki asks.

"The people who broke my window."

"I didn't see a broken window outside, Mrs. Lewis," Ruben says. It wouldn't be the first time she's exaggerated something over the phone. Probably a bird just collided with her window.

"Oh, dearie, it's not out front." She shudders as she settles into her armchair. "Whoever it was, they smashed my bedroom window while I was taking a nap."

That's fucking nuts, he wants to say, but remembering where he is, he says, "Unbelievable."

"Could you take a look at it, baby?" Vikki asks.

Outside, the evening air is balmy and pestilent with mosquitoes. He walks around to the right side of the house where he sees the wound in Auntie Nicole's window, the broken glass seeded around the brick that made the hole. He picks up the brick—there's something carved into its side: a circle with a squiggly line wrapped around it. No, not a circle, the moon, the full moon enfolded by a snake, or a worm.

He's setting down the brick when he hears a raspy voice behind him. "You're on private property, mister."

He knows that voice, and knowing it's Mr. Wallace, he stands up slowly, puts his hands up, and turns around. At least Gene Wallace isn't carrying a rifle, just pointing a grill scrubber at him.

"Oh, it's you, Raul," Gene says, the menace in his crusty old face relaxing into something like friendliness as he lowers the grill brush. "You here about Nicole's window?"

Ruben has long since accepted that Gene, Auntie Nicole's neighbor and the founder, president, and—to date—*only* member of the street's "neighborhood watch," will never get his name right, and has settled for him at least remembering its first letter.

"Yeah. You doing all right, Gene?"

Gene's got a bad sunburn, so deep it even shows lobster-bright in the gloom. He's wearing a shirt emblazoned with the sentence *I Voted for Jesus, Did You?*

"No, I'm not," Gene says. "Doped-up kids are making a mess everywhere. Saw it on the news just now. Got something to do with the supermoon or whatever."

"You seen the moon?" Ruben asks.

"No, sir. I ain't looking up at the sky when dopeheads are on the streets and on people's lawns."

Whatever misgivings Ruben has about the strange behavior of the people he saw on the streets, he's more worried how a nutjob like Gene might respond. He tries, as gently as possible, to suggest Gene hunker down for the night.

"Then who'd protect the block?" Gene asks. "Can't give them an inch. You oughta know this is how it starts."

How what starts? Ruben almost asks, but decides it'd be more productive to crumple his own skull with a hammer than carry on this conversation.

He turns around to assess the window, while Gene walks back into his screened porch where he's got a little camp chair set up, along with his rifle and a cooler full of beer on ice. Like he's tailgating before the "looting" or the "communism" starts.

A few minutes later, Ruben heads back inside. "Window's not too bad," he says, "but the crack's bound to spread. I could replace it tomorrow."

No answer. Vikki and her aunt's faces flicker with the white-blue strobe of the TV as they watch, transfixed. Ruben removes his toolbelt, sets it aside, and sits down on the couch beside Vikki.

"You don't do that, you just don't," Auntie Nicole mutters, twisting a rolled-up magazine in her hands. Vikki has her hand over her mouth.

They're watching the local news. The chyron sprawls across the lower half of the screen in ugly red letters: N. MIAMI CHURCH ARSON.

"Who the hell would do that?" Ruben asks as he watches the live footage of a little church in North Miami—the one he used to pass on his daily commute when he was working on the new Burger King—crumbling into itself, collapsing as a ball of fire, orange and black all at once, spewing cinders.

That Auntie Nicole doesn't chastise him for his language says everything. But more stunning is the lack of firetrucks around the church. No police cars either. Just people, standing in clusters; some of them seem to be watching the church, but most are looking up at the sky.

"You don't do that," Auntie Nicole says. The magazine begins to tear in her grip.

The reporter gets the church's name wrong, but that hardly matters at this point.

"The man who claims responsibility for this shocking arson is standing with me," the green-eyed lady says, and the camera pans over to a guy who looks like he stepped out of the back room of a bank with his pressed suit and the gold pin in his tie.

"Where are the firetrucks?" Vikki says. "Where are the cops?"

"Why isn't anyone grabbing him?" Auntie Nicole mutters.

The reporter asks the man why he set fire to the church. He doesn't answer at first, staring blankly past the reporter before turning to the camera. He doesn't look dangerous, but then Ruben's seen enough psychopath's mugshots to know how easy it is for evil to hide in meek, plain-as-oatmeal looks.

"We burned this empty box because it was a temple to a false, voiceless god," the man says. His Brooklyn accent clashes with the elevated register of his words. "The true God has shown Its face to us, sung to us from above, and we can no more turn away."

The reporter does a beat, takes the slightest step back like she's reevaluating whether a guy in such an expensive suit might get violent, and asks him, "Sir, was this arson racially motivated?"

"You don't understand, you haven't seen," the arsonist says, his jaw clenched. "Have you seen the Moon tonight? So pretty, so bright?"

Ruben's guts clench and churn, but whatever dread he feels is exploded into a panic as he watches the man become enraged by the reporter asking him again if the arson is a hate crime. The blow is so sudden, the camera barely captures his fist striking the reporter across the jaw, and in the next moment the camera tumbles and starts filming the news van's hubcaps—orange flame dancing in the rims—as the cameraman cries out.

"You must see," the arsonist says, his voice cracking with a high, bright anger. "You must all see." The camera turns, the screen fills with the man's face, wide-eyed, pale, and fanatical. "Let me share what we have seen."

Every instinct in Ruben tells him to lunge for the remote and change the channel or turn off the television before the Moonhead can turn the camera toward the sky—but a bright light shines on the Moonhead's face, his pupils dissolve, his face slackens, and the camera falls from his hands and the feed cuts out.

"Kelly, Kelly?" the anchor calls, somehow calm, not sounding at all like someone who just saw his coworker get assaulted. And then the newsroom disappears, and the screen goes dark. Ruben shuts off the TV. Neither Vikki nor her aunt protests.

What could happen to the moon that would do this to people? Ruben thinks back to the little whisper of a migraine he felt looking at its light, and the weird doodle scratched into the brick that broke Auntie Nicole's window. When he tries checking his Twitter feed again, it doesn't load, and it's nothing to do with the internet. He can't remember the last time it crashed.

"Maybe you should come with us, back to Ruben's place," Vikki says.

But just as she says it, police sirens scream in the distance, and in their wake follows a welter of gunshots, some remote, some maybe as close as a block away. One police siren passes through the street, recedes, and then is cut silent with a screech of tires and the riotous crunch of two cars colliding. In the ensuing quiet, a noise starts up, warbling, eerie, unmistakably human: dozens of voices singing in close harmony, far away but not nearly as distant as Ruben would like.

Ruben stands up, gets his tool belt, and clips it on. "Mrs. Lewis, you got any scrap wood I can board up the doors with?"

"Just Jack's old bookcases," Auntie Nicole says, and then her eyes crinkle. "Filled with all those filthy books he liked."

She means the spy novels with the bosomy, swooning women on their peeling covers.

"You need my help?" Vikki asks.

Ruben thinks about it. Normally he'd tell Vikki not to get her hands dirty, but she probably needs a distraction—something to do with herself—as much as he does. "Sure," he says. "But first, I need some things from my truck."

He sneaks out through the back door like he's avoiding sniper fire because, for all he knows, he is. His truck is waiting for him. Under the tarp in its bed are some of his heavier tools—his nail gun, for one thing. Ruben has his nail gun in hand and is about to head back inside when something appears on the waters of the canal. An empty rowboat, drifting unguided along the gentle current. A dark, wet stain smears the boat's middle thwart. Watching the rowboat, Ruben also catches the wild pale glint of the moon on the water. He doesn't see the moon itself in the wake of the boat, only its light, but it's enough to make him feel like his skull is in a pneumatic press, and as much as he wants to look away, he can't. His vision becomes a narrowing tunnel, one he feels himself stepping into, even as invisible, insistent tethers drag his eyes skyward. Clouds muffle the moon, and Ruben falls back into himself. His head throbs, his eye twitches, and he tastes copper and smells fire.

Once inside, Ruben does his best not to think of the moon and whatever's happened to it, whatever he might have seen had he looked all the way up. With Vikki's help, he smashes up her Uncle Jack's bookcases. With the nail gun it's quick work to board up the back door, the flimsiest entry point to the house. Most of the windows are barred and don't need boarding up, but they do need covering. Although Vikki offered to help with the work, mostly she just scrolls through her phone, her forehead crinkled with dread.

"Anything useful?" Ruben asks her.

"Nothing," she says. "None of the news sites are saying anything."

"About the Moonheads?"

"About anything. No updates in hours."

"When's the moon supposed to set?"

She checks. "Four A.M."

Shit. Five more hours of this? That's assuming this craziness ends when the moon's gone.

Vikki gets a call on her phone. He knows it's her parents calling from Fort Lauderdale because Vikki's accent leaps from Manhattan boardroom to Kingston in a flash. The conversation lasts a few minutes, and while Ruben boards up the bathroom window he thinks of his own parents, his dad in Staten

Island and his mom back in San Juan. Hopefully it's raining where they are, no moonlight at all.

He checks his phone—no new texts or updates in over an hour. Matter of fact, no service at all, or Wi-Fi either. This dawns on him just as Vikki yells *Shit* with both barrels of her voice and hurls her phone against the wall.

By the time Ruben gets to the living room, Vikki's eyes are watery but more furious than scared. "They're trapped in their apartment," she says. "Mom said there are National Guard guys in the streets who barricaded the boulevard. Or, there were, anyway. I guess when Mom peeked just now the soldiers were gone, only their trucks were there."

"They'll be okay," Ruben says. "They're tough. And they've got each other."

It's his own parents he's worried about.

Outside, the harmonious, wordless drone of the Moonhead choir comes and goes, in and out like a tide. Every so often Ruben peeks through the curtains and sees people running, sometimes chased by others. Once or twice over the next hour, a brick or a stone clatters against the house, or a gunshot reports from somewhere on the block. After one such shot, Gene Wallace's raspy voice warns a "goddamned anarchist" to stay off his property. Gene can't see the moon because it's on the other side of his house, and he probably doesn't realize how lucky he is for that.

Do the Moonheads still remember who they are? Do they recognize their friends and family, or are they so changed they become something completely *other*, the molds of their minds melted away by the silver poured from the moon's crucible?

Just make it to moonset, he keeps muttering to himself as he drives nail after nail into planks securing the unprotected windows. It's nearly midnight when he finishes the last window. The house is dark and quiet except for the glow of the kitchen appliances and the hum of the air conditioner. Vikki and her aunt have made tea and reheated some rice and pigeon peas. Too much Scotch bonnet pepper, but Ruben is grateful to have something in his stomach.

When Auntie Nicole's landline telephone squawks, Ruben almost drops the bowl from surprise. The phone rings, once, twice, and Ruben watches it as Auntie Nicole waddles from her chair to answer.

"Mister Wallace?" Auntie Nicole says. "Slow down, dearie, no no, I haven't been—say what?"

The mention of Gene Wallace is enough to make Vikki narrow her eyes and Ruben to groan inwardly, but Ruben's close enough to the phone to hear Gene's voice—hesitant and afraid.

He can also hear the muffled hubbub of voices chattering next door on Gene's lawn. Ruben goes to Auntie Nicole's bedroom and peeps through the curtain. At least a dozen people, probably more, have assembled in an almost military formation on Gene Wallace's lawn. A few are in cop uniforms. Even from the odd angle he can see the silver in their eyes. He can't see the porch from there, but if Gene's on the landline with Auntie Nicole he must have fallen back from his screen porch redoubt. He imagines Gene, cornered and penned, hyperventilating, searching for his heart pills...

Ruben starts thinking of how many Moonheads he can take on if they catch him. He's armed with his hammer and nail gun, and that's enough for two, maybe three if he's lucky. Shit odds, shit night. Still, there's no helping it. He's always been a helper and a doer.

When Ruben steps back into the living room and glances at the boarded front door, Vikki knows what he's thinking right away.

"No," she says, jaw set, eyes hard.

"No what?"

"No to whatever you're thinking of doing." Vikki follows him to the back door. "You think he'd risk his neck to help you?"

Hell no, every part of him says. Ruben shrugs. "Sure, he's an asshole, but..."

"But what?"

But he's human, One Love and all that, Ruben wants to say. Instead he just starts prying nails off the boards on the back door with the claw of his hammer. As he works, he feels Vikki's silent fury burning his neck.

Finally, she sighs. "Fine." A pause. "But I'm going with you."

Now it's his turn to get angry. "No."

One look at Vikki's face and he knows there's no point arguing. Still, he tries. "What about your aunt?"

But Auntie Nicole hollers from the kitchen. "You get Mr. Wallace, dearie. I'll shut myself in the bathroom till you soon come."

A long sigh. "You can hold the flashlight."

"Fuck that," Vikki says, low enough that her aunt won't hear her, "give me the hammer."

They go out the back door. Ruben doesn't bother with the lock, because the cheap MDF the doorframe's made of is so flimsy that locking it won't make a difference to a determined attacker. Vikki's behind him with the hammer, while Ruben holds his nail gun in one hand and his flashlight in the other. Contrary to the name, a nail gun can't "shoot" anything, but if a Moonhead gets in arm's reach, Ruben will stamp a nail through them.

"Follow me," Ruben whispers, and they sneak around the back yard, past his truck, toward the low chain fence separating Gene's property from Auntie Nicole's. On the other side, the Moonheads are still holding their vigil.

"Come out come out, brother," some of them chant, while others hum the strange harmony of the choir from earlier. "Let the good light in!"

Ruben and Vikki get to Mr. Wallace's back door and Ruben tries the knob. Locked. Ruben's no locksmith, but he knows enough to see Gene locked the knob but didn't close the deadbolt. Easy enough. Ruben sets the muzzle of his nail gun against the knob and blows out its aluminum cylinder. Ruben almost opens the door right there, but then he freezes, imagining Gene—scared and jumpy—on the other side with his rifle.

Ruben knocks three times. "Gene?" he says. "Gene, it's just me, it's *Raul.*"

"Raul?" Vikki murmurs.

No answer. His hand on the broken knob, Ruben mouths a short prayer and pushes the door open. The house is dark. Ruben takes a cautious step in, Vikki close behind him with the hammer.

"Gene?" Ruben calls into the darkness.

No answer.

Ruben walks with a half-crouch, his flashlight whipping around, shining on framed photographs of astronauts and generals and a signed Georgia Bulldogs Herschel Walker jersey.

Finally, Vikki points out a pale scrap of flickering lamplight spewing from a doorway.

"Gene?"

"I'm in here," Gene answers, calmer than Ruben can ever remember him sounding. "Come on in, Ruben."

Ruben's sweat runs cold as he steps slowly toward the office doorway, Vikki moving like his own shadow behind him. When Ruben comes to the doorway, he finds Gene with his back turned, standing beside a beautiful leather-paneled writing desk, in a room blanketed in football memorabilia—

Dolphins and Bulldogs—and illuminated only by the light of a desk lamp. That and the moonlight slithering through the blinds.

He knows what's coming even before Gene turns around. He knows, and yet it still slugs him like a fist when Gene Wallace turns his head and his eyes glimmer with silver flecks.

"Shit," Vikki says.

"Neighborly of you to come," Gene says. "But I'm fine. Really."

Ruben takes one step back and Gene, hands at his sides, takes one step forward.

Ruben lifts his nail gun. "Stay back."

"You haven't seen it yet. But you will, both of you will."

"I mean it, Gene," Ruben says. Another step back, while Gene claims two paces of his own. Ruben shines his flashlight at Gene, and Gene recoils, the pupils of his eyes shrinking to nothing before he covers his face and shrinks back. Ruben switches to the strobe setting, and Gene starts stumbling back until his back is against the window casement.

"Stop," Gene says, his already raspy voice becoming a hiss, "your fake light can't chase away the truth."

Gene seems to shrink into himself, balling up to protect himself from the strobe, and Ruben thinks he sees something wriggling under Gene's skin, or perhaps the skin itself is warping and blistering as if held to a plasma torch. Without thinking, Ruben steps closer to get a better look. Gene's hand swipes out fast as anything and the flashlight tumbles from Ruben's grasp. In the next instant, Gene slams into him, hitting much harder than any man his size or age should, and Ruben is pushed flush against the wall.

Gene's hands, Ruben's wrists, the nail gun between them. For a moment, Ruben feels like he's in a tug of war with a truck winch, and then the tension of their grappling breaks as Vikki levels Gene with a perfect strike of the claw hammer to his skull.

Gene falls limp onto the dark walnut floorboards. Where the hammer crumpled his skull, something like mercury seeps out, while more of the stuff leaks from his ears and puddles on the floor. Vikki finds the flashlight and shines it on Gene's face, and both she and Ruben jump back when Gene's pupils turn to little beads and his head turns partway and his lips peel back in a rictus smile.

"It's coming," Gene says. "You think daylight will save you?"

Gene's mouth opens wider, jaw unlatching, and something barely audible, like a dog whistle, splits Ruben's ears. Almost immediately the thrash of frantic footsteps starts up, and Ruben knows they must run, but he's only started turning when a man launches from outside, crashing through the office window. Cut in a dozen places, leaking tears of silver, a latex-gloved EMT throws himself at Ruben and Ruben doesn't think about it, just puts his nail gun between them, and after the loudest crack of his life, two hundred pounds of meat collapses and Ruben doesn't have any time to consider what he's just done. He's running, Vikki out in front of him, both hurrying for the back door.

Glass shatters from the force of bodies. He glances over his shoulder as people spill into Gene's living room through the windows, crawling over each other and over drifts of broken glass glittering in moonlight. The hesitation of that glance is all it takes for one of the Moonheads—a girl, maybe fourteen years old—to catch him, grab his ankle, and trip him just enough for a web of hands to grip every part of him and drag him back in a dozen directions as if they're about to tear him to pieces.

But the mesh of hands melts away as the strobe flashes, and the Moonheads wriggle off and cover themselves with their arms and make sounds that only barely register as human. His heart in his mouth, Ruben stumbles back up to his feet and picks up the nail gun.

There's Vikki, holding the flashlight in one hand and the hammer in the other. The Moonheads' shadows writhe in a flickering flipbook show on the walls, and as with Gene it looks like their skins are trying to crawl from their bodies and hide from the light. As long as the strobe shines on them, they're pinned, incapable of advancing further. There are cops, old folks, kids, a nurse in scrubs...

"Ruben, baby," Vikki says, "go on now, make sure Auntie's safe."

He doesn't understand at first, but when it clicks, he can't believe what she's suggesting. "No way. Fuck no. I'm not leaving you."

But there's that look of hers, that clenched jaw, flared nostril, hard line in her forehead that says she's made up her mind and she won't change it. She's got her foot on a landmine and she knows she can't move. As long as she's got the strobe on them, the Moonheads are trapped.

"Ruben," she says, "I'll be okay." She always blinks three times when she lies; it's why she never lies, he can always see through her. "You go back, lock the house up, keep Auntie safe."

What about you? he wants to ask, but his words are like paste in his mouth.

"I'll find my own way back. Just go, now."

Some of the Moonheads are peeking through the gaps in their fingers, some are trying to force themselves to move, to spread out, escape the reach of the strobe. How long can the batteries on the flashlight last? How long since he replaced them?

Vikki's life is now a factor of however much charge is left in two lead-acid cells.

He wants to stay with her. He wants to pick her up and carry her back to the house. He wants to be more than just a guy with a nail gun. But that's what he is, and he knows there's not a damn thing he can do for her now. She has her foot on a landmine, and if he's with her when it goes off, they'll both be fucked. He understands this. Warm tears roll down his face and mingle with icy sweat.

"I love you," he says. "I love you so much, Vikki."

"I'll be right behind you," she says, forcing a smile and blinking three times through her tears.

He forces himself to turn away, and then he has to force himself to start moving. Even after he wends the corner the strobe's flash follows him, almost in rhythm with his chaotic heartbeat. He runs out the back door. The back yard is clear.

When he gets back to Auntie Nicole's house, he hesitates at the door. He could still go back. He can still save her...

The clouds begin to part. Ruben rushes into the house.

Auntie Nicole is where she said she'd be—locked in the bathroom.

"It's okay, I'm here, it's safe to come out." A lie.

As she unlocks the door and shambles out, Ruben thinks of what Gene—or what Gene had become—said: *Do you think daylight will save you?*

Auntie Nicole's telescoped eyes ripple with all the hurt seventy years can store in a body when she sees Ruben and only Ruben. "Where's my niece?"

"She's coming," Ruben says. "She's right behind me."

It's another lie, but he's not wrong. Ten minutes later, as Ruben and Auntie Nicole sit in the dark living room listening to the angry night outside, the symphony of car alarms, intermittent gunshots, and the low drone of the Moonheads' singing hushes, a voice calls from outside.

"Auntie? Ruben?"

Ruben stands up from his chair and hurries to the front window, but stops himself before peeling back the curtain. Where is the moon right now?

"Ruben, baby, I see your shadow through the curtain."

It's her voice. But it's too calm to belong to a woman standing in the middle of the end of the world, trapped on the wrong side of a barricaded door. He doesn't answer.

"Ruben, just look at me. I've got something to show you."

Suddenly, Auntie Nicole is beside him, her hand on his arm. "It's not her," she whispers. "That's not my sister's baby."

He knows. A stupidly abstract part of his brain wonders how they got her—if the batteries died or if a Moonhead got her from behind.

Auntie Nicole tugs on his arm. "Come away from there."

But he doesn't respond. When she tugs again, he shrugs her off. Without Vikki, what's the point of any of this?

"Ruben, I don't want you to be alone," Vikki says, and her voice is so sweet, so much velvet that he almost believes it. "This isn't the end of anything. Open the curtain and look at what I have for you."

Auntie Nicole is backing away. She knows what's coming, and Ruben knows it too, even as every rational part of him screams at his hand to let go of the curtain. But he opens the curtain anyway, and puts his face to the window to peek through the gap between two boards.

There's Vikki. If not for her bare feet and a small gash on her cheek, she'd be ready for a business meeting. She holds the moon in her hands, trapped in the silver pane of the side mirror Ruben recognizes from his own truck.

The light breaks through him. The migraine that gnawed at him earlier fits its entire jaws around his skull and he feels cold, then hot, then cold again, and then numb. Something has entered him, something at once solid and intangible.

But Ruben is still himself—the only thing he's lost is his fear.

He sees it now, and knows—even before he hears the seraphic voices of every other soul on the planet now united in a great living circuit—that what Gene said was true. The daylight would never have ended anything, for the many-segmented body that grasps the moon in its thousand legs is only a shadow, and the true thing Itself must be coiled around the sun. Everything is all right. When morning comes, Ruben will meet God.

ELMREACH

Daphne hangs up, her boss's voice still ringing in her ears. Ethan has been waiting patiently. The Christmas tree lights flash on the shadows of his cheekbones, dance on his irises, this good and simple man, her new fiancé.

"Well, there's good news and bad news," Daphne says.

Ethan frowns. "How about the bad news first?"

"I'm out of a job."

Ethan winces. He apologizes—she did this for *his* town, for the Christmas tree farm—and says maybe, just maybe, Maury will have a change of heart.

"I don't care if he does. I'm sick of working for Maury, and with my CV I can get a job at any firm in the city."

"Well, what's the good news then?"

"My holiday schedule is clear."

He smiles. She leans forward, he meets her lips. There's something so wholesome in how he kisses with his lips shut but fluttering partway open, politeness on passion's threshold. Everything in Elmreach has been so wholesome, so kindly, so complete. The handpainted signs over the shops on Main Street, the cheerful banner over the tree farm where Maury wanted to develop his stupid stripmall, the exuberant light displays on every house, the neatly shoveled driveways, the little droves of children caroling door to door. And Ethan's family home—the Olmwood family home—is the microcosm of Elmreach's charm: a cozy cottage aesthetic, a crackling fireplace, frosted windows glowing red and green.

Ethan pulls away from the kiss, but lets his hand linger on her hip just a moment. He says he has to help finish making the Christmas dinner. She asks if he needs help. No, no, you just relax, he tells her. The smell is already overwhelming, sweet potatoes caramelizing in the oven, gravy reducing in saucepans, fat dripping from a pair of ducks on spits into troughs of roasted potatoes, and that's not even touching on the pies or the eggnog or the mulled wine.

Ethan disappears into the kitchen, and Daphne walks with her mug from the den to the living room to sit by the fireplace where the Olmwood family has hung their handsewn, monogrammed stockings. Near the fireplace is a bay window, and she curls up on the sill. Outside the snow comes down in exhalations of silver flakes electrified by moonlight, as bright as the diamond on her engagement ring. There is never such pure snow in the city. It falls on the lawn, on the doghouse, on the trees.

Daphne's tranquil mood sours when she notices the trees. Three skinny dead pines. They bother her somehow. She can't remember seeing them before.

Heavy footsteps—too heavy to be Ethan's, who despite his robust frame has a dancer's grace—sound behind her, and when Daphne turns, she expects to see Ethan's father—her future father-in-law. But it's not Mr. Olmwood in his customary red velveteen robe, it's a younger man with the same stocky build and the same cornflower-blue eyes, only none of Mr. Olmwood's mirth. This man is a sour note to the symphony of the Olmwood home, and yet she can tell from a glance he's Ethan's relative, like if Ethan were ten years older and had spent those ten years drinking and smoking to excess and sleeping in a culvert.

"Oh, hi there," Daphne says. She tries to smile, but the expression crashes against this man's grim, appraising stare.

"You must be the newest girl," the man says. "You're prettier than the last one, that's for sure."

He's dressed in a thick blue robe over what appears to be an ugly sweater, with a pair of moccasins on his feet. In one hand he holds an open can of processed pasta, in the other a crusty fork. Flecks of orange sauce stick to the little gold-white bristles around his mouth.

Daphne looks away from the man and his dead-fish eyes, glancing for a moment out the window. The snow is still swirling, but the trees are gone, and she wonders if she didn't imagine them completely. But why would she imagine trees that weren't there?

"I'm sorry, I don't think we've been introduced."

"Of course we haven't; they don't like me talking to people like you," the man says. He stands rigid like a Coldstream Guard with his canned pasta in hand, and spears a piece of ravioli with his fork and then shovels it into his mouth.

"It's good to meet you."

"No it's not," Carter says through a full mouth.

Daphne tries to keep a polite face, tries not to wrinkle her nose from the stale cigarette smell wafting from Carter, but it's difficult. So far, Carter is the first person she's met in Elmreach she hasn't immediately liked. He's the first person in Elmreach who's made her feel uncomfortable, or reminded her of the cheerless city.

Carter swallows. "So, out with it, how'd you meet my kid brother? And how'd he rope you into accepting his ring?"

The bluntness of the question from this stranger—even if he is Ethan's brother, like he claims—stuns and rankles her, but thinking back to her first meeting with Ethan the week before soothes her hackles.

"Well, your brother was—is—a perfect gentleman."

Carter grins, showing a row of nicotine teeth. "Sure is. Always the charmer, that one. But how'd it happen?"

"Excuse me, but what does it—?"

"Tell me."

Daphne is again struck by his blunt tone. "Well, if you must know..."

She recounts the events of the last week. There she was, a lawyer from the city come to Elmreach for her firm, to scout a location for a new commercial development for a major client of her boss, Maury Leitner. On the outskirts of town, her car broke down, and—

"—and a dreamy tow-truck driver showed up to tow your car to the family shop, Olmwood Auto, where the nice bearded guy offered to fix your belts for free because it's almost Christmas," Carter says, interrupting her.

For reasons she doesn't understand, her guts knot up. He sounds so certain, and what he says is so uncannily true. Maybe Ethan told him...

"Well, yes..."

Carter chuckles. "You hit it off with the dreamy tow guy, he shows you around the town, you start feeling at home. Then after a few days, after you've fallen in love with the guy and his town, he brings you to his favorite spot in the world, an old treestump in the woods he used to pretend was his castle, and he promised to always be your knight, and you promised to always be his queen. Etcetera, etcetera." Carter shovels some more pasta into his mouth. "You're wondering how I know, and the answer's easy: They don't change the script, not when it works so well bringing in new blood."

She can't keep the edge out of her voice anymore. "What are you talking about? Who is 'they'?"

"It's not really a stump, you know. That's just what it likes for you to see it as."

"It?"

"The *Ear of the World.*" The words seem to shudder out of his lips, and they hang in the air long after he's shoved another forkful of canned pasta in. He glances around, like he expects someone to be standing behind him, but there's no one there.

"No one to bundle me away? Heh. Course they wouldn't let me out if it wasn't already a done deal."

Is he a drunk? She sees the silver of a flask in his robe pocket, and smells whiskey on him. Daphne wants to get away, wants to find Ethan. She can hear him whistling to the Bing Crosby music in the kitchen, can hear him chopping vegetables. How she wishes he were here with her now, how she wishes she could be far away from this strange, smelly, dumpy effigy of the man she loves. But Carter's wide frame fills so much space, and she feels strangely afraid to move. Why should she? He hasn't done anything other than be rude, and she's in a safe place—her fiancé is just a room away.

"I don't know what you mean," Daphne says. "Now, if you'll excuse me—"

Before she can uncross her legs to stand from the sill, Carter holds up a hand. "Wait. Maybe it isn't too late; maybe they're slipping up."

"What are you talking about? Not one thing you've said has made sense."

Carter puts the can to his lips and drinks what she can only imagine is lukewarm sauce, some of which dribbles down his stubble. When he finishes, he smiles. "Have you eaten or drank anything they've given you? My family, I mean."

"What does that matter?"

"Don't you wonder why I'm eating this shit on Christmas Eve?" Carter asks, pointing to the empty can. "It's not for the flavor, that's for sure. It's because it comes in a can, a can that's been filled and soldered thousands of miles from Elmreach. That's the only way to be totally sure."

She doesn't say what she's thinking, but Carter seems to read it from her eyes.

"Nah, I'm not crazy. Now, answer my question: Did you eat anything my family offered you?"

She thinks about it. Mostly she ate fast food or the hotel breakfast, until yesterday when she finally spent the night Ethan in his home, the night he proposed to her. Her stomach grumbles at the memory of the oven-fresh pumpkin pie Mrs. Olmwood baked and served with the home-pressed apple cider.

"A slice of pumpkin pie," she says. "And a glass of your family's apple cider."

The look that flashes over Carter's face frightens her because it's so unexpected. He looks sad, distraught even, but only for a moment, then his face hardens into a flat pane of indifference like before.

"Well, you're fucked then."

The words, ridiculous and random as they are, still frighten her. "What?"

Carter begins to move, shambling toward her, and she almost screams, but her voice catches in her throat, and before she can think to call out to Ethan for help, Carter sits down next to her on the windowsill, his large bulk taking up most of the space and forcing her to sidle closer to the fire. She thinks he might grab her, might do something, but his attention is elsewhere. She follows his gaze to the window, where the skinny trees—four of them now—are swaying in the wind and snow.

"The children are playing," Carter grumbles.

She doesn't ask what he means. The trees transfix her. They look wrong somehow. Move wrong. Not swaying stiffly as trees do against the wind, but flexibly, rapidly, like men who shake their limbs to keep warm in the cold.

Carter reaches into his pocket and Daphne gasps as he pulls out of a knife, but he only uses this knife to saw open the top of another can he has in his robe—a can of beans this time. He slurps beans from the jagged edge of the can. "When I was a kid, this was a nice town. Poor as shit, but nice."

"It's..." She finds her voice again. "It's a nice town now."

She's relaxing again. Carter isn't violent, isn't dangerous, just a little spacy. Maybe bitterness and sibling jealousy can drive a man crazy.

Carter shakes his head. "Nah, what this is isn't natural. Think about it, how is it that someone like you, a successful professional from a big city, completely changes her priorities and gives up her big salary and the world she knows for some handsome hick and his little nowhere Upstate burg? How is that possible?"

"It's— I haven't..." she trails off.

It doesn't make sense. Oh, all the joy felt real. The comforting change of pace, the sincerity of the small-town people, their infectious, benign obsession with all thing Christmas. Maybe she was tired of working for Maury, tired of her job, maybe she wanted someplace that reminded her of her childhood in Glenn's Falls.

But still, it doesn't make sense. No matter how much she wants it to. Daphne fiddles with the ring, the pretty slender white gold, diamond-studded ring on her finger. It doesn't budge.

"Like I said, Elmreach was normal once, when I was little." He gulps down some cold beans. The firelight ribbons through the water in his eyes. "Normal in that, like so many little towns, it was near dead. Paper mill shut down, put half the town out of work. Maybe it would have ended up bankrupt, but then Father Tannehill, the old priest, saved the town. See, he found something in the woods, those same woods where my brother proposed to you. He found the Ear of the World."

Daphne doesn't speak, but she wants to ask what it is.

"It's the physical representation of the Mother of Many in our world. It's an ear, and also a mouth of sorts. It's how *She* listens, how She communicates with the people."

Now she can't resist asking. "Mother of Many? Who— What is that?"

"You'll know soon enough."

She shudders. "This is all bullshit. You're trying to scare me."

"I wish I were. But the Mother of Many is real, and the whole town worships Her. In exchange for that worship, she makes the people feel happy and productive, keeps the despair that's swallowed so many towns away. This power is most pronounced around Christmas time, in the cold months. Don't know why—maybe Her power is strongest when it's cold. They work harder, scrape by better. Apart from the worship, the people help the Mother grow Her children, and sometimes she lets them harvest Her children—for fuel, for food, for a lot of things."

"These children. What do they look like?"

"I thought you said this was all bullshit."

"Tell me."

Carter slurps some beans. "Well, they don't look like much in their larval state. They blend in real well. Before their needles fall out, they look like pine trees. They never quite smell the same though. There's a hint of iron in the scent; maybe you've smelled it."

Daphne doesn't say, but her eyes must betray her again the way Carter smirks.

"Now, I mentioned that sometimes the Mother lets the people harvest her children. It's not just to help them out, it benefits Her too. You see, when a person eats the flesh of Her flesh, they commune with the Mother. It's like part of Her becomes part of them, and vice versa. The ones who eat the flesh of Her flesh, they can hear Her even without being close to the Ear."

"Hear *Her*? What, this Mother-thing speaks to the people? What's Her voice sound like?" She tries to sound incredulous, but she sounds tremulous instead.

Carter shakes his head. "I have no idea what She sounds like, and I don't expect to ever know. I've never eaten Her flesh, and never will, God-willing. The others have never forced me; I don't think they can. For whatever else they are, they're not violent."

From the kitchen, Ethan calls out, his voice a welcome raft thrown to her. "Daphne, dinner's almost ready! Maybe help Mom set the table?"

Now, at last, Daphne gets to her feet, and almost bolts toward Ethan's voice, but she stops herself. It takes so much to stop herself, to keep her feet anchored.

"What you waiting for?" Carter asks. "Your prince is calling."

Daphne grinds her jaw. "I don't know," she says. "I don't know why I'm scared. Nothing you've said makes any sense; none of it can be real."

His nicotine smile—a row of yellow headstones—flashes again. "Do me a favor. Take a gander at the spread and come back and tell me what you see. Tell me what's for dinner, because all I smell is stewed grime."

Daphne watches her feet moving in front of her. She wends the hallway, into the kitchen, where the smell of cloves, rendered fat, butter, and sweet potato washes like a wave over her. Her mouth waters, her gut grumbles. She looks around, but Ethan's not there.

Old Mr. Olmwood is half-dozing, half-stirring his bowl of fresh eggnog. "The boy's down in the cellar, Miss Daphne," Olmwood says.

"The cellar? What for?"

"Oh, fetching a jug of our apple cider, I'd imagine. We press it down there in the cellar."

Daphne's gut gurgles. She's never been this hungry, and nothing has ever smelled so irresistible. The ducks are out and glistening, the plates of veggies and the basin of mashed potatoes and the gravy boat and the foil-wrapped yams all steam, waiting to be dug into. She hovers over the ducks and it takes all her willpower not to peel a strip of golden crackled skin from the flesh. The old joy from yesterday, from before she met Carter, resurfaces, and she's grateful for it, for this delicious feeling of belonging, this certainty that she is now where she is supposed to be, where she was always meant to be.

But the elation flickers. She thinks of Carter again, of what he said. Tell me what's for dinner, because all I smell is stewed grime.

Her nose wrinkles as it did when she smelled Carter the first time, but the sour fetor that now assaults her is so much worse than his odor. It's a sulfurous, mildewed bouquet of rot, overripened fruit, and ammonia, and it's made so much worse—accentuated, even—by the overlaid presence of the original smells of Christmas dinner. And just as she smells two things at once—comingled and convergent, both true and both false—she sees two things simultaneously. She sees the sumptuous feast, and she sees its hideous abnegation. Where the ducks are, there are also steaming spools of tarry black coils halfway between roots and sausage links (or entrails). Where the mashed potatoes steam in their casserole dish also puddles a gray gruel with the consistency of grits. Worst are the sweet potatoes, because these are still *moving*, dandling their tiny, tarsi-tipped appendages through tears in their tinfoil membranes.

This only lasts a second, the time it takes for her to breathe in and then bite her tongue to keep from screaming.

She hears Ethan coming up the staircase from the cellar, but she doesn't want to see him anymore. That's not true; she wants more than anything to see him, to feel his hands enfold her shoulders, to rest her head against his broad chest, but she knows—or at least the part of her that still knows who she is knows—that she has to get away. None of this is right.

As Ethan's footsteps quicken, Daphne hurries out of the kitchen. Out in the living room, Carter is waiting for her, a hateful expression of amusement on his face.

"So, what did you see?" Carter asks. "What's for dinner? I've never been able to see the pretty lie. Are there sweet potatoes? God, I miss eating yams." He chuckles.

"Why?" she says. She feels like she might collapse.

"Daph? You there?"

"Your prince calls."

"Stop it. Why are you like this? Why do you— Do you think this is funny? Nothing about this is funny!"

For just a blink, the regret she glimpsed before etches itself into Carter's features. He looks away from her, out the window. There are seven—no, eight—of the trees waiting in the snow.

"Sorry," he says. "It's just, the first time this happened was a tragedy. So was the second time. But now... What are you, the fifth girl? Well, now it's just like a bad joke."

Footsteps approach the living room. *Ethan.*

"You can stop this," Daphne says. Her voice is a little wraith of smoke barely escaping her lips.

Carter closes his eyes. "You can't stop what's already done. Soon you'll hear Her calling to you."

"Daph?"

Ethan's approaching, and her body aches for him.

"Hey, little bro," Carter says. He looks at his feet, like he's afraid to look Ethan in the eye.

"This stranger isn't bothering you, is he?" Ethan asks, draping his arm around Daphne's shoulders. Her skin tingles under her sweater at the weight of his arm, the press of his muscle. Her body is telling her to go limp, like a bird in a dog's mouth. Ethan's touch is joy, simple warmth and kindness. Why not unspool herself, why not melt into that joy, into his touch, into his flesh and bones?

No. *Run.*

Daphne breaks away from Ethan and bolts. Not that there's anywhere to run. Ethan doesn't even chase her, doesn't even speak a word. Like he knows there's no point.

Daphne gets as far as the den where, like a doe spotlit by a truck's headlights, she's arrested by the dazzling coruscations of the Christmas tree. An immense specimen, it towers to the very ceiling, twelve, maybe fourteen feet high, decorated from top to bottom in lights, tinsel, and ornaments. Steeped in the tree's shadow and its glow, Daphne can feel her resolve dissolving. She's reaching out. She watches her hand reach out. The tree smells like pines and blood, like spruce and iron. Her finger grazes a branch, and the sensation is uncanny, like the odd tingle when the hairs of the right arm brush against the hairs of the left.

As she ponders what that might mean, Ethan comes from behind and puts his arm around her, tighter this time. Daphne looks behind them, as if Carter might come charging to her rescue, but of course he doesn't, and most of her is glad for that, glad to melt again to Ethan's gentle grip around her wrist.

"Come to the dinner table, Daph."

She lets him take her. Or her legs do. They don't listen to her when she tells them to run again, nor do her arms heed her command to shove Ethan away.

At the table, she doesn't see the lie anymore, only the hideous assemblages of pulpy, stringy flesh. But she still smells the good; smells the joy and bounty of a Christmas feast, and her mouth waters despite all that her eyes can't escape.

The fifth girl, Carter called her. Not a tragedy, a bad joke; a farce.

Ethan has put a fork and knife in her hands. The Olmwoods—Mom and Dad—beam at her from across the table, encouraging her to try this or that first.

"Go on, Daph, it's getting cold."

Ethan, so handsome, is showing his teeth, straight and pearly and perfect, framed in pink gums. Daphne stares at his teeth and then stares at a little pulsing vein in his throat, the same artery she feels chugging under her own jaw.

Maybe Carter is right. Maybe it is too late. *Soon you'll hear Her calling to you.*

But she hasn't heard a voice yet, no voice other than her own, the voice telling her all the better things she could do with her fork and knife than cut into the putrid flesh on her plate.

GOT THE SPIRIT BUT LOSE THE FEELING

Ned Cobb pulls the mortuary van into the parking lot, his tired body shuddering with relief at the sight of Sheriff McCaskill's cruiser parked under the tacky red neon sign that proclaims TIFFANY'S DINER - BEST CHICKEN FRIED STEAK IN TOWN. Tiffany's is the furthest outpost of Crumb, Texas, the last stop before the ramp to 380 and the rest of the world.

There's a good amount of cars in the lot, and Ned can see people in the booths, and that relaxes him somewhat, as much as he can relax given what he's been through the last—how long has he been up now? Twenty-eight hours? Thirty-two? He takes a deep breath and closes his eyes. Breathes in, breathes out.

He turns the key and kills the engine. Crickets in the roadside bushes fill the new silence. He checks under the tarp again. Harriet Winthrop is still there, her body inert again with the wire severed; that translucent thread like fishing line laced through her spinal cord and into her brain. He checks his face in the mirror. With his eyes bruised and ringed from exhaustion and his nose busted and swollen, he looks like a raccoon with a coke problem. His lip's cut too. Winthrop—or the thing that turned her into a deadly marionette assassin, rather—really did a number on him back at Doc Landers' office. But at least he's alive. At least he's still in control of his own body. It's been six hours now since he's heard from either Doc or Deputy Barron.

"If something happens to me, find the sheriff, tell him everything," was what Deputy Barron said before driving off to investigate the Chapek farm.

So here Ned is, at Tiffany's, where the sheriff always spends his evenings.

The bell jangles as Ned steps in. He's barely set one foot down before a familiar, pale face studded with piercings and crowned in royal purple hair fills his vision. Doreen greets him with a smile: black lipstick, white teeth, pink gums.

"Howdy, Ned," Doreen says. "You look like dogshit. Want the usual?"

He shakes his head. Doreen's been waiting tables here since they were in high school, back when Ned had dreams of doing something more stimulating with his life than driving a van—not even a proper hearse—for a funeral home, and back when Doreen was supposed to go off to art school and be the butterfly who breaks free from her small-town chrysalis. Ned and Doreen— always a little more than friends, never really a thing; just the only two kids in town who listened to Joy Division and dared believe President Reagan was a senile shit-for-brains.

"I gotta talk to the sheriff, Dor," Ned says, brushing past her.

It's the usual small crowd of regulars in the diner. Mrs. Tiffany, the proprietress, a slender, fifty-something auburn-haired woman who more resembles a high school principal or bank attendant than the owner of a greasy spoon, sits at her booth highlighting figures on a spreadsheet. The next booth over, Old Lyle Rook, knife salesman, is sharing a meal with his friend Johnny Deale, lawyer. But the man Ned's after is at the counter, sitting high on his stool, nose buried in the day's paper. PRES. CLINTON'S 100 DAY RATINGS LOWEST EVER, the headline reads.

"Sheriff?" Ned says, coming to lean beside him.

Sheriff McCaskill lowers his newspaper and scowls. With his iron gray hair and pouting lower lip, the sheriff's always reminded Ned of a somehow-grumpier Lee Marvin. The look in the sheriff's eyes tells Ned that even all these years later, Ned's still the longhaired, pierced-nose troublemaker he caught selling weed to the other kids on prom night. Weed he got from Doreen, of course.

"Yeah?" McCaskill grunts.

Ned hesitates. He's not sure how to begin, or how not to sound crazy. Better to just show him Harriet Winthrop and the wire still dangling from her brainstem.

"Sheriff, if you'll follow me outside, I've got something I need to show you."

"Follow you? Outside?" The sheriff's already squinty eyes narrow to slits. He has such a leathery face. "This some sort of game, Cobb?"

"No, sir. *Deadly* serious. Deputy Barron told me to come to you."

McCaskill looks even more annoyed. "Oh, did he now?"

Ned glances around. The other patrons are watching him intently. The most irksome thing about small towns: no privacy anywhere. Doreen is smiling at him as she freshens Old Lyle's coffee. All circumstances aside, Ned can't help but smile back. How is it she's gotten prettier the further into her twenties she gets?

"Is this about the alien nonsense again?" McCaskill asks.

Ned's not sure how to respond.

"It's that alien shit, ain't it?" Old Lyle calls out, leaning over the back of his booth, his nicotine-yellow teeth shucked like an ear of sweetcorn.

"Language, Lyle," Mrs. Tiffany chides without looking up. She's finished with her spreadsheet and moved onto a crossword puzzle.

"Dan came around here a couple hours ago, spouting nonsense," McCaskill says. "Some high-blue bullmess about alien puppets and wires in folks' heads. Near about had him committed on the spot, I'll tell you."

Ned's hands are cold and clammy. The deputy was already here? But then where did he go after stopping here? Was that before or after he went to the Chapek farm?

"Ridiculous, all these rumors," Johnny Deale says, his shoulder-length gray mane flopping as he shakes his head. "Those two rotten Dufresne kids go out to shoot bottle rockets at steers and say they see a meteor, next thing everyone's seeing aliens and U-F-Os."

"There *was* a meteor," Lyle says. "I seen the pictures like everyone else."

"*Meteorite* if it hits the ground, you ignoramus. And anyway, you didn't see pictures of any meteorite, you saw pictures of a crater."

"There was no meteor when we checked it out," McCaskill says.

"*Meteorite*," Deale and Mrs. Tiffany say.

"It was just a burnt hole in the ground," McCaskill continues. "You ask me, them damn troublemaking kids just blew something up in the woods and spun a tall tale."

Ned leans against the counter and pinches his forehead. Like sharp fingers poking the inside of his skull, a headache's flaring up. It was nine days ago when the Dufresne brothers told their story about the meteor.

"What about what Mr. Chapek saw on his farm?" Doreen says.

A week back the whole town was buzzing with the story that Mr. Chapek, respected farmer and rancher, had gone crazy. Chapek said he'd watched a slimy, gray, legless creature—something like an obscene tadpole—flop its way across the pasture toward the barn.

McCaskill scoffs. "Oh, that nothing-burger. Chapek was drunk, he admitted so to me himself after we searched his barn the next morning. Nothing there."

"I've been drunk once or twice. Drunk doesn't make people see aliens," Ned says.

McCaskill's leathery face cracks with a rare smile. "For what it's worth, I wouldn't be surprised if ol' Chapek was doing heavier stuff than Jim or Jack."

Ned's anxiety and exhaustion give way to frustration, and he pounds his fist on the counter, an action that hurts more than he expected. "Look, I don't care what you think you know, I've seen it for myself."

"Inside voice, son," McCaskill says. "Now what is it you've seen?"

"Those wires Deputy Barron told you about, the ones in folks' heads? I've seen them, hell, I can show you if you'll just take a look."

"Seen them where?" McCaskill asks.

"On Harriet Winthrop and Craig Peterson."

"What about Harriet, now?" Lyle asks.

"It's just horrible what happened to Craig Peterson," Mrs. Tiffany mutters. "Forty-two years old, two kids, beats cancer only to die in a pointless car wreck."

"Drunk drivers, the bane of all civilization," Johnny Deale says, shaking his head.

If a drunk driver hadn't slammed into Craig Peterson's car two days ago, no one would have ever found out what was going on. Ned was the one who drove the body to the funeral home, the one who found the severed wire, a translucent cord coiling from a little hole in the dead man's spine. Ned showed the body to Doc Landers, who performed a—very much unsanctioned—autopsy with his friend Deputy Barron in attendance. Landers was tracing the path of the threads through Peterson's skeletal system and musculature when frail Harriet Winthrop, the friendly old post office worker, barged into Doc Landers' office. She was maybe eighty pounds and well past seventy years, but she threw Ned across the room like he was made of packing peanuts. She'd have strangled Doc Landers were it not for Deputy Barron putting two bullets through her skull. The wire that held her in thrall then detached and burrowed its barbed tip into Barron's arm, and might have threaded into his bones and taken control had Ned not burned it out with a scalpel heated on an alcohol flame, because as it turns out, the wires play by the same rules as deer ticks. In the eight or so hours since, Ned's been surfing a tide of adrenaline interspersed with crashes, and right now he's crashing again.

"We're not talking about drunk drivers, we're talking about aliens," Ned says. It sounds so silly, spoken out loud.

"I don't believe aliens could come here," Mrs. Tiffany says. "I'm no astrophysicist, but it seems to me we're too far away from any other star for travel to be feasible. It would take hundreds of years to get here."

"Nothing saying aliens couldn't live a really long time," Doreen says. "I mean, aren't there trees and jellyfish that live for a thousand years?"

"Trees and jellyfish can't make spaceships," Mrs. Tiffany replies. "Have you ever heard of Fermi's Paradox?"

"Oh, that's the one where you should believe in God because of hell, right?" Lyle says.

"That's Pascal's Wager," Johnny Deale says.

"If there's so many stars with so many planets in the universe that can bear life, and so many of those that can develop intelligent life, why haven't we ever made contact? That's Fermi's Paradox in a nutshell," Mrs. Tiffany says.

"Aliens been here, just the government won't tell us," Lyle says.

"That's one explanation for the paradox," Mrs. Tiffany replies. "Another is the Great Filter—that intelligent life destroys itself before it can reach the stars."

"Could we please focus here?" Ned says, clapping his hands, as much to rouse himself as to get the others' attention.

"Maybe we should listen to him," Doreen says. "Ned isn't the type to just make shit up."

"Thank you!" Ned says, louder than he means to.

"Well, I think I've had quite enough of this silly talk," McCaskill says, turning back toward the counter with an air of finality. "You'd think we'd stop hearing about this alien stuff after two months."

"Two months? It wasn't even two weeks ago that that meteor hit," Ned protests.

"*Meteorite*," Mrs. Tiffany, Johnny Deale, Doreen, and Lyle all say.

"What do you want us to do, Cobb?" McCaskill asks. "You want me to believe there's some space aliens turning people into puppets? You want me to get on the horn and call up President Bush and have him send the army?"

"What do you mean President Bush? It's President Clinton now," Ned protests. "And all I want is for you to come look—"

"I think I know who the president is," McCaskill replies with an edge.

Ned is about to argue when he realizes this is pointless, they're drifting from the point again. But then he sees something that makes his heart lurch.

McCaskill straightens out his newspaper. The headline is different now: IRAQI ARMY INVADES KUWAIT. And the date is different; wrong by three years.

Isn't it?

"If aliens were coming, they wouldn't come here," Johnny Deale says. "Who the hell would want to take over Crumb, Texas? No offense, Sheriff."

The sheriff only grunts, flipping his newspaper.

"Closing time in half an hour," Mrs. Tiffany announces, checking her watch. "If you want something, Ned, now's the time to order."

Ned doesn't answer.

"You know, Mr. Deale, why *wouldn't* aliens come here?" Doreen asks, leaning on the counter beside Ned now. "It's quiet, small, an easy place to start."

At least someone in here has a brain. Ned turns to her. "Dor, why don't you come and see? I need someone to believe me. I need someone to help me—we're all in danger, and Deputy Barron—"

The door jangles just as he's speaking. And in walks Sheriff's Deputy Daniel Barron, a tall, young man with a neat crew cut and the ropy, rangy look of a wide receiver—which he was, back in high school.

Ned's gut relaxes, his jaw unclenches, he almost sighs audibly in relief at the sight of Deputy Barron.

"You're back," Ned says. "Thank God you're all right. When you didn't call the payphone at six like you said you would, I thought—"

"Easy there, friend," Barron says, waving his hand. His expression is relaxed, not at all the look of a man who's been up for about as long as Ned has. "You look agitated, Ned."

"I'm agitated because the sheriff won't listen," Ned says, pointing at McCaskill, who barely lifts his nose from his paper to nod at his deputy. "Why don't you tell him?"

"Tell him what?" Barron asks.

"He wants you to tell us what you already told us, I guess," Mrs. Tiffany says.

Barron chuckles. There's something weird in the sound, something not entirely organic, the rhythm too regular, the pitch too uniform. The relief in Nat turns rancid, becomes a high, bright apprehension again.

"Oh, Ned, I hope you haven't been telling that joke to these people," Barron says. He rolls his eyes.

"What joke? What are you—?" Ned stops. His words congeal on his tongue as he stares into Barron's eyes and recognizes the same hollow, lusterless nothing that was behind Harriet Winthrop's when she attacked Doc Landers' office. Ned's eyes track over Barron's head, looking for the slight glimmer of the diner's lights on a wire, but he can't see anything.

"You look queasy," Doreen says, her hand touching Ned's shoulder.

"He's one of them," Ned says, pointing to Barron. "They got him—*it* got him."

Barron—or the puppet, rather—smiles, the folding of the skin around the lips too symmetrical to be human. "Doreen's right, Ned. You look like you need to sit down."

Ned swats his hand away. "Don't fucking touch me."

"Ned—" Doreen tries to hook her arm around his and he reacts on instinct, shoving her away. Doreen strikes the counter, and the way she grunts and the hurt, shocked glimmer of her gray-blue eyes sends a jolt of remorse through Ned.

"I'm sorry, Dor," Ned says. "I'm just—it's not safe here, we need to get out of here. Come with me, we'll drive somewhere safe, we'll..."

His words fail him, his chest contracts, painfully, his breaths become leaden and painful, like he's breathing from an exhaust pipe. His trembling hands feel heavy as dumbbells, and he can't feel his tongue between his teeth, while the walls seem to be closing in, the people around him with their bland pink faces and gawking expressions spinning spinning spinning.

Is this what a heart attack feels like?

A hand grasps his wrist. Mrs. Tiffany. Her eyes look into his, glinting with the shine and depth that speak of a real McCoy human.

"You're having a panic attack, Ned," she says.

Another soft feminine hand takes his other wrist. Doreen. "Easy, Ned. Breathe in and out. Slowly. Calm yourself."

"We need, we need to—" He tries to form a sentence, but it's taking everything he has not to fall over or shake to pieces.

His ears crackle and hiss like old record players. Under that white noise, he hears Mrs. Tiffany's voice. "Look at the apple in my hand, Ned," she says. "Just ground yourself by looking at the apple in my hand."

He looks. She holds a bare palm to him.

"There's no—there's no apple in your hand."

"Sure there is," Barron says, his hateful dead face grinning.

"A shiny red delicious," Mrs. Tiffany says.

"Dark, round, and crimson, like a human heart," Lyle says.

"Hearts are gray, you dunce," Johnny Deale snaps.

He blinks rapidly. There's an apple in her hand now, and then there isn't, and then it's there again, its glossy, waxen red curves shimmering under the overhead lights.

"No, it's not, this isn't—"

"Everyone sees the apple, Ned," Mrs. Tiffany says.

"Don't you want to see the apple?" McCaskill asks, his newspaper folded on his lap now, the headline once again gloating about Clinton's low polling numbers.

"Stop it!" Doreen shouts, pulling Ned away from Mrs. Tiffany. "God, what's up with you freaks? There ain't no goddamn apple."

Ned holds tight to her, and she anchors his feet to the ground, and helps him to a booth, where he sits down. "In the van," he mutters, tears rolling down his cheeks, "in the van, there's a body, there's proof..."

"Shh," Doreen says. "Ned, you're delirious. You're not talking sense."

"I oughta head out, the missus will be expecting me home soon," McCaskill says, standing up and walking to the rack where his coat is hanging.

"I better be going too," Barron says, walking behind him. "Take care, Ned. You oughta go home and catch some sleep. I can tell you need it."

Don't go with him, Ned wants to yell at McCaskill, but his voice is a little shy grub in the trunk of his throat.

Doreen squeezes his hand. "Feeling any better, Ned?" Beautiful little dimples form around the silver stud piercings in her cheeks when she smiles.

Looking at her, feeling his heartbeat steady and the hairs on his arms settle, Ned remembers hot summer afternoons with the two of them sitting in her old '77 F150 Explorer, passing a joint between them, eating bags of gummi bears half-melted by the summer heat and the truck's greenhouse effect, his hand exploring the soft, fuzzy skin of her stomach, breasts, and inner thighs, his fingers sticky with sweat and sugar. She might have tattoos all over her throat and arm now, but she hasn't really changed otherwise. Her eyes are as sweet and bright as ever, and the twinkle of light in them says she's still her.

Lyle and Johnny Deale are paying their check, getting ready to go. The light is out in the kitchen behind the counter—the cook's gone, if the cook was ever there to begin with.

"You all right to close?" Mrs. Tiffany asks Doreen.

Doreen nods in answer. And now it's just Ned and Doreen. Doreen wipes down the counters and turns out the lights. "So tell me about these aliens. What are we dealing with?"

Her tone is serious, sober.

"Do you believe me?" he asks, tracking her as she wipes down the counter with a rag. As he watches her cleaning, he wonders when they—it?—got Deputy Barron. Wonders if McCaskill is a puppet by now. And what about the rest? Probably all of them are, or will be soon.

Doreen tosses the rag into a cleaning bucket, then removes her apron and folds it up. "Don't know yet, but I figure you wouldn't make an ass of yourself if you didn't believe something was happening, and I don't think you're on anything. Are you?"

Ned shakes his head. "No. Three months sober."

She sits down across from him in the booth, leaning forward on her elbows. "Clean too?"

"Yeah, uhh—" He stops, wondering why she's asking about him being clean. Her eyes still shimmer, human-like, and yet... "Dor, I need to ask you something."

"What?"

"Can I...feel behind your neck?"

She tilts her head, like a cat. The dimples appear again around her cheek studs. "This some kind of put-on?"

"I'm serious."

She rolls her eyes. "Sure. Knock yourself out." His hands tremble as he reaches across the booth, grazing her cheek and flicking past the fleshy lobes of her ears with their huge black gauges. He feels the bumps of her neck and spine, up to the base of her skull, down toward the neckline. "Feel anything interesting?"

No wire. No wire in her. He sags with relief. "Oh God, you're still you. You're still—"

She leans in, presses her lips to his. His tired eyes flutter. He tastes the menthols she smokes on her breaks.

His eyes open, and they're not in the diner anymore. His shoes crunch into a litter of old receipts and empty cigarette packets, and his back sinks into the familiar seat cushions of Doreen's old Ford. From the truck's crummy stereo, "Disorder" by Joy Division threads out grainy and faint, like he's listening to the song through a seashell.

Doreen sits beside him, in the driver's seat. Whiskers of pale smoke waft from the tip of a lit joint tweezed between her tattooed fingers. "You feeling better?" she asks.

He nods his head, slowly. Yes, he feels better. Safe, relaxed, all the aches gone.

"So, why do you think these aliens came here, Neddy?"

He shrugs his shoulders. "I don't know. To conquer, I guess. Isn't that what invasions are about?"

Doreen slips the joint into Ned's lips, and Ned takes a puff. It's nasty stuff that makes him cough, and that discomfort is almost enough to make him believe this is real.

"I don't know, Neddy," she says. "Maybe they think they can help. Maybe they see a reckless species going off the rails, and they're here to steady the proverbial wheel. Or maybe that's just some bullshit they tell themselves. Maybe it's just fun to see what you can do to lesser creatures."

Doreen brushes her hand through her hair, and when her fingers emerge, delicate silver wires slither from under her black nails. The song on the stereo hits its crescendo: Stephen Morris starts massacring the drums and Ian Curtis launches into immortal refrain.

"What will it feel like?" Ned asks.

"What do you mean?"

"I mean, will it hurt when the wires burrow into me?"

She rests her hand on Ned's wrist, her fingers sticky with the grime of evaporated soda that coats the armrest. The wires coil around Ned's arm; they're not smooth as they appear, rather edged in tiny bristles like what grow on cat's ear leaves.

"Oh, Neddy." Her voice is so perfectly inflected, so unmistakably her own. "Haven't you figured it out? They already have."

"But when? When did they, when did you—?"

She presses a finger to his lips. "Relax. Just listen to the music, and don't worry about what your body's doing without you."

A WILD GREEN TIDE IS SOON COMING—NOTES ON A PLANNED STORY

Because every trope must be resisted, and because a triangle is a stronger shape than a star, there are only three, not five teenagers in the banana-yellow Jeep. First to be introduced is the unfortunately named Carlsbad—"Bad Carl" to his friends—whose appearance and ethnicity the writer leaves open, except that his hair is an unruly, dark bramble crown. He swishes dip in his cheeks as the Jeep judders and bounces on the dirt road that split off from the highway that knits Calrose, Florida, to the little gas-station-hamlet of Oliff Branch. Bad Carl hates dip, that much is clear from the face he makes if this is a movie, whereas if this is not a movie the prose relates in pithy strokes of narration the bitter, pungent expectations set upon North Florida country boys.

When the Jeep, artfully spattered with mud, pulls up, the driver is the first to get out and step into the shadow of the grim and gothic Bellamy House. We hate Big Al as soon as we meet him, with his half-unbuttoned Banana Republic shirt (the writer has channeled all his distaste for the Prepneck kids—Preppy Rednecks—he knew in high school into a homunculus of obnoxious traits and attitudes that wears the name Big Al), his wavy bleach-blond surfer hair, and his perpetual sunburn that will make him look 40 by the time he's 23. We hate him even more when he pours out the dregs of his bottle of Keystone Lite and then flings it at the house that looms ahead, the missile smashing through a dusty pane on the second floor.

Now the hypotenuse of the lust triangle climbs out of the Jeep, her pink, coltish legs a stark contrast to the earthy tones of the dirt road beneath her sandals. Zoey is tall, skinny, and pale, with frizzy red hair she ties with a hairband and thick librarian glasses. She scolds Big Al for his senseless vandalism, or maybe she doesn't because she's dumbstruck by some indefinable menace radiating from the backwoods manor's dilapidated façade, half-swallowed by six varieties of wild vines. Either way, Big Al hooks his arm around her waist and pulls her close to him to plant a sloppy kiss. In prose,

Bad Carl watches the kiss and remembers when he and Zoey went to Dillon's Arcade for her ninth birthday party, and then thinks what a tragedy it is that someone as smart as her is letting her grades go to shit and wasting time with Big Al, forsaking nursing school for a future of stretch marks and TV dinners and bags upon bags of crushed aluminum cans taken out to the curb every week. Meanwhile, in a screen treatment, an extreme closeup on Bad Carl's eyes conveys his disgust and ambiguous jealousy.

Bad Carl tries one last time to talk Big Al out of the planned mischief. The usual reasons: cops, Judeo-Christian morality, respect for sufferers of suicidal depression like Mr. Bellamy. Big Al refutes and/or dismisses his concerns with practiced competence and assuredness. The police don't ever come out this far unless someone calls them, and anyway, the land belongs to Big Al's dad—the house is getting knocked down in a few months so he can build a new hunting lodge, so what difference will a few more broken windows make?

Bad Carl attempts another tack—What about tetanus? What if they get hurt?

What are you, a pussy?

Call me a pussy again, Alphonse.

Big Al's chapped lips are shaping the word when Zoey calls the boys' attention.

Out in the unruly woods, swarming with vines and undergrown by a carpet of pine litter and deer moss, a whitetail buck is watching them from between two skinny slash pines. A beautiful eight-pointer, the kind of deer men in these parts love to parade from the beds of their trucks to show the world they get to decide when and how beautiful things leave.

The deer shows no fear of the three teens, and stands stock still while watching them, an antlered harbinger to the terror that all such stories as this must deliver. Bad Carl thinks he sees a green glimmer in its eyes, while Big Al squints and pantomimes holding and pointing a rifle at the animal.

The deer turns from them and calmly slinks back into the woods. The teens don't speak of it, or maybe they do, it depends on word economy up to this point (if a prose story) or various factors in a screen treatment.

Inside the house, fading afternoon light shunts in through cracks and holes in the walls, while cobwebs trace beautiful, elegiac veils around the chandelier light fixtures and the long-forgotten chairs of the parlor. In a film version, the camera pans past forgotten framed photos of the Bellamy family, some in black-and-white or sepia, including one of a bald man dressed in strange particolored robes. In prose, Bad Carl notices the photos but doesn't dwell on these pointillistic narrative particles.

Zoey asks aloud—and goes unanswered—if it's termites that create all the little puncture wounds that pepper the walls.

We follow Bad Carl as he goes off on his own to explore the home. There is still plenty of light infiltrating the structure, but he uses the flashlight on his phone and minds his steps as he ascends the creaking staircase. Maybe this is the time we learn more about Bad Carl's past and his character. The narration might offer insights into his home life, the aunt and uncle always watching cable news, or maybe it doesn't. Maybe Bad Carl remains a cypher because the writer likes him that way. Maybe interiority and backstory are extraneous to the real meat and gristle of a story, optional choices made *de rigueur* by decades of homogenized workshop instruction that relies on canned aphorisms like "give every character one interesting, memorable physical trait." All of this is tentative, all of this is ephemeral, all of this may never get past the strobing black line at the top of the white word processor page; maybe this is just a momentary discursive diversion to distract from the novel that was coming along great until it wasn't.

Bad Carl follows a harsh glare into a room on the second floor, one cluttered with bookshelves and mirrors. The mirrors are dusty and fogged and tarnished but some still cast Bad Carl's face back at him, albeit altered in subtle or grotesque ways. Past the gauntlet of mirrors, Bad Carl finds a bookcase stuffed with paperbacks with peeling spines, and next to that bookcase is a writing desk upon which sits a mechanical typewriter. A cobweb whorl surrounds it, almost as if some spider wove a protective charm around the machine. Bad Carl dispels it as easily as he'd blow out birthday candles. A single page, yellowed with age, sits atop the paper rest. Someone has typed a single line on it: A WILD GREEN TIDE IS SOON COMING.

A sound attracts his attention and he turns his head. Something taps the broken window, and a serpentine shadow slithers behind the illuminated drapes. Bad Carl approaches the window and almost stumbles on a bottle—the bottle Big Al chucked—and when he looks up the shadow is gone, and all he can see outside the window is an air potato vine crawling up the house's wall.

We cut to another room if this is a visual form like film or a graphic novel, or possibly an RPG-maker indie horror game you can download for $2.99. If this is prose fiction, Bad Carl overhears the other two and investigates the sounds they're making.

Here, in what appears to be a trophy room—bursting with mounted sport fish, heads of buck, elk, and hog, geese and other waterfowl hung from wires as if they're still flying—Big Al and Zoey are making out, Big Al with gusto, as if he's biting into a juicy nectarine, while Zoey is more tentative, her bespectacled eyes roving around and alighting on the sharp antlers and the glass eyes of the game animals, and the rusted, gossamer-wreathed barrels of shotguns and hunting rifles.

Big Al slides his hand up her stomach and lifts up her cropped shirt, uncovering her bra and a mild red rash on the skin of her ribcage. It's now that Bad Carl walks in. Zoey's eyes meet his before Big Al notices him standing in the doorway.

Wordless tension, punctured by descriptions of Bad Carl's metabolic responses—preferably something not too cliched, nothing about "boiling blood"—before Bad Carl turns around and stomps off.

Carl, Zoey manages to say, but he's already gone.

Bad Carl heads back to the room of mirrors and old books. The sun has fallen beneath the pines, ruddy now, bloodshot and darkening to a bruised glimmer. In the rapidly darkening space, Bad Carl finds Big Al's bottle and picks it up. He faces his nearest mirror-self, a dusty, warped semblance, and flings the bottle through it. Delicate mirror shatters against the sturdiness of mass-produced brown glass. In the immediate aftermath, something taps on the window. *Tap-tap-tap.* It sounds like a person's finger on a windowpane. But when Bad Carl investigates and peels aside the tattered drapes, there's nothing outside except a lush air potato vine that's crawled up the house's face.

Bad Carl's own bewildered, frightened face stares back at him from a dozen tarnished silver puddles. Picking up the bottle again, Bad Carl smashes every surface where his face dares see him, and as he breaks mirror after mirror, he thinks back to childhood again, shared birthday parties with Zoey, bug hunts in the fields and pine woods outside the middle school, simpler days when they weren't expected to be anything but friends, when they both hated Big Al and his shithead land-developing, wetland-draining, pillar-of-the-community dad. This sudden flourish of interiority works in prose, while in a screen treatment the shots of mirrors splintering are interspersed with micro flashbacks of halcyon childhood times with Zoey before she took up with a boy who hates her only a little less than he hates himself.

In the last intact shard of a broken mirror, Bad Carl sees Big Al watching him from the doorway.

Blue balls work up a fury, don't they?

Fuck you.

Bet you'd like that. Guys say you're jealous of Zoey and me; maybe that's right, but not how they think.

Bad Carl balls up his fists, ready to speak the only language his family and community cared for him to learn fluently.

Big Al steps into the room, his muddy boots crunching over shards of glass. Bad Carl squares up, ready to drop his sunburnt ass.

From downstairs, Zoey calls up to the boys, Hey, guys, something weird's going on here.

They don't answer or even acknowledge what she's said, like two opposed magnets on an inexorable course. The writer worries Zoey might be "flat," or "passive," or that she "lacks agency." Maybe that's so. Like too many women or girls in too many horror stories, maybe she's been created only to be sacrificed. Much like the deer harbinger, she's only a token of terror, a symbol of something more than the thing in itself. But then the writer remembers "agency" is a buzzword, a conversation filler in workshops that can't meet a story where it wants to be. What if her agency is her passivity? What if she's here because it seemed as good or bad as any other choice? What if she couldn't imagine a life less empty than what her parents have lived, and her being here in this strange place, forgotten by the men who are supposedly fighting over her, is just the inevitable result of that fatalism? Or maybe the writer gives himself too much credit.

Either way, back to the duel that isn't a duel, Bad Carl's all squared up for a fight, except Big Al doesn't want to fight.

She tell you it was my idea to invite you out here?

It's the only thing he could have said that Bad Carl isn't ready for. Just like he isn't ready when Big Al comes all the way into his personal bubble and leans in. Big Al's breath smells like the bottom of a beer bottle, while his hair and skin smell of styling mousse and sunscreen—that second one's surprising, given the condition of his skin. Bad Carl's immobilized. He can't hear his own thoughts, let alone the slither of something serpentine crawling through the broken glass. He can't control the flow of his own blood, can't control the sudden burning heat in his ears or the tumescing cock in his jeans that even now his childhood nemesis' rough hand is digging under his belt for.

But then the scream. In a prose version, Bad Carl thinks of that time his uncle ran over a cat and it took ten minutes to die. In a graphic novel, the vowels—bold, embossed, red-orange—splatter across the panels. In a film treatment, the actress who wears Zoey's skin dredges up every cubic inch of air in her lungs to let loose a queen of a scream.

The writer worries again about Zoey, if there's enough of a character here for anyone to care if she lives or dies. He also worries—even though he knows Aristotle's narrative rules are more taste than tenet—that the story as a whole lacks a suitable anagnorisis, and if this lack is why he hasn't finished it, why it still feels empty. Is there no wheel or reversal, no sparkling recognition to exert its fascination on the audience? Unless the anagnorisis already came, before the "monster" even showed up, or unless the recognition comes not between two characters but between the characters and the setting (realizing this world doesn't want them) or between the characters and the narrative itself, when they realize what kind of story they're in too late to save their friend.

The boys scramble down the stairs, all enmity and eros dissolved. In the rapidly occluding parlor, their phone flashlights find no sign of Zoey, only eight long, jagged crimson streaks, the grooves her fingers carved into the floorboards as they were ground to pulpy stubs by an overwhelming pull. The front door hangs ajar, rattling on its rusted hinges while the dark jaws of the universe lurk beyond its frame.

Bad Carl is the first to rush out and shout Zoey's name, and in answer Zoey screams again, somewhere out there, somewhere in the trees. Bad Carl and Big Al call again, but they've heard the last of Zoey. And so have we. The only reply is the rustle and squirm of something among the trees, a leafy susurrus most of the way to laughter.

Only now do the two young men—the little boys lost—notice how the various vines swathed over the Bellamy house are moving, tendrils snaking in every direction as if in search of prey.

They argue, both conscious now of the menace all around them, but at cross-purposes on what to do about it. Big Al wants to get the hell out of here and drive back to Calrose where things make sense (the *Ordinary World*, if we're riding with Campbell, and we'd prefer not to). But Bad Carl thinks they should search for Zoey, hoping against hope there's still something left of her to find and save. He has passion, courage, and morals on his side. But Big Al has the keys, and more importantly, Big Al isn't afraid to save his own sunburnt ass whatever it takes. He shoves Bad Carl and makes a dash for his Jeep. Bad Carl catches him by his ankle, and Big Al falls.

A melee ensues, the two boys grappling for the keys, for each other's throats. Knees, elbows, teeth, blows below the belt, all on offer here, while all around them the kudzu (three-pronged, voracious), muscadine (spade-shaped, cunning), and air potato vines (round, sturdy) slither ever closer from their dark marches in the shadows of the slash pines.

Big Al comes out the victor. Two things can happen, depending on which the writer finds more convincing when he actually sits down to write it in-scene. Either Big Al escapes from the scrum, or he really starts giving it to Bad Carl, hammering him with blows or closing off the flue of his life with his callused hands. Either way, the vines get him. In scenario one they snag his ankle just as he's almost to the Jeep, while in scenario two they wrap around his waist and lift him off Bad Carl. In both scenarios, the vines enter through the mouth, nostrils, and through new orifices they create in his ribs and back. They wriggle through every soft passage and branch their tendrils in search of something new and interesting all in the space of a second. A medically fascinating vivisection from the vines' perspective, but from Bad Carl's view on the ground it's like watching high tension steel cables shred through a blood bag.

Anointed with his nemesis/would-be paramour's blood, Bad Carl is lucky that the keys fall into his hand. He runs for the Jeep while the vines are still sorting through Big Al's parts as a watchmaker puzzles over a clock's complications. The yellow Jeep roars to life, and the radio playing Pantera when the teens arrived now blares static. In his panic, Bad Carl doesn't pay any attention to this little detail.

Even as Bad Carl turns the Jeep around and angles it toward the dirt road—that humble, ruddy viaduct to civilization—the vines swarm over the Bellamy house and over the lawn. Under their mass the old house groans, shudders, collapses, decades of lost memories and old secrets imploding in an instant, its serried ghosts left now to wander the unpeopled wilderness.

The vines make a go at the Jeep, and an enterprising shock of muscadine even manages to wrap around its bumper but only manages to come away with a plank of chrome as the vehicle veers off to freedom.

In prose, Bad Carl's lack of interiority is the writer's boon now—terror is the hardest emotion to convey, except by direct action, and here Bad Carl's mind-numbing fear manifests in him nearly driving Big Al's Jeep into a ditch while he stares uncomprehending at his phone, trying to remember his own passcode before he realizes he doesn't need the code to call 911.

Call the cops and tell them what? He doesn't know, and it's just as well because he doesn't have service anyway. In the cinematic version, a high-altitude tracking shot shows the Jeep as a garish yellow beacon blazing through the nighted arteries of the vast North Florida pine flatwoods, while in the prose Bad Carl observes the dark silhouettes of trees shuddering and squirming as he bullets past them, off the dirt path and onto the paved state road.

Bad Carl drives without a destination in mind, not even sure he's headed the right way. Anywhere but where he's coming from. Eventually a gas station appears from the nightscape, brightly lit, a bastion of commerce and civilization in a suddenly hostile wild.

There are no other cars in sight, something he barely notices as he pulls up under the station's metal canopy, just as he hasn't really noticed that the radio is still shedding a froth of static even though he's closer to Calrose now, almost on its outskirts.

Bad Carl leaves the engine on and rushes for the door. Of course we know how this ends—civilization's glow never chases the monster away; at best the light of a watchman's lantern or the cone of a streetlight buys the hero some time. At worst, the light is like the phosphorescent lure of an angler fish.

The door doesn't open, and Bad Carl jostles the handle and pounds the glass barrier, shouting his throat to pieces, before noticing the button to the side of the door labeled: *Please Ring for Entry After Dark*. He rings the bell, once, twice, thrice, but nothing happens.

Like the slow, oily drip of a cracked egg, the realization seeps in that there's no one behind the counter. Inside the gas station, hot dogs turn on a cooker, the slushy mixers churn, one-gallon cans of "authentic, local" boiled peanuts gather dust. But no one's there to let him in.

Bad Carl wonders what that means, wonders why he still has no service, and as he's trying and failing to process his predicament, the gas station's lights flicker and then fail. Bad Carl runs to the Jeep while vines reach out from the forest. He shifts into drive as muscadines twine around the concrete pillars that support the station's canopy, and a kudzu strand tears off the driver's side mirror.

Bad Carl drives toward nothing, toward a town that may not exist anymore. Drives because there's nothing else he can do, no one he can go back to save, no one he can call for help.

The way ahead, the Jeep's high beams shine off the dewy edges of lush leaves, while in the rearview mirror twin onslaughts of vines swallow the road, erasing the black scar humans traced through nature.

Up ahead it's the same as behind. The vines close in, spill out from the woods that hem either side of the road. Bad Carl can do nothing but scream, an angry, defiant roar that cracks and stumbles into something small, something plaintive. Why me, the scream asks. Why any of us? As far as the writer is concerned, every revenge story centers on a consequentialist moral argument, but this argument can assume two divergent forms. The first: *X Did Y, So Must Suffer Z.* The second: *I Don't Care If X Did Y or Not, I'll Exact My Z On Them.* This is the second kind of revenge story, where X is the world's ghost/nature's hauntology/anima mundi in the form of animate vines, Y is the three teens selected as representatives of the human race, and Z is a balancing of the scales, a hard reset to factory settings.

A wild green tide washes over the Jeep and Bad Carl within it.

Cut to black. Epilogue time. Bright light of morning glistens off dew rolling down the curve of a vine's leaf. Pan down to a verdant forest floor, a crisscross lattice of various vines protecting the callow saplings of a new global carbon sink. Pan up. Three pairs of dirty human feet tread softly over the tender vines. The sun rises, and three young naked people, two boys and one girl, glimpsed only from behind, explore an Edenic paradise of majestic greenery. Vines of impossible dimensions branch into explosions of voluptuous flowers and succulent fruit of every color.

Above, a black monolith strobes in a tract of white.

DISTANT FIRE OF WINTER STARS

Five miles from town, just me, my rifle, the deer blind, the white field getting deeper the more powder falls. Here's me in a pile of myself, one foot corked at a ninety-degree angle, still caught in the bottom rung of the slick ladder. There's the vast pale dark held up by the skinny pines reaching into the nowhere.

All the whistling, all the roar, my rifle already buried in the fresh white, my face windburnt, hands like lifeless fans of coral under my gloves. Get one free, pull the heel of the glove by my teeth. Search for my phone, bite tongue, taste iron, stay angry, don't let the dark in the corners of my vision spread. Phone's dead, of course.

What was it Dad always said? *You can borrow time, but only from yourself.*

My backpack gathers snow a body's length out of reach. Inside there's handwarmers, a roadflare, bullets, a first aid kit, Dad's flask. The first step of this delicate procedure must be agony: lifting my twisted ankle from the rung. How can something numb hurt so much? Frozen crust of flesh around a core of molten pain. How can a leg be so heavy?

I recall when I was nine, the first time I found Dad ragdolled on the floor of the garage with one of his weird books splayed on his stomach, and I tried to turn him over, tried to lift that continent of surly fat and muscle and beard.

Life doesn't like being played with, is what he said when he woke up.

Dad could fix everything. Car radios, bicycle chains, eyeglasses, shoes, everything. Just not himself. At twelve years old he told me from his hospital bed, *Everyone has their time,* and then he breathed into his silver flask, just a blink before he died.

The snow and my own weight fight me for every inch on the way to the backpack. My thumb sticks to the zipper, and the zipper takes its tithe of skin when I rip it free. Here's the handwarmers.

Funniest thing, when I find Dad's old flask under the granola bars. It's warm. Shouldn't steel be cold? Shouldn't it stick to my hand like the zipper?

I've never drunk what's inside, what he passed to me in secret from his hospital bed, what I kept from the nurse and the doctor and Mom and hid first in my box of secret treasures and then kept in my first car's glovebox and then dropped in my hunting bag for whatever luck such trinkets bring.

I've never even twisted the top. Dad was a Kentucky bourbon man, so that must be what's inside. But now when I unscrew the cap—stubbled with just a salting of rust—the smell that oozes out surely isn't bourbon. And what leaks into the snow isn't the sweet amber of corn mash.

Darkness fattens around the corners of my eyes. How do such skinny pines hold up so much sky?

I remember to open my eyes. The world has turned, or rather I have, sat up now, my back to a tree. Fireglow kisses the feeling back into my face. Resin hisses and branches whine as they bend and snap.

There's a man across from me. Big as I am, just my same age or thereabouts. Even looks like me, except his beard is wilder. He tends the small fire with a pine branch. It's when he smiles, and mirth etches little white crinkles around the rims of his eyes, that I know.

What are you doing here?

He smiles wider; shows a wall of nicotine yellow. I'd ask you the same, kiddo. Seems pretty stupid to come out alone in this weather.

Who do you think you are—my dad?

We both laugh; me weakly, he with vigor and so much fire in his belly that a dead man shouldn't have.

You built this fire?

And splinted your leg. You should be able to walk on it, just favor the right.

How are you here?

It's like I always said, you can borrow time, but only from yourself.

Dad reaches across the fire and hands me the flask. He shakes it so I hear there's still a little something left in there. Some of his life, reserved for a time of need.

Son, there are always ways around these things, if you know what you're doing, and you're willing to give something up.

I think about how Mom raged after he said no to chemo, and suddenly my hand finds feeling enough to make a fist.

You left us. You let the cancer take you away from us.

He doesn't reply straight away, like there's years of silence needs sifting through. I gave up a little time, he says. Gave up a little of what I had left so I could be there when you got grown and needed me. Listen. I can keep this fire going till morning, but when dawn comes, you're on your own. There's the Fish and Wildlife office a mile from here, due west. You know your directions, don't you? I taught you that, at least.

I blink to keep the dark away. Outside the fire's reach is nothing but a ravenous dark. Above my head is all black except for a few cold stars. I see me mirrored on his eyes. There's me, grown man but still a boy so much smaller than this man my same height.

I won't make it that far, Dad.

Hush, boy. You'll feel stronger in the morning.

What if I don't?

You'll have to. Now rest up. I'll keep this fire tended; I'll keep the dark off you till sunup.

I rest my head against the tree and let my eyes flutter shut while the hissing resin sings from the wood. Against the weight of my lids I peek open a last time, expecting it to be nothing but dark, but the fire's still there, and so is he.

THE LITTLEST FISHY

* Glimmer

It's almost like Eva's alive again. Her YouTube video about acclimating new fish to an already populated tank plays in the background as Sherri lowers the bag with her newest acquisition to bob on the water. Entropy will do its work, and the water in the bag will equalize with the temperature of the twenty-gallon tank. Listening to Eva, Sherri almost expects that any second Eva's voice will turn shrill as she tells Sherri to pick up her socks and panties from the bedroom floor. Only Eva had ever been able to arrange her messes into a semblance of order. She smiles to think how proud Eva would be to see her taking care of her own tank now, a community tank no less, with mollies, loaches, killies, even a giant halfmoon betta named Gaspar.

Sherri's newest fish is a mystery.

It's a cute little doofus with googly eyes, a translucent pale belly, and one pectoral fin smaller than the other. When Sherri saw it in the tank at the aquarium store, it was swimming pathetically in circles. None of the attendants at the store could tell her what type of fish Fishy—that's what she's decided to name it—is, nor could they remember stocking it in that tank. They sold it to her for one dollar.

Once she's added the prime and made sure it's adjusted to the tank water's temperature, she releases Fishy into its new colorful home. Fishy is surprisingly cold to the touch, and doesn't swim so much as tumble free of her hand, then sinks all the way to the substrate and settles on its belly. At first Sherri worries the other fish will bother it, but they don't. Even the mollies, who are always so curious about new arrivals, keep their distance, hiding behind the plants and the plastic castle.

Gaspar is another matter. Gaspar, a mustard gas halfmoon giant betta, is the king of the tank. Sherri gave him that name because she wanted to hate him, because he was the first fish she bought, only a week after Eva was killed, mere days after she scattered Eva's ashes into Biscayne Bay as per her wish, when Sherri wanted to have control over something living; when she wanted to be the one to decide what lived and what died. Gaspar Hernandez, his namesake, was a classmate of hers at art school, the guy who talked to her, the only woman in the class, as if she wasn't also there getting a master's degree. The worst thing he'd done was try to poke holes in her thesis paper on the mid-20th century Haitian artist Yvonne Etienne, arguing that Etienne's aquarelles were just inferior copies of the watercolors of the 19th century German artist Fabian Kastl. What made her hate Gaspar Hernandez more than his patronizing tone was that, after some study, she was forced to conclude he was right. Etienne's most famous work, *Orijin Lan* (*The Origin*), was like a crude, blurry forgery of Kastl's *Der Seekaiser* (*The Sea Emperor*), where in place of the murky Triton-figure with his fearsome trident was only a vague, dark hole in the ocean.

But Gaspar the fish was not like Gaspar the human. Sherri's early intent to murder the beautiful betta with neglect failed when Gaspar persisted despite terrible conditions and little food. Soon she had a change of heart and, though it was painful to start, began watching Eva's how-to videos on fish care from her channel, AquaPastelGothique. Unlike her more controversial vlogs on oceanic microplastics, defunding police, and abolishing prisons, these videos had meager views in the dozens or low hundreds—and a good portion of those views were Sherri's. Soon Gaspar thrived, and now Sherri loves him.

"Who's my perfect little murder-bean?" Sherri would coo as he attacked a black worm or flared his fins at his own reflection on the tank.

Now when all the other fish hide from Fishy, it is Gaspar alone who boldly ventures out to investigate. Investigate and then some. Gaspar violently darts at Fishy, striking the defenseless little thing and dragging it by its bigger fin. It's so sudden, Sherri has to reach in and shoo the betta off with her hand. From that moment on, she fits a glass divider in the tank separating Fishy from the others. The loaches, mollies, and killies seem grateful, but Gaspar just pouts, swimming side-to-side, glaring at Fishy from beyond the glass.

* * *

In the early days, when grief was overwhelming, Sherri couldn't watch TV or use the internet because the gunman's face and name were everywhere. All the sappy bullshit about his troubled childhood and his struggles with mental illness—as if everyone else isn't mentally ill in some way, as if that makes killing six innocent strangers understandable—all the thoughts and prayers pablum, and the tired "we can't say for sure it's a hate crime" tripe; she couldn't take it. She still can't. Fuck him, fuck his lawyer, fuck his parents who "can't believe our boy would do that," fuck the cops who fed him Pollo Tropical, fuck the FBI who put him on a "watchlist" and called it a day, fuck the entire city of Miami for being able to sleep at night while people like *him* were everywhere, waiting for their chance to kill people like her.

But at least now Sherri can watch TV again, at least now she can check the news on her phone without her skin crawling.

* * *

As Sherri's preparing for bed, the light in her bedroom starts flickering. That on its own wouldn't mean anything, but she also feels the hairs on her arm rising as if from a static charge.

Then the lights go out. Not just the lights; the AC stops blowing. Her power is out. She glances out her window. Next door, the windows in Mrs. Fuentes' townhouse are still brightly lit. Just as she's drifting to sleep, the power comes back on, and she's bathed in obnoxious light. Weird. She makes a note to herself to talk to her neighbor Randal tomorrow; maybe he'll know what's up.

She switches off the lights and gets back into bed. In the living room, the fish tank gurgles.

* * *

In her dreams, Sherri can be with Eva again. Feel the hair on her arm brush against hers, their warmth comingling, Eva's breath in her ear. In this dream she is swimming in the sea, pushing stones around on the ocean floor, forming strange patterns with them. She whispers something to Sherri from deep down.

Sherri can't understand her. Because she's underwater. Because she's speaking an unfamiliar phrase. "*Orijin Lan, Orijin Lan, Orijin Lan.*" The origin. The origin. The origin. She rises from the bottom and approaches. When Sherri looks into Eva's eyes, they are wrong; changed. Amber glimmers of copper foil with wide black pupils.

Sherri wakes before Eva reaches her.

* * *

Morning light. Her bedsheets are stuck to her back; the air is stale and humid. Sherri's alarm clock didn't go off. She checks her phone. A bit past seven; work is in two hours. There's a fishy smell in the air. When Sherri rolls out of bed and trundles out into the living room, she doesn't see the dead fish scattered on the laminate floor—she feels them first, their cold, slick scales under her toes. The sound she makes is half gasp, half scream.

Twelve dead fish glimmer like bits of dull tin foil in the slanted light that trickles through the blinds—mollies, killies, loaches littering the floor, some in tiny puddles of tank water.

When she turns on the tank light, there are only two fish left in the tank, one on each side of the divider. Gaspar and Fishy. Fishy tumbles through its side of the tank, blinking its googly eyes and yawning with its idiotic round mouth. On the other side, Gaspar swims furiously across the length of the divider as if searching for ingress.

Sherri has no answers; she's heard of mass die-offs, but never mass suicides among aquarium fish. It couldn't be Fishy, could it?

The lights in the kitchen flicker on and off. Crying intermittently, she collects the dead fish into plastic sandwich bags and places the bags into the freezer—she'll give them proper burials after work. She gets dressed, and forces herself to care about the need to get on the road and make it to work on time, or at least acceptably late. On the way out, she writes a note on a Post-It and leaves it on her neighbor Randal's door. ELECTRICITY WONKY. TAKE A LOOK LATER? He's an electrician's apprentice, maybe he can help.

* * *

Work is long. Work is somehow dull and hectic at once. An office manager's job is always that way—you spend six to nine hours every day explaining things to coworkers that they could find out for themselves by just two minutes of looking through their old emails.

Sherri thinks about her poor fish; about Fishy. About the lights. She thinks of Eva, and the dream she can't quite remember. She wishes she could call her; she wishes her phone would start buzzing with a steady stream of choice memes.

"So wat u wearing?" Eva used to text, that same tired old joke that somehow got funnier every time.

When no one's around her workstation, Sherri plays Eva's videos on her phone with the volume so low that it sounds like Eva's whispering a secret to her.

* * *

It's late. Sherri's digging little holes on the lawn behind her townhouse with a spoon. Tiny graves for all the little fish. In front of her, the rising moon gluts into the canal water. She's halfway done with the burials when a shadow falls over her.

"Hey, I got your note," Randal says.

Randal has been her neighbor since before Eva moved in with her. He's tallish, skinny, always looks sleepy. He has a voice as soft as a polite cough. He is kind; his sad-dog eyes make Sherri uncomfortable sometimes.

Sherri tells him what happened, shows him into the apartment. He gingerly steps around the empty yogurt cups and other bits of trash strewn around the floor. A big, fat German roach skitters from out of an empty bag of corn chips; Sherri hopes Randal didn't notice. She can see he wants to say something about the state of the place; she's grateful he doesn't.

He checks the fuse box, says everything's all right. Sherri asks if it could be wiring; he doesn't think so.

"Sorry for taking up your time," Sherri says, but she knows he was grateful for the invitation.

He shrugs it off. "Hey, that's what neighbors are for."

On his way out, he asks what happened to all the rest of the fish. Sherri says nothing, and he lets the question die.

"I like the new one," Randal says, pausing a moment to inspect Fishy.

Sherri thanks Randal for his time and sees him off, wearing her nicest smile. After Randal leaves, she inspects Fishy. Its pectoral fins are no longer mismatched—they are identical in size and shape now. Has Fishy grown? Maybe, but it's hard to tell.

* * *

Night comes, sleep beckons. She dreams.

* * *

She's in the ocean. An ocean without bottom or shore. She kicks and paddles with her arms to stay above the surface, but something is pulling her down. Nothing solid, nothing she can feel. No, she understands somehow that it is an invisible net that holds her, a biological mesh of a quadrillion plankton bound in inexorable strands of vibrant, striving matter. An individual cell is powerless, but taken all together the strength is enough to move mountains. She fights; she loses; she plunges. Her scream is a whorl of silver bubbles erupting from her mouth. Darker darker deeper deeper, and there is something swimming around her now, something of tangible shape. She can't see it, only feels it displacing the water, feels it thrash closer and closer. Close enough it comes that in the bathypelagic gloom sinister geometries reveal themselves—claws and teeth and eyes like disks of amber foil. She would scream were any air in her lungs.

The horror is abolished. Light, glorious light. The weight lifts from her, and she swims not in dark water but in a sea of violet light. There is Eva again, swimming to her, and Sherri embraces her. She knows what Eva wants: to be fertile, for you to be fertile together. She touches Sherri and Sherri's skin melts, Eva's hand reaching into hers as her own reaches into Eva's; intersection, not penetration. Skin, bone, myelin breaks down, cell membranes dissolve, cytoplasm bleeds to cytoplasm. Eva to her, her to Eva; in the gulf of rosequartz light, two becomes one, one becomes many, many becomes a species, becomes a clutch of eggs, becomes a numerous and numinous brood, becomes a future, becomes a second chance at life and everything.

** Shudder

The alarm works this time, and Sherri wakes when she should. Awakens content. She's not sure why. The feeling doesn't carry for long, not after she looks at the bedroom floor and sees the mess again. Clothes, knickknacks, food packaging; two months of depression distilled into a leaf-litter of plastic waste and clutter.

And then when she pushes herself out of bed and goes into the living room, her heart becomes a greasy lump bobbing in her throat.

Fishy is on the other side of the divider now.

Fishy has changed again.

What she doesn't see if more significant—Gaspar. Floating around Fishy is an ethereal flake of mustard-yellow cellophane—a scrap of Gaspar's tail, the sole remnant of her favorite pet.

Fishy seems to hear her sobbing and swims to the edge of its tank to look at her through the glass. Its belly is veined, its fins are silver and very long, edged now in what look like clawed digits. Fishy's eyes are as big as ever, but the rest of its cranium have grown to their proportion. Fishy is five or six times bigger than when she purchased it a few days ago. Sherri realizes Fishy is still hungry; Gaspar wasn't enough, not nearly enough.

* * *

Sherri doesn't go to work that day. Nor the next day. Nor the day after that. She ignores the texts and voicemails for a while, then turns off her notifications and forgets her phone entirely. It's not fear, not quite, but something holds her, compels her to know just what this creature that killed all her fish could be. She camps on her bed with her laptop and researches. The research she's doing now is more intense than any she ever did in the MFA. She only takes breaks to check on Fishy, fetch a new can of soda, or get snacks.

Hours and hours of scrolling through aquarium keeper blogs, online encyclopedias, fishkeeping YouTube channels, none of it yields anything like Fishy. Fishy is a chimera—its bony jaw resembles that of an angler fish, its rotund body has passing similarities to a puffer, and its clawed pectoral fins resemble something between a pleco's fins and the appendages of a clawed frog. When Sherri approaches its tank to feed it, it swims toward her and presses its pale belly to the glass. When Sherri touches the glass, she feels a static charge, and little concentric ripples of pale violet light appear on Fishy's belly.

There is nothing like Fishy in the world; or nothing she can find on the internet. She wishes she could bring herself to venture out to a library—maybe a big one in an old city—and find the old books that might speak to such a creature.

All she can find on the web that approaches what she's looking for is a two-hundred-year-old German poem by a familiar name: "Der Fisch mit den Händen" by Fabian Kastl.

This poem leads her to once again survey Kastl's paintings, his oil works like *Der Neffe des Malers, Schwarze Rose unsterblich,* and *Bernadette,* but also his watercolors: *Sole von Rügen, Der hungrige Wind,* and *Der Seekaiser.* These lead her to strange conspiracy theory websites talking about something called the Science of the Old Dark, a 19th century order called the Brotherhood of the New Dark, and a supposed government program called "Project Red Door"—somehow Kastl is connected to all of this. And this leads her back to her old muse, Yvonne Etienne, and her most storied works: the supposed forgeries like *Kòk Mouri, Kalma Pal,* and *Orijin Lan.*

Interspersed in this she finds herself reading somnolently about connections between ray-finned fish and terrestrial life, neural nets in jellyfish (they're just water with a self-preservation instinct, but aren't we all?), the labyrinth organ in anabantoid fish, trophic cascades, microplastics, ocean acidification and mass coral die-offs, mermaids, ancient fish-worshipping cults, oceanic oil spills...at one point she dozes off and wakes up to find she's written *"They learned to breathe air and walk once, they'll do it again"* on her word processor.

Mixed with her research are dreams from the little time she spends asleep. At a certain point it becomes difficult to discern what she gleans from research and what she sees in her dreams. On the third morning, as she searches her bare cupboards for anything edible, she dazedly watches Fishy—now the size of a bullfrog—climb out of its tank and crawl through the trash on the floor with well-defined amphibian arms. The roaches flee, but Fishy finds them in the trash as a pig finds truffles, and devours them before retreating to the safety of its tank to breathe again. Did this happen or did she dream it? There are no more roaches now, so it must be the former.

This new development frightens her.

The disturbing realization that Sherri doesn't know what Fishy is—and less still what it's turning into—spurs her to new action. Clove oil is considered a humane and effective way of euthanizing injured fish, so she administers a large dose to Fishy's tank. When nothing happens, she pours in the entire bottle—all two ounces of the numbing extract. She watches a whole lot of nothing happen; Fishy swims in its tank blithely, regarding her with eyes that now look small and beady in its huge, froglike head.

She raids the cupboard under the sink. Bleach powder, ammonia, detergent, leather polish, whatever noxious chemical she can find. She dumps it all into Fishy's tank. Dumps so much that the water turns a turbid gray and

Fishy thrashes angrily, so angrily that Sherri stacks two huge art encyclopedias on top of the tank lid and then weighs it with a dictionary for good measure. She watches until the thrashing in the tank stops, but she doesn't remove the books from the lid.

* * *

Another dream. Eva again, but she has changed. It's not just her eyes now; her entire body is altered. She is still beautiful; perhaps more beautiful now than ever she was in life. Her skin is radiant, a rainbow swirl like the nacre of abalone in every one of her scales, a long graceful swirl of translucent protein-silk like a betta's tail ribbons in her wake as she darts after Sherri. Her teeth are sharp, her clawed hands webbed and potent. She will grasp her; she will have Sherri.

Sherri swims away from her, but she'll never escape, not with her clumsy limbs so ill-suited to the surf and brine. She'll bind Sherri in a net of plankton weave and drag her to the hole in the bottom of the deepest trench from which all life emerged...

* * *

Sherri's pretty sure she's lost her job by this point. It's been six days since she last left the house. There's very little left to eat in her fridge or pantry, but she's never really hungry anyway. The last time she checked the fish tank, there was nothing inside, as if Fishy had just dissolved in the noxious soup of household poisons. But she notices that the larger rocks in the substrate have moved—been arranged into geometric patterns. Sherri has seen these patterns somewhere...

She's just beginning to consider what this might mean when someone knocks at her door. At first she ignores the knock, but it comes again.

"It's just me," Randal says.

Sherri opens the door just a crack. She doesn't want Randal to see her house right now. Politely, she asks him to go away.

He says he's worried. Says he hasn't seen her car move from her driveway. Has Sherri been fired?

How is that any of his business?

Well, it's not, but, well, don't you think people will get worried? What if someone calls the cops for a wellness check?

Then they'll waste some pigs' time; she's okay with that.

Randal isn't looking at her anymore. His attention has shifted—he's looking toward her bedroom window. He asks her if one of her sister's kids is visiting.

No.

Well then who's that kid behind the blinds?

Sherri doesn't answer him—from inside her bedroom comes a scurrying noise.

She shuts the door on Randal. She's frightened—she doesn't want Randal to go, but she doesn't want him here either. She can still see his shadow in the crack of the door—he's not leaving.

Sherri steps away from the front door. Something is moving inside her bedroom—sounds of claws scraping the floor and dripping water. How long has it been since she's eaten? What if this is a hallucination? No—Randal saw something, didn't he?

She moves toward her bedroom door, and as she takes slow, measured steps, she hears ragged breathing and water dripping.

She reaches the door, turns the knob, opens it.

Sherri perceives parts of what she's seeing before she comprehends the whole—long, gangly limbs that end in hooked claws, a head like a toothed frog with bulbous, amber eyes, a translucent belly, and two odd pink, glistening-wet organs extruding from that belly. These organs swell and contract and make a wheezing noise. *Lungs*, two primitive lungs.

The thing is two feet tall; the thing is struggling to reach the knob of her bathroom door; the thing is looking at her in terror. It opens its jaw and lets out a gurgling noise, and that's when Sherri screams. She backs away just as the creature—oh, for fuck's sake, Sherri *knows* what it is—just as *Fishy* cringes against the wall and covers its eyes with its clawed hands.

Sherri's not even done screaming when she hears Randal call out to her from the front door. He tries the knob and then starts pounding the door with his fist. Fishy has collapsed into a ball of sorts, its budding legs curled up as its more developed arms clutch its still-forming lungs. Somehow Sherri senses that those exposed lungs are very tender and that they ache being exposed to the air. Just as she didn't comprehend her impulse to kill Fishy a few days ago, she doesn't understand the equally powerful impulse to hide it now. Whatever happens, Randal can't see Fishy—Fishy must be protected from him.

Randal calls her name again. At the top of her lungs Sherri tells him to fuck off and mind his own business.

What happened?

She stubbed her toe. Now fuck off, Randal.

* * *

Sherri carries Fishy in her arms into the bathroom and draws a bath. Lukewarm water—the same temperature as the tank it once occupied.

No, not it, *She.* Sherri realizes that when she touches Fishy's stomach and feels the swell of an egg sack. When her fingers alight on the belly, concentric ripples of pale light shimmer, and Fishy shudders and lets out a croaking sigh. Sherri lowers her into the water and immediately her dull gray scales come alive, attaining a brilliant, nacreous iridescence. She looks at Sherri with love and endless forgiveness.

She is hungry just like Sherri is. A long gray tongue snakes out from her mouth. Sherri knows what she needs, intuits it somehow. She only wants a little bit from her—what could it hurt?

Sherri shows her throat, and Fishy's tongue latches onto her skin. Little barbs on the tip of the tongue saw through the top layers of Sherri's skin and coax a trickle of blood to the surface; it's all Fishy needs for now, just a few drops.

* * *

Fishy gets bigger every day. Sherri's not eaten much. Just a cracker this morning and some water. She should eat more, but she doesn't want the food she's used to.

Why is it Sherri can see her veins and capillaries through her skin? Why is her skin so itchy?

* * *

Yvonne Etienne was not an unimaginative plagiarist. This Sherri now knows for certain. She experienced the same visions as Fabian Kastl before her, but perceived them and painted them more faithfully, more correctly. Where Kastl's prejudices projected the shape of Triton and his phallic trident onto the canvas, Etienne perceived instead the yonic origin point of all life, a fissure in the bottom of the ocean, an aperture, an orifice in the deepest trench from which the first fecund particles of organic life emerged. This living matrice, this origin point, Orijin Lan, still lives and still feels all the world through trillions upon trillions of sensate organelles; every plankton, every coral, every algal cell an eye, an ear, a mouth, a nose for Her to experience all the poisons the proud human species has dumped into Her oceans.

*** Shimmer

How many days has it been now? Sherri's head is swimming when she hears the police call her full name through the front door. It's late; dark out. Their flashlight beams cut through the gloom of the living room.

They knock, at first politely, then more insistently. Call her full name again.

Randal is with them. He calls Sherri by her first name, says he's worried about her. Sherri want to tell him to leave and take his fucking pigs with him, but her voice is so weak from disuse that she can't form even one word.

Fishy emerges from her bathtub and stalks on her now-developed legs toward Sherri, tracking slimy water from her webbed feet. Fishy is almost as tall as her now. Her second eyelids are down—that means she's agitated.

"Shh," Sherri whispers to her, stroking her now-engorged belly. The egg sack is swelling; it looks painful. At least her lungs have retracted into her body.

The police call again. Sherri wobbles to her feet. Her clothes are flecked with blood, the last time she looked in the mirror she resembled someone going through heroin withdrawals—and her skin has the track marks to match.

"Go away, I'm fine," Sherri manages to croak.

They don't hear her. She watches shadows shifting under the door jamb and shields her eyes when a blinding flashlight shines through the window into her face.

A voice from outside, male, uncertain, "There's someone else in there with her."

From behind her shoulder, a growl rumbles from Fishy's throat.

They must have a locksmith with them; a jangling in the keyhole, like someone's feeling it out.

Now Sherri finds her voice. "Fuck off, all of you, leave me alone!"

Fishy cringes.

"They're here to help you," Randal says.

"Ma'am, you sound agitated."

"Agitated? You're breaking into my fucking house!" Each word like a glass shard.

Fishy begins cringing back, but too late. The door swings open, flashlights flood the living room, and shine on Sherri and Fishy.

She can't see Randal or the cops' faces, but she hears the gasps. Sherri thinks she sees one cop go for his holster.

How like men; how like humans to hate the unknown, to want to kill what they can't and won't understand.

"No!" Sherri throws herself between Fishy and the men, and Fishy darts away. She blunders through the living room and smashes through the window into the back yard, where the canal beckons. Sherri follows.

The police are running after, one of them has drawn his pistol. *Jesus Christ*, Randal shouts.

With strength she didn't think she had left, Sherri vaults through the opening Fishy made in the window and tumbles onto the grass. Fishy is flopping clumsily, her legs are not meant for the land, but she is moving closer to the edge of the canal, the canal that leads to the intercoastal, to the bay, to the ocean.

The world explodes behind Sherri, and something like a hornet whizzes past her shoulder.

Fishy stumbles, struck in the back. Sherri's shriek is almost as loud as the gunshot.

A hard, rough hand reaches Sherri, seizes her by the wrist, pulls her back as Fishy flops into the canal.

Sherri pulls away. Pulls until her wrist dislocates and her hand slips limply from the cop's grasp. She doesn't look back; she runs for the canal.

And in those moments before she plunges into the dark, still water, a light appears in the canal.

From the turbid patch where Fishy fell in, little luminous bubbles—no, not bubbles, *eggs*—bob to the surface and shimmer with inner violet light.

Sherri trusts herself to the water and leaps in.

As she plunges into the water illuminated by the shimmering spawn, she sees, clearly now, a face she knows, altered but still hers to love. Fishy is gone, awakened by the water to her true and honest shape.

Eva looks at Sherri with amber eyes and whispers her name through the water. Sherri's broken wrist ceases hurting, healed by the water's kiss. Eva reaches for Sherri now, and the touch she strove away from in her dreams she now leans toward. Webbed, clawed fingers gently trace the curve of her cheek, and her skin detaches. Clothes that no longer fit; a skin that no longer fits. All slough away, revealing beneath them Sherri's pristine armor of nacreous scales that drink whatever meager light the moon can smuggle through the dark throat of the city.

Sherri parts her lips and releases the air her lungs greedily protect, but she doesn't drown, for new gills emerge on her throat to thresh the water. Hand in hand, claw in claw, she and Eva rise to the surface where the flashlights converge.

Randal and the police regard them with horror—the two things that breach the surface of the canal. And Sherri, for her part, stares back at them with pity. Eva gathers her clutch into a weave of algae and together they kick off, dragging the clutch behind them.

Their powerful finned limbs are well-suited to navigating the water; soon they've found the intercoastal. Soon they'll find the waiting mouth of the bay, and the ocean beyond. They leave the bright, false lights of the city behind them, but they'll be back. Sherri and Eva and all their children will return to the land one day to fulfill their purpose.

They are the world's hope now, the hope of everything living—the one and final chance to drown mankind and its poison empire before all life dies forever.

THE RUMOR

Nobody sane knows what the Rumor is, so how would you know when you've heard it whispered in a crowd or seen it spray-painted on an overpass or scribbled on a paper airplane? You don't, not until it's inside you. That's what Dud knows anyway.

As he pedals his bicycle, he reads the graffiti on the side of what used to be a radio store—back when it was legal to own one—and wonders if he's just been infected.

THE CROWMEN USED TO BE PEOPLE, the message reads in fresh, dripping red.

Nat, seated in front of him on the edge of the seat, sighs. "Remember the malts we used to share?" They point to Ma Trencher's Quicktime Diner, boarded up now. As they point, the bike wobbles, and Dud shifts his weight to balance. Even as lithe as Nat is, two people on a bicycle is a hard play, especially with how lousy the road is. Still, there are worse experiences than having Nat's body flush to his, the fruity smell of the pomade in their neon-yellow pompadour forcing open Dud's sinuses.

"I remember you always forgot your billfold," Dud says.

Nat glances back and winks. They have thin, pale lips, moss-green eyes, and a pointed, elfin chin Dud loves to cradle between his thumb and forefinger. "You've always been good for it."

They first met at the Black Summer riots, when Dud was a first-year scholar and Nat was a photographer for the radical press. Dud got his head cracked by a police baton, and if Nat hadn't dragged him out of the riot gas, he'd have asphyxiated like so many others. That was three years ago. Not long before the Rumor started. He was a scholar with parents, a future, a working radio, all that blam and dazzle.

Now Dud weaves around concrete roadblocks and potholes. Behind derelict homes and shops looms the inner barrier, twenty meters of concrete separating the unclean Outer District from the Inner District where the Barons of Industry and their ilk live. But it's not that wall Dud and Nat want to get past. They want egress beyond the outer barrier separating the city from the countryside where Dud's parents live.

"Who's our contact?" Dud asks.

"A woman named Yaa," Nat says.

"Fuck. Now you tell me?"

"What's the big deal?"

"I know Yaa," Dud says. "By reputation anyway. She works for King Lugo."

"We're trying to smuggle ourselves out of the city—can't avoid dealing with the Smuggler King."

Isn't much he can say to that.

This morning, Nat showed up on Dud's doorstep with a wild handful of news: they'd gotten a ticket out of the city, but they needed to leave today. Dud was game. There's a hitch though.

"Why are the Crowmen after you?" Dud asks.

"You know how it's illegal to photograph a Crowman?"

"You idiot."

"You don't get it—it was the perfect shot. Two of those big honking bozos pulling a kid out of his mother's arms. For all the good it will do—not like there are newspapers to publish the snaps anymore."

Two-meters tall, built like linebackers, mute, dressed entirely in black leather with cloaks fringed in dark feathers and beaked rubber masks with opaque, reflective lenses for eyes, the Crowmen are impossible to miss, and even now as Dud glances at an alleyway he sees one of them watching he and Nat pass by.

"Look out!"

Nat's warning comes just in time, and Dud swerves around what looks at first like a discarded winter coat, but which a quick glance behind reveals as a human being sprawled on his face, in the helpless way of the Mords.

"Poor bastard," Dud mutters. Truth is, if he gets infected, he'd rather become a Mordant than a Manic; at least Mords don't hurt anyone.

"Where are we going? The train station's the other way."

"I have to punch in at the factory first," Dud says. "If I don't show up, they'll put my name on a watchlist, maybe send cops to my apartment."

"Sure, but won't they get suspicious when you punch in and then disappear in the middle of your shift?"

"They won't notice until everyone clocks out."

Nat sighs again. "Man, I'd kill for a smoke."

"Check your right pocket."

Nat purrs when they find the cigarette Dud slipped into their pocket before they left his apartment. "You sneaky devil—never even felt you slip into there."

Pickpocketing; just one of the skills a scholar picks up when the world falls apart.

Approaching the factory zone, the smog and vapors thicken. Ash flakes drift down and gather in the stormdrains and on the hoods of cars left in the streets to rust. Dud pulls his shirt over his mouth while Nat coughs from their cigarette.

"Just think," Nat says. "This time tomorrow we'll be in the country, breathing clean air—a disgusting thought, isn't it?"

Dud doesn't answer. They pass a line of hooded people—Saints—about a dozen of them all walking as one segmented creature joined by the rope they carry. Blindfolded and with wads of wax and cotton stuffing up their ears, Saints preach by example the virtue of closing oneself to the Rumor.

Then, more disturbing, they arrive at the biscuit factory. There, alongside the queue of haggard workers waiting for the day-shift to begin and the parallel line of even more wrung-out laborers filing out from the small-hour-shift, is a pair of Crowmen.

"Shit," Nat says. "Shit shit shit."

"It's all right," Dud says. "Probably just a new precaution."

No one knows who gives the Crowmen their orders, or if anyone does. Hard to ask questions when the Rumor's floating around. When they first appeared on the streets after that first terrifying week of ordinary, meek people bludgeoning their friends to death and citizens collapsing in droves into sudden catatonia, everyone assumed the Crowmen were sent by the government, but that seems unlikely now. Even the police, always despised in the Outer District for their strikebreaking ways and lickspittle loyalty to the Barons, stay out of their way. What happens to those the Crowmen take? Is there a camp somewhere in the city? Maybe in the shuttered bootball stadiums, or maybe the infected are simply crammed into giant incinerators. Or meat grinders.

"They're looking at us," Nat says. "They're looking at me."

Dud wants to say otherwise, but Nat's right. The Crowmen seem to have turned their heads this way. Nat's shudder rattles through the bike's frame, and

Dud gives them a quick kiss behind the ear. The little brass studs in Nat's lobe are startlingly cold against his lips.

"We're okay, they're just looking," Dud tells them. "They're just—"

And then the Crowmen start walking, the line of workers parting nervously to get out of their way.

So much for punching in to keep off the list.

Dud pushes with his feet to turn the bike then starts pedaling. Nat lifts their camera and aims it over Dud's head. He glances back while the bulb goes flash, and maybe it's just his imagination, but the Crowmen seem to squirm, as if in pain.

They zip down the way and wend the corner onto Pockrus Street. Before the Rumor started, Pockrus was a place where people could scratch their most obscene itches.

Police sirens start up. Less than a block away, it sounds like. Could be for anything, but it only makes Dud's already out of control ticker crank up to the next gear. Only thing worse than being chased by Crowmen is being chased by Crowmen *and* coppers.

Nat points. "Turn into that alley."

"Why?"

"Trust me, I know these streets."

Dud banks hard right, swerving the bicycle off Pockrus into a narrow alleyway between a flophouse and what looks like it might have been a school building. Graffiti scrawls along the walls hemming the alley, and though he tries not to read, the messages slip through the membrane of his vision.

THE RUMOR IS THERE IS NO RUMOR.

THE CROWMEN WERE ALWAYS HERE.

THE BARONS MADE THIS HAPPEN.

A CRACK IN THE SKY.

SEX SEX MONEY DEATH SEX AGAIN.

At the end of the alley they come to what looks like an access road behind a large building with a blue corrugated metal roof. Dud doesn't recognize the Daily Avenue Cinema from this side, not without the flashing neon marquee proclaiming the featured pictures.

"Let's hide the bicycle behind the dumpster," Nat says.

A good idea. Once the bike's hidden, Nat takes Dud's hand and pulls him toward the theater's backdoor. Inside the cinema lobby, the familiar scent of popcorn butter and cinnamon pellets recalls simpler times, back when he and

Nat would go with friends to see the newest features, when there were new features to see. The lobby is barren, just a single concession booth open, and the man behind the counter is snoring. They sneak past him and into the theater. As they slip through the doors into the dark, slanted space, the police sirens fade, replaced instead by the sultry brass instruments of the main score to *Immortal Hearts*.

There, in stark tones of gray and black, private investigator Dexter Parlay (played by perennial heartthrob Lin Chang), with his perfectly pressed coif, stares wistfully at the audience and at his beloved, played by the smoky-voiced bombshell, Dorianne Mendy, who rolls her eyes and lets out her trademark husky laugh. It was one of the last pictures to premiere two years ago, before everything changed. A two-year-old picture, and yet the flickering light on the screen reveals a sea of heads in the seats, a near full house.

Dud and Nat find a pair of seats third row from the front. Nat's head rests on Dud's shoulder and their hand slips into his.

"How long before they give up?" Nat whispers. They mean the police.

"I give it five minutes before they have to respond to a ration riot," Dud murmurs.

The screen fills with Dorianne Mendy's full, pouting lips and eyes like two puddles of molasses. Goddamn, what a woman.

"If you're gonna kiss me, kiss me, damn it," Nat says, speaking in perfect sync. They stroke Dud's jawline just as the woman on the screen traces the sharp angles of Lin Chang's cleft chin.

"Sorry, doll," Dud says, in time with Dexter Parlay. "I was caught up thinking about the rest of my life."

Unlike Dorianne Mendy's Dee Summer, Nat slips a little bit of tongue with their kiss.

Music swells, scene closes, credits roll. The lights come on in the theater. Most of the people rise to their feet and start shuffling out. A few linger and quietly chat with whomever they came with.

Then there are those who don't move at all. They sit, eyes glued to the screen, bodies slumped in their seats, mouths hanging open. It makes Dud shudder to think of it, how these people walked into the cinema, possessed of their own wits, sat down to watch *Immortal Hearts*, and then fell into an inescapable hole within their own minds. Mords now, listless husks waiting for the Crowmen to collect them. No one really knows how long it takes after exposure for the Rumor to take you—they could have gotten infected days ago. It's a thought Dud tries not to dwell on.

"Think the heat's died yet?" Nat asks.

Before Dud can answer, a welter of mutters and whispers bubbles up from the lanes of people exiting the theater as the doors open. A curious thing happens to the lights. They don't go out, not exactly. It's more like a dark gloss clouds over them, dimming the theater.

From the doorway, instead of the light of the lobby, darkness invades and coalesces into the forms of two Crowmen. The people rush out and the Crowmen pay them no mind, their beaked masks and glass eyes fixated on Dud and Nat.

In a blink, everyone else has left, and it's Dud, Nat, the Crowmen, and the Mords rooted to their seats.

"Oh fuck me," Nat says.

In retrospect, a room with only one entrance and exit was a poor choice of hiding place.

"They're slow," Dud says, squeezing Nat's hand as they both stand from their seats. "They can't get to us without giving us an angle on the exit."

And that's true enough, but then one of the Crowmen does something that throws all Dud's assumptions out. It lifts its gloved hand, and from their seats, the Mords rise to their feet and turn to regard Dud and Nat with wide, blank eyes. There's only a second's pause before the Crowman points, and the Mords throw themselves forward.

The first of the Mords, a middle-aged red-headed woman, is only a few seats away and launches herself at Dud, but Dud ducks his shoulder and uses her own momentum to fling her away. He tugs Nat's hand and the two leapfrog over the chairs, row by row. Another Mord comes from Nat's side, but Nat bats them down with a hard swing of their camera bag, while Dud kicks away a pimply kid who tries to tackle him by his ankle. Even as they negotiate the rows, the Crowmen stand resolute in front of the only exit. Even as slow as they are, there's no way Dud and Nat can get around them.

Unless...

"Nat, take a snap!"

Dud guards Nat's back, shoving away an old man and then bashing the red-headed woman with his elbow, while Nat fumbles with their camera bag. The Crowmen know what's coming, and to Dud's satisfaction, they begin to move, easily climbing over rows of seats in their inexorable march toward Nat.

But Nat gets their camera out, and just as the pimply kid has gotten his arms wrapped around Dud's waist and the old man is closing in from one side and a teenage girl with thick glasses is coming from the other, flash goes the bulb on Nat's camera.

The Mords collapse. The Crowmen's forms change. For just a second, the solid shapes of black leather, rubber, and feathers turn oblong and amorphous.

It's a narrow window, but Dud and Nat don't waste their chance. Three blinks and ten furious strides later, they're dashing out the exit and into the lobby, the Crowmen and Mords behind them.

"Straight for the train station!" Nat shouts as Dud pulls the bicycle out from behind the dumpster. "Don't stop for nothing!"

"How do they keep finding us?" Dud mutters as he pedals up the access road toward the main street.

"It must be the photographs. Maybe they can *feel* them, like a piece of them is trapped in the picture."

They cycle under an overpass. Overhead, on the overpass, a man is laughing hysterically, holding his sides. He sees them and shouts something, and Dud is grateful a sudden gust of wind intercepts and scatters his speech—nothing good comes from hearing a Manic speak.

* * *

The train station is four blocks from the theater. In the old days, it was a busy place, being the hub for all the city's subway lines, as well as freight and passenger trains going out of the city. Now, with the subways out of commission and all passenger trains indefinitely suspended, there wasn't much point in anyone going there other than the workers who unloaded the precious freight shipments—the city's only lifeline to the world outside.

The train station looms ahead. It was a beautiful old building once; now the honeycombed glass façade is opaque with soot. Dud pedals to the edge of the stairs and stops.

"Where are we supposed to meet Yaa?" Dud asks as Nat climbs off the bike.

"In the loading bay, bottom level."

"Great. Perfect place to get shivved."

"Don't be silly, Dud, they wouldn't shiv us—they have guns."

"Right."

At the top of the stairs, a pair of men in the gray coat and fur hat uniform of the Outer District Police guard the main entrance. Dud has just noticed them, and his heart quickens at the realization that one of them is putting a two-way hand radio to his mouth.

"Yeah, I think it's them," the policeman says.

"Relax," Nat says, squeezing Dud's arm. "Who do you think pays them? Not the city."

The copper puts his radio down and points at Dud and Nat. "You're late," he says. "She doesn't like being kept waiting."

Nat pulls Dud along and they race up the steps. "Our apologies, officers."

Dud takes one look over his shoulder at the empty streets behind them before Nat tugs him through the revolving doors and into the train station terminal. Even in here there's graffiti. Somehow, although it defies logic, someone's managed to spray a message over the angelic mural on the terminal's vaulted ceiling thirty meters from the floor—

THESE AREN'T MY THOUGHTS.

They hurry through the terminal, past the ticket booths, to the staircase. An overpowering stench of mildew fills the stairwell. At the bottom of three flights is the loading bay, a cavernous space dug into the very crust of the world, part depot, part warehouse. There are a dozen rail lines leading into a dozen different tunnels, and in the old days there would have been mountains of freight in long containers. Now, though, there is only a single train.

A team of five workmen are loading one such crate into a car while a woman watches them. She's not tall, nor is her appearance especially fearsome, but there's a quiet competence in her round face, her short, businesslike head of pressed curls. She wears not the green overalls of the workmen, but a floral suitcoat and a pair of glossy leather shoes. Doesn't take Dud more than a second to spot the bulge of a large pistol in her pocket. So this is Yaa, Smuggler King Lugo's righthand woman. People say Yaa carries an 11mm revolver with a grip carved from human shinbones. They also say she never misses a shot with it.

"Which of you's Nat Lubeck?" Yaa asks.

"This one is," Nat says.

"Payment up front."

Nat opens their camera bag and takes out a roll of ration tickets, a thicker spool than Dud has ever seen—enough to feed a big family for a year, easy. As Nat hands the tickets over, they give Dud a smoldering bit of side-eye to cut off any stupid questions. Thing is, Dud wouldn't ask—Dud doesn't want to know the things someone has to do to get that kind of spool.

Yaa pockets the tickets and then gestures with her head toward an open crate about the size of a coffin, packed with straw. "Your first-class accommodations await."

Seeing the crate, Dud's gut drops. "How the hell are we going to fit in that?"

Yaa's grim face crinkles with amusement. "*We?* You thought you were going too?"

Nat grabs Dud's arm. "He *is* going. I'm not leaving without him."

"That was never the deal."

Already, the workmen are adjusting their postures, watching with wary interest. They're just waiting for the signal from Yaa to goon up.

"Fuck your deal," Nat says. "I'm paying you a fortune—make room for him."

"There's no room," Yaa says. "And even if the two of you could cram into that little toy chest, it would never get past the inspectors. They weigh every crate."

"What about other crates?" Dud asks, keeping his voice down in a way Nat hasn't bothered with.

Yaa spits. "Buddy, you want out of the city, come back next week."

Dud has often wondered what it feels like when the Rumor takes over someone and turns them into a Mord. He imagines it's something like what he feels now, a creeping hopelessness, a rising tide of gelatinous despair, a calcifying certainty that there is no escape. But Nat can still make it.

Nat's getting themselves in Yaa's face, and Dud can see the hair trigger of Yaa's restraint flickering with each word.

Dud grabs them by their camera bag and pulls them back. "Stop," he says. "Just go. At least one of us can make it."

Yaa's hand radio crackles with an incoming message. "What is it?" she growls into the radio.

Another crackle of static, and then, "...trouble. Some Crowmen coming..."

"What the hell are *Crowmen* doing here? What do they want?"

Shit. *Shit shit shit.*

"...I...I don't know, I think—"

The radio crackles, but nothing more comes through. Dud looks to Nat, and their eyes meet. "They're after me," Nat whispers. "The photos. You go,

Dud. You go on the train; they won't stop chasing me as long as I have what they want."

"You're going on that train, not me."

"But—"

"But nothing," Dud says, and fans out with his thumb the photographs he pinched from Nat's camera bag just a moment ago. "Heat's on me now. You go somewhere better."

"Dud, you stupid, sneaky—"

Dud shuts them up with a kiss, pulling Nat against his chest, breathing in one last time the scent of their pomade.

"Get them in the crate already!" Yaa shouts, as the workmen grab hold of Nat and drag them into the crate. The last glimpse Dud gets of Nat before the workmen close the lid over their face is a look of total, absolute devastation. It's how Dud should feel right now. Why, then, does he feel so good? Maybe because for the first time in two years he's done something with purpose. The workmen load the last of the crates and Yaa gives a signal to the engine, which starts up with a monstrous belch of diesel fumes.

The elation of watching Nat's train pull out of the loading bay and disappear into the tunnel doesn't last, because just as soon as the noise of the train subsides, a new sound fills the dank air. It's not the sound he expects, not the slow, plodding footsteps of Crowmen coming down the stairs.

No, it's coming from the tunnels. It's the sound of feet sloshing through puddles, of shoes clopping on railroad tracks, and the sound of laughter. Syncopated, febrile laughter from a dozen throats.

The workmen shine their flashlights, raise their shotguns and pistols. Leering faces darkle at the very edge of the flashlights' reach.

"Manics," someone hisses.

"We gotta get outta here..."

Yaa says nothing, only draws her revolver, which looks comically large in her small hand. The grip looks like ivory—or maybe shinbone.

A voice from one of the tunnels, "Hey, wanna hear a good joke?"

Yaa's pistol barks in answer, its thunder a catastrophe of echoes in the cavernous space of the loading bay. The Manics pour out from their holes. Yaa and her men open fire, and as it turns out the stories are true: Yaa doesn't miss; skulls burst like rotten red pumpkins. But there are only six shots in her cylinder, and so many Manics.

What happens next is a muddle, not least because Dud conks his head on the platform edge when a Manic pulls him down by his ankle. Kick, grapple, run, bash, duck, kick again, run again, hide behind a crate, run some more. Laughter fills the loading bay and hoots of infernal glee and shrieks. Maybe he sees a workman's intestines dragged out from his belly like silk from a magician's hat while two other Manics twist his legs off. Maybe a Manic whispers something into his ear, something quick and muddled, just before he bashes the thing's head into a crate.

Kick, grapple, dodge. Hands grip his leg and jaws crunch into his ankle.

Kick, stomp, limp. A set of jagged, dirty nails rake at the skin under his eye.

Duck, hobble, hop. Laughter behind him, the stairway ahead.

* * *

Dud drags his leg with each step he ascends, doing his best to keep weight off the ankle, where a Manic tried to bite his tendon but only managed to tear away a scrap of flesh and bruise the bone. His knuckles throb, his jaw aches, his hair is matted with blood—some of it his, some of it from the Manic whose brains he bashed out against a crate. They're still down there, he can hear them laughing and howling and playing their demented games with whatever's left of Yaa and her men. They're not following him, but then their job wasn't to catch Dud, only flush him out.

Dud pulls himself by the railing. One step after another, until at last he emerges into the dark expanse of the terminal, where the Crowmen are waiting.

They stand near the ticket booth, regarding him through their mirrored obsidian eyes, their gloved hands fisted at their sides. Dud wants to say something snappy and defiant, like what Lin Chang's Dexter Parlay would say to the thugs trying to rub him out, but all that comes out is, "Go fuck yourselves."

The Crowmen stride forward. As slowly as they walk, Dud can't hope to outrun them on his bum leg. Dud slips out the photographs and holds them up. "This what you want? All this mayhem for some snaps?"

The Crowmen hesitate. Dud can't see their faces—if they have faces at all— and yet he knows the posture of fear, the suddenly rounded shoulders, the hitch in their stride. Dud draws his lighter from his pocket, and the way the Crowmen quicken their pace, how their slow strides become glacially frantic—

like men drowning in honey—suggests he's got the right idea. He flicks open the lighter and a little beacon of light kindles from the tip. The Crowmen are coming, but fire is so much faster.

As the photographs accept the rapturous touch of flame and cellulose bubbles and combusts, the Crowmen bubble too. Their definitions blur, their clothes and trappings slump and slough away as dark gouts of shadowy fire dance from the cracks in their shells. It's all so quiet, like the silent films of his boyhood. This is the first time Dud's ever watched an idea burn. If only Nat were here to see it.

* * *

It's in the way he walks. The way he's covered in blood and a sticky black substance no one can identify. The way he laughs to himself. Where Dud walks, the people move away to give him space. Whispers reach his ears, *What's a Manic doing out in the light? Where are the Crowmen?* But he's not a Manic. He is himself. He is perfectly sane, and he's only laughing because of how stupid it all is. All the rules, all the imaginary lines people draw, all the walls they build to keep the dark out when the dark was always there inside even the brightest, buzzing lightbulb.

The Crowmen won't come near him now. They've had days to find him and nab him, but they're scared. They see him and edge away, these homunculi of terror terrified of one who knows how to unmake them.

He walks to the edge of the district, to the inner barrier of steel and concrete, and he starts climbing. The wall is almost vertical, but like everything manmade it's crumbling, and in the gouges and cracks he finds hand and toeholds. Searchlights follow his ascent, and loudspeakers from the watchtowers shout warnings that fizzle to radio static in his ears. At the very top, where the concrete is edged in a silvery lace of razor wire, Dud tears open his belly to haul himself clear, and then he looks out over the bright, orderly avenues of the Inner District, where the cars still putter and hum, the sidewalks are full, the parks are green and lush, the air is clean, and the people are well-fed and happy, untroubled by any Rumor.

And over his shoulder, past the long, grimy tract of the Outer District and the outer barrier's dour cheek, stretches the world beyond: the nighted farmlands, the sloping hills, and the cupped hand of the vast valley and the mountains that gird it, where a ganglion of lights shimmers, the other cities and smaller towns, enclosed by their own walls and watchtowers, their searchlights errant threads of spiderline swinging through the void.

DRUCKTEUFEL

Izzy Duverne doesn't relax when the state trooper returns her license and registration, does not relax when he writes a warning for a broken taillight and wishes her—or rather wishes FM, in the passenger seat—a pleasant stay in Mississippi and a safe trip back to Texas. The muscles of her shoulders and back stay knotted and her heartbeat lingers in her throat until the slate gray car with its blue stripe peels off the shoulder and cruises onto I-20 and out of sight. She takes deep breaths, in, out, in, out; she repeats the mantra she learned from therapy: *My body is my body, my mind is my mind.*

"Asshole talked past you," FM says. "Like I was the one driving."

That wasn't what bothered her. She learned from a young age that if a cop ignored you, that was about as good as you could hope for.

They didn't speed. Just a broken taillight on her beat-up Honda, which may not have been a problem if FM had been the one driving. What it was, simple enough, was that the cop saw a Black woman driving with a white man. The trooper was ruddy and towheaded, young enough to be one of Izzy's freshman comp students. "Good deal," he said when FM answered, "We're PhD students, meeting up with a classmate," to his question of what FM and "his girlfriend" were doing visiting Mississippi. *Good deal,* as if to say, *Good deal for you.* As if to say, *I can let this go.*

"Like, am I crazy? Was he not completely ignoring you?"

"You're not crazy, but—put that fucking joint away!"

FM's nervous fingers drop the joint he's taken from his pocket. If the cop searched their car, he'd have easily found more than just a little weed among FM's possessions. What would have happened to them then is a question better left unexplored.

"I'm already sick of this state," FM says, shaking his head.

FM (that's his whole first name, not his initials) Burnside is a squirrely guy. Not ugly, exactly, more funny-looking. Thin, round-shouldered, buggy blue eyes. He wears longsleeve shirts to hide the track marks in his inner elbows.

He's a brilliant writer, but in the most annoyingly self-aware way, considering himself a "Gnostic," whatever the fuck that means. The sort of guy who looks for opportunities to quote Kierkegaard in ordinary conversation, and who smokes blunts rolled from pages of the Bible.

"We're almost there," Izzy says, as if he's the one who needs reassuring, as if he's the one whose best friend got paralyzed by a cop's bullet in the spine.

The fast-food restaurant where their friend Sam said to meet at is in Pelahatchie, a little nothing town just to the east of Jackson. It's been a while since either of them have seen Sam—six months, by her reckoning, since Sam's apartment caught fire and Sam dropped out of the program and left North Texas. Sam's changed some, but it's impossible not to recognize them.

Sam Lutz is a big person. No other word for it; despite Izzy's trove of more evocative adjectives, "big" is what leaps out to her. Halfway to seven feet, built like the Michelin Man. Their face has always been a gentle and round resting place for their thick glasses, but the wooly black beard is a new twist, hiding what has always been a weak chin. They're wearing a long-sleeved shirt, despite the summer heat, and when Izzy and FM's eyes meet, she can tell he's thinking the same thing as her.

When Sam sees Izzy and FM enter, they smile, but it's a brittle smile. When they hug Izzy, Izzy searches for some spark of their quiet, casual old intimacy, but instead she feels from Sam a hesitance, like she's covered in something they don't want to get rubbed onto them.

When they sit down to eat, Sam asks Izzy and FM if the two of them have complied with their requests, the "terms" Sam set out when asking them to drive to Mississippi.

"No words or letters or numbers on your clothes, that's good," Sam says. "What about the tags? Did you cut them out?"

Izzy has. This morning, before leaving with FM for the eight-hour trip across the armpit of the south, she took care to cut off whatever tags remained on her clothes. FM assures Sam he's done the same.

Sam nods. When the food arrives, they eat voraciously, as if they haven't had anything to eat—or anything appetizing—for days, if not weeks. The burger is okay. The root beer is good, even exceptional. The fries taste like the most delicious seeds of colorectal cancer, hot and crisp and rich and loaded with iodine—proper fries, Izzy believes, *must* have a slight chemical aftertaste.

While they eat, Sam asks little questions about their friends' work, about their studies, lives. They ask about Izzy landing an agent, about FM's first novel—the nine-hundred-page doorstopper of baroque, florid philosophy masquerading as a novel, what he and Izzy both affectionately call "the beast"—going to print. They reveal, casually, that they've recently come clean to their folks about their enby identity and preferred pronouns.

"That was fun," Sam says, unironically. "Boy, Mom was pissed, but you can't really disown someone when you're broke like she is."

For a second, a little of Sam's humor creeps into their haggard mien, but it sags again, and Sam returns to looking troubled.

It gets to be too much for her not to ask, so Izzy breaks and comes out with it. "Why did you disappear, Cupcake?"

Sam half smiles. "You haven't called me that in a while."

"I haven't called you *anything* in a while. Why didn't you say something before leaving?"

She's surprised by how hurt she sounds. Why should she be hurt? She and Sam were over for months before the fire happened and Sam dropped out of everyone's lives, so it can't be the ire of a forsaken lover. Is it her anger at Sam turning away from a promising career? Can't be that either; brilliant a poet they might be, it's not as if Sam—or any of them for that matter—could say they were destined for greatness within academia or otherwise. Was it anger that Sam's vanishing had cost her sleep, had convinced her yet another person close to her had been swallowed up by the world?

"You could have sent a text once in a while, bud," FM says.

Sam nods. "The reason I left is the same as the cause of the fire, and the same reason I couldn't really communicate with anyone. I had to go off the grid."

"For your own protection?" Izzy asks.

Sam shakes their head. "It was for the *world's* protection."

"How's that?"

"What are you talking about?" FM asks.

Sam glances around. There are few other people in the restaurant, and none sitting especially close, but even so they look nervous. "Not here," they say. "Follow me to my place. Then we'll talk, and I'll show you what stole me from the world."

Stole me from the world. Izzy almost smiles despite her irritation, despite her misgivings at Sam's strange behavior, for in their words are the cooling cinders of the poet she knew.

"So where is the place?" FM asks.

"Nearby. But before we go..." Sam hesitates, as if dreading a difficult conversation, and then takes from their pocket two nondescript paper bags. "I need your phones before you get onto the property."

"Why?"

"What the fuck for?"

Sam sighs. "Like I said, I'll explain when we get there. Please, just trust me when I say it's for your own safety. For the world's safety."

Sam holds out their hand, passive, expectant, offering no more argument. Maybe it's their sad puppy eyes, the look of sincere terror that compels Izzy to give Sam her phone. FM follows suit. Sam does not answer when FM asks when they'll be getting their phones back.

Sam pays for the meal. Pays in quarters, which is odd enough, but Izzy can't help but notice the coins are all scuffed. Deliberately so—every letter and number scratched and made illegible.

* * *

Izzy follows Sam closely. Without her phone, she knows she has no hope of navigating these backroads and finding her way back to I-20, especially now that the sun is getting low on the horizon and night approaches. The billboards around here are vomit-inducing. "Real Men Love Babies," "What if I was aborted?" and the most cringeworthy: "Jesus knows what you did last summer."

It's about ten minutes into the drive when Izzy first notices the mud-spattered sky-blue pickup riding on her tail. The truck is on a lifted body with big tires and has a bright Gadsden flag front license plate, two youngish men sitting in the cab. At first she thinks they just want to pass her, so she drifts toward the shoulder to give them easier ingress to the other lane, but they don't pass, they just rev up and shrink the distance between fender and bumper to less than a golf cart's length.

"What the hell are they doing?" FM grumbles.

"Whatever they can get away with."

If she were still in Texas, Izzy might be tempted to pump the brake and check them, but she's not in Texas, she's in Swampass, Mississippi, and right now she doesn't even have a phone (thanks, Sam). So she plays it as calmly as she can, keeps to the same speed, doesn't look back, doesn't even look in the mirror to see the men's inevitable grins full of sanguine menace.

Mercifully, when Sam slows down and Izzy slows as well, the truck brakes and doesn't plow into her. Sam pulls their car off the main road and noses it onto a red dirt driveway, and Izzy follows. The truck, too, grumbles toward where Sam has stopped, and for an instant Izzy imagines the men stepping out of their vehicle with shotguns or AR-15s or whatever, but that doesn't happen. Instead, Sam gets out of their car and looks out past Izzy and FM at the truck and the men in the truck, and though Sam's glare isn't meant for her, Izzy still feels the withering force of it. Maybe it's the beard or maybe it's something else, something imperceptible, but Sam, the sensitive poet Izzy once called Cupcake, looks *dangerous*. The men in the truck must see it too, because they peel off and speed down the road.

Sam has parked their car just outside of an old wooden gate secured by a rusted chain and a heavy padlock. Most of the paint has peeled from the gate, but the name "Lutz" is still legible. Izzy gets out as Sam stands impassively by the gate.

"So, is this it?" Izzy asks.

Sam nods.

"What's the hold up, bud?" FM calls from inside the car. "Forgot your key or something?"

Sam seems to consider the padlock, then looks to Izzy and then to FM. "Wallets," they say. "I need your wallets." Sam gestures to a mailbox a few yards off. "Put them in there, they'll be safe."

Izzy feels her irritation rising. "Jesus Christ, what is this?"

Sam sighs through their nostrils. "Necessary precautions. Trust me when I say it's in all our best interest that you do not bring anything with legible text past this gate. That includes dollar bills, credits cards, licenses, and anything else."

Izzy recalls the scuffed quarters.

"Why don't you tell us what's going on before we do anything else?" FM asks.

Sam clenches their jaw and grumbles. Once again there's the sincere terror in their eyes. "The short of it is that there's a demon who feeds on words. There, now please put your wallets in the mailbox."

* * *

Sam's double-trailer overlooks a vast stretch of skinny pine trees and tall grass where behemoth grasshoppers lurk. Inside, it doesn't look like the home of the off-the-grid paranoid wingnut Sam now appears to be. There is a remarkable absence of the clutter and disorder Izzy expects to find. Instead, it's clean and sparsely furnished, with just an old couch, a small card table with a few chairs around it. The kitchen is small and features a gas stove and an ancient refrigerator that looks like it should be in a forgotten bomb shelter.

"Make yourselves at home," Sam says, without any irony.

Izzy sits herself down on the couch, which smells so thickly of cigarettes as to recall the tap taps she rode in during her visit to Port-au-Prince. There's a yowl as she sits down, and something dark and shaggy wriggles out from under the couch and glares at her before stalking away to the next room.

"That's Sugarplum," Sam says. "She was Uncle Ralph's cat."

"She seems nice," Izzy says.

"She's an asshole. Don't let her boss you around."

FM is drawn to one of the only decorations in the room—an ornate silver dagger (short sword?) with a hilt made of carved antler, secured in a gold-tipped leather scabbard mounted on the wall.

"And I shall call you *Sting*," FM says, affecting a faux British (Hobbit?) accent.

"Careful, that's an heirloom," Sam says.

"Badass is what it is. Is it a dirk?"

"*Hirschfänger*," Sam says. "German hunting dagger. German nobles used to carry them on hunts for putting wounded game out of its misery."

"I thought your folks were Jewish."

"The Lutz half was. But on my grandmother's side, the von Neustadts were old Prussians. I have relatives who died in Auschwitz on one side and relatives who served in the Waffen S.S. on the other."

"Y'all, can we talk about what actually matters?" Izzy snaps.

Sam looks to her with something like embarrassment. "Well, to tell the truth, my family history is relevant to what I'm about to show you."

"How's that? And what are you about to show us? Is it really something you couldn't have told us about over the phone? Where's the *demon* you mentioned?"

There's the anger bubbling to the surface again. Old anger from old wounds. Anger at Sam who shut her out, broke up with a text message, then disappeared, and then months later called her from a payphone begging her to come to Mississippi and to bring FM with her.

"You think I'm crazy," Sam says. Before Izzy can say anything, they continue, "You're not wrong to assume that. I'd think I were crazy too in your position. But I'm completely sane. And sober too, for the first time in years. Sobriety is a must when the fate of the world is in your hands."

"Delusions of grandeur much?" FM says, sitting down at the card table.

Sam remains standing, looking between FM and Izzy. They sigh. "I guess I'd better show you."

When Sam walks, the floorboards creak and the trailer shudders. They disappear into an adjoining room, what looks like a study. While they're gone, it dawns on Izzy for the first time what truly bothers her about this house, more than the sparse furnishings.

No books. No newspapers or old magazines or notepads, none of the composition books a poet like Sam—even a lapsed poet—would certainly keep around. More than that, there's no writing at all. Curiosity compels her to get up from the couch and search the cupboards in the kitchen and the contents of the fridge. What she finds is both disturbing and expected: no printed labels on anything. Canned goods stripped to the aluminum, affixed with makeshift labels with hand-drawn pictures of the contents: beans, beets, asparagus, etc. The fridge is the same, full of foods divested of their packaging, contained in nondescript baggies and plasticware.

She is still searching the fridge when Sam's heavy footsteps reenter the sitting room.

Sam's got heavy workman's gloves on as they carry a heavy metal box in their arms. They set down the box on the card table, insert a key into the lock, and crack open the metal shell. Izzy comes behind Sam to get a good look at what's inside and is struck by a sudden eruption of that marvelous, heady redolence that old books produce, a smell that Sam—in one of their poems— had once called "*paprichor.*"

After an initial rush of dopamine from that fond smell, Izzy experiences a flutter in her chest and a momentary shortness of breath. And that's before she sees Sam lift the heavy tome from the strongbox.

When she sees the midnight black binding of the cover and embossed, intricate mandala of fractalizing leaves leafing to yet more leaves, and the silver plate at the center with its grinning face—a countenance half the likeness of Medieval depictions of the moon's face and half that of a human skull—her heart jumps, and she feels a powerful itch at the spot high on her back, between her shoulder blades. She reaches back and scratches the spot—the spot of her new tattoo—and after a moment the itch is gone.

Sam holds up the book for Izzy and FM to see. It is as thick as a Bible, its vellum pages sere and yellow and notched at margins as if by the teeth of time. Gingerly, as if even with the gloves they're wearing touching the book is dangerous, Sam flips through some pages and Izzy catches glimpses of heavy Gothic text that might be Old English or something else, and strange images—what look like astrological charts and mathematical formulae.

"Back in Germany, my family name was Lutznau," Sam says, shutting the book.

"Like the filmmaker, Klaus Lutznau?" FM asks. "The one who started the death cult?"

"He and his sister, Rachel, were occultists, students of the Science of the Old Dark. This book must have belonged to one of them, but somehow it found its way to the hands of my great-grandfather, their cousin, who was very much not in the know pertaining to matters of forbidden lore. It crossed the ocean with him when he fled the Nazis, and then it sat in a trunk, forgotten, for decades, until the day my parents sent it to me along with some family journals and photo albums—research for my dissertation project, you know. That was a week before the fire, before I left town."

"But what is it?" Izzy asks.

"This is *Der Wortgaunerleid. The Tale of Hrotger the Word Thief,* written by Aloysius von Erfurt," Sam says. "This is what stole me from the world. This is why I need your help."

"Whoa," FM says, on the literal edge of his seat. "Shit, man, I've never even heard of this. How old is it?"

"Six centuries, give or take," Sam says. "But the thing that lives inside it is much older."

"Thing?" Izzy asks.

"The demon I told you about," Sam says. "Hrotger."

"Why haven't I ever heard of this book?"

"Never mind that, FM," Izzy says. "Why the fuck do they think there's a demon in this book?"

"Things I've seen have convinced me," Sam says. "And I can very easily demonstrate this is no normal book." Sam walks to the wall where the dagger—

the *hirschfänger*—hangs and draws the shimmering blade from its scabbard. Sam returns and holds the blade over the splayed pages of the book.

Before Izzy or FM can ask what they intend to do, Sam buries the dagger into the tome's pages. Izzy is not prepared for the glut of dark ichor that wells up from where the steel bites vellum, a viscous treacle that might be ink or might be arterial blood. It flows from the pages, and dribbles onto the table. FM nearly falls out of his chair to avoid it touching him. When Sam pulls the dagger from the book, the liquid slides off the blade and rolls off the pages, revealing an unblemished page without any sign of violence, as if the dagger never touched it. Sam puts the dagger away and wipes the dark flow with a rag that turns from gray to black. Sam dumps the rag into a garbage bag.

Izzy isn't sure what to say. Isn't sure how what she's just seen can be real.

"That's one demonstration," Sam says. "Here's another."

They reach into their pocket and draw out a crinkled piece of paper. The receipt from the fast-food place. Sam holds it up so Izzy can see.

It looks entirely wrong. For one thing, the text has changed from the staid font of a cash register to the heavy Gothic script of the book. For another thing, there are little dancing ink devils on the margins. Little imps with leering grins.

"This is what the book does to printed text," Sam says. "It consumes it. Assimilates it, takes control. Whatever text it assimilates becomes an extension of its being."

"Whoa, that's fucking cool," FM says.

"No, not cool," Sam says. "What's touched by the book becomes the book, and the book is dangerous, its will is malevolent. Imagine if the book was everywhere—imagine if it spread to a library, to a bookstore, to the *internet*. That would be it for us, for civilization."

"If it's so dangerous, why not just burn it?" Izzy asks.

"I tried that after it infected my personal library. All I managed to do was lose my apartment."

Sam walks through the ensuing silence to the gas stove, turns on a burner, and burns the receipt in the open flame. Izzy and FM are still silent when Sam thumps back over and shuts the book, releasing another bloom of paprichor.

* * *

Maybe it's the fact she's on the verge of disassociating, maybe it's the smell of the couch she was just on, but Izzy needs a smoke for the first time in over a year. All Sam had was a plastic bag with a few old stale menthols—Izzy's old flame. Izzy steps out onto the trailer's porch. The sun's final squeeze coruscates over the bristle tops of the slash pines. Izzy lights up with the last vapors of a plastic lighter and breathes in, out. In, out. *My body is my body, my mind is my mind.* The menthol helps, but nothing could make this moment feel real. Izzy watches the dying sun, feels the sweat beading on her forehead, listens to the susurrus of grasshoppers, but none of it can ameliorate the wrongness that now hums through her as if she's a tuning fork. A mosquito alights on her forearm, and rather than swat it, Izzy watches as it plants its legs and plunges its sawed proboscis through her skin. The pain is miniscule, but welcome, and the world solidifies at the point of entry and then expands until the world is the world and her skin is her skin and her body is her body and she stops humming and lets out a menthol sigh.

The door opens and FM steps out. She tilts her chin in greeting.

"I saw it," FM says. He's trembling again. "Saw the thing bleed, saw what it did to the receipt. And I still think that motherfucker's crazy. Or we are."

"It's the second one that worries me," Izzy says. She takes a deep drag. How much simpler it would be if they'd found Sam as she expected to find them, neck deep in bottles and needles, clinging to life by a hangnail. Instead, they're clean and sober, more lucid and alert than they ever were when Izzy knew them. And in possession of what seems to be a cursed book. "When Sam took our phones, I didn't know what to think," she says. "And then they took our wallets and I figured something bad was about to come. I guess I should be relieved they aren't going to murder us. That book might though."

"You think so? How dangerous could a book be?"

"It's not a book, FM," Izzy says. "Not really. If what Sam says is true, it's more like a virus. Like an analog version of a computer virus, and any printed language is a vector. I would think you of all people would see how terrifying that is."

FM nods and frowns. "Well, let's hope Derrida was wrong then."

Izzy snorts.

FM reaches into his pocket and pulls out the joint he'd been fiddling with after the traffic stop. "Can I get a light?"

Izzy takes the joint and touches the tip to the cherry on her menthol until it ignites, then passes it back. The smell is like vanilla if vanilla could go rancid. Familiar, comforting, and just a little nauseating, recalling muggy Miami afternoons in high school spent sneaking beers from her stepdad's garage fridge and getting baked with her cousins, Eva and Loulouse.

"Mind if I get a puff?" Izzy asks.

"Go for it."

The first taste, the initial infiltration of pot, has always been an unpleasant one for Izzy, but in this case the aftertaste is foul. She starts coughing, painfully.

"You okay?" FM asks, just before he takes another drag.

Her throat burns and pulses, her lungs tingle, and then with the next breath of fresh air the discomfort ceases; she can breathe again. It occurs to Izzy that this must be one of FM's Bible joints. Last he'd spoken of his little project, he'd smoked his way to Leviticus 23 using paper from a Bible printed on acid-free paper with soy-based ink.

"Wait." It dawns on her what she and FM have just been smoking. She snatches the joint out of FM's lips and stubs it out against the porch rail. "Please tell me—"

She unwraps the joint, ash and charred fannings of weed sprinkling out. Once the paper unfurls, she sees what she hoped she wouldn't.

There's no scripture on the paper, at least not Christian scripture. She's not even sure what language the writing's in. What she does recognize is the little capering imp that had appeared on the receipt. Her heart quickens and her lungs startle, and she drops the paper as she wraps her arms around herself, feeling a panic attack coming on again, fighting it down as best she can.

"Oh shit," FM says. "Wait, if we smoked it, what, what does that mean?"

In. Out. In. Out. *My body is my body, my mind is my mind.*

"Izzy, what does it—?"

"I don't know," she says, her voice a stranger in her own throat.

"I don't feel any different," FM says. "I feel fine..."

Izzy isn't sure how she feels. She's not disassociating; not quite anyway.

"Izzy? FM?" Sam calls from inside the house, and their heavy feet start thumping toward the door. Izzy's foot falls on the singed blunt wrapper and sweeps it away, off the porch, just as the door opens and Sam sticks their head out. "Dinner's ready," they say.

Izzy looks at them. FM lets out what sounds like an involuntary giggle.

"Something wrong?" Sam asks. "I mean, besides—well, you know."

Izzy forces a smile. "Just a little rattled is all."

It's both true and a lie.

Inside, they sit around the card table. The book and its strongbox have been removed, and the room feels warmer, more wholesome for its absence. Dinner is simple, franks and beans. Izzy's not hungry, but she forces herself to eat. They eat in silence, eyes on their plates. Izzy is afraid to speak, and perhaps FM is too, for as long as they keep quiet and Sam says nothing, she can pretend she still lives in the ordinary, solid world she lived in before where books don't bleed.

Sugarplum rubs against Izzy's ankle, but when Izzy reaches down to give a scratch the damn cat bites her hand and scampers off. Sam was right about her.

When dinner's over, Sam puts the plates in the sink to soak.

"I really appreciate you being here," Sam says. "Really. I never expected you'd actually come."

"We're friends, aren't we?" FM says.

Izzy, for her part, isn't sure what to say. She wishes she'd never come here, but it's too late now. They're here.

She wants to know what might be happening to her and FM, but she's not sure how to ask without raising Sam's suspicions. She's not sure what Sam might do if they think Izzy has been...is "infected" the word?

"I know that look," Sam says, looking right at Izzy.

She keeps a straight face despite the little voice saying *fuckfuckfuck.* "What do you mean?"

Sam sits across from her. "It's the look you get when someone's not telling you the full truth. I got used to it, being as full of shit as I was."

She smiles. She recalls what Sam told her once, the reason they liked Izzy so much, and why they were so close to her and FM: because in all the program, the two of them were the only ones who were actually honest with Sam. When Sam had been in their fiction workshop—the only poet there— everyone else had mollycoddled them. Izzy had explained in great detail why Sam's stories failed, the coincidences they hinged on, the stilted dialogue that pervaded them, the anticlimaxes they finished with.

"You want to know why I need your help."

"Can't blame me for wondering," Izzy says.

"No I can't. It's simple, Izzy: to destroy the book, you need to conduct a ritual, and this ritual takes three people, people that I trust and care about. You and FM are the only ones I could have asked, the only ones who qualify."

Izzy feels touched, and yet at the same time, experiences the quiver of doubt she'd always get when Sam lied about not using or drinking when they were together. What is Sam hiding this time?

"Where'd you learn about this ritual?" FM asks. "And what is it exactly?"

"I learned of it from the same source as I learned about the book itself: from Rachel Lutznau's *Tagebuch*. She was the only one who knew how to destroy it but, for reasons she doesn't explain in her journal, decided not to."

"Does she explain how the book got like this?" Izzy asks.

"It didn't *get* like this. It always was. Rachel said in her journal that Aloysius created the book as a weapon. A weapon designed expressly to destroy the Holy Roman Empire and the Catholic Church, which he viewed as a backward and repressive hierarchy. In turn, the Church saw Aloysius as a dangerous heretic and sorcerer, and they weren't exactly wrong, though the brutality in how they arrested and tortured him before putting him to an *auto-de-fey*—you know, burning him alive—would almost vindicate him.

"Anyhow, according to my cousin Rachel, the Church took possession of Aloysius' book and tried to destroy it. They burned it a few times, but it always came back; there's even an anecdote about it reconstituting from the flesh of a church summoner, who died only after the other priests peeled every last page from his back. Eventually, having no better option, they locked it up and buried it under the Cathedral of Cologne. It stayed there for a few centuries until—of course—some stupid Nazi, a classicist professor slash eugenicist named Wilhelm Friedl, came along and found it. This Friedl guy fancied himself a latter-day sorcerer, but he didn't know what he was doing any better than the Church had. Rachel doesn't say how she got it from him, but I get the sense Friedl was grateful when she took it off his hands.

"The funny thing about the book is that it calls itself a story, but there's no story at all. I tried to read it when I first discovered it in the chest my folks sent me, but even if I had been fluent in German at the time, none of it would have made sense. The few sentences I was able to parse out almost read like they'd been written by a predictive algorithm: asymptotic to, but falling short of, real syntactic sense. The alchemical diagrams and the astrological charts are nonsense too: either they depict bogus alchemy and astrology, or else they reflect sciences native to a different reality than ours.

"But there are patterns, and one word does repeat. Over and over: Hrotger. If you try reading the book for more than a few minutes, all you'll start seeing is that name. Just pages on pages of "Hrotger, Hrotger, Hrotger," and then you'll get the headache of your lifetime. These aren't mistakes, they're part of the book's design. Aloysius summoned Hrotger and imprisoned him in the book because Hrotger was a spirit of chaos. It would have been the perfect means of destroying the Church, to take over and assimilate their books. Think about it, back then the Church had a near monopoly on the written word. It also wouldn't have impacted most common people in those illiterate times—they never would have noticed anything had happened.

"Now, though..." Sam shakes their head. "I don't know what would happen. It's best we never have to find out."

Silence. Izzy glances at FM, who's tapping his foot like he always does when he needs his fix. She can't really blame him; right now she'd welcome chemical oblivion too.

* * *

Izzy can't sleep. She has the couch, while Sam snores in the bedroom, and FM has nodded off on his side in the corner of the room, on top of the ratty old flokati rug. Sugarplum sprawls like a rug herself in the middle of the room, glaring in turn at Izzy and FM, the invaders.

Part of it is the heat. Even with the AC running, the air in the trailer is a soup. But heat wouldn't be enough to keep her up—she slept so many nights without AC in Miami, when her folks were tight on money.

What's keeping her up is obvious, even if she won't admit it.

Izzy gets up from the couch. She's going to do what she's always done when sleep won't claim her: go for a walk. She gets up as quietly as she can and slips on her shoes. Then she pads like a thief toward the door, passing FM on the way.

She also passes the fishbowl on the dresser by the door where she left her carkeys. For an instant she imagines getting in her car and driving away from all this insanity. But that would mean leaving FM behind. FM will be out of it for hours—lucky bastard—and though he isn't the biggest guy, she has little confidence in her ability to pick him up and drag him the thirty or so yards to where her car is parked.

And what if she's carrying something in her that would destroy the world if it got out?

No. She'll take a short walk in the woods and then come back. That's all. She leaves her keys in the fishbowl.

Outside, the night is already yielding to dawn. She doesn't have her phone to check, but she guesses it's somewhere past 5 am. She walks toward the dense wall of pines that forms the wood behind the house, in the opposite direction from the road. She loves pines, their lizard-scale bark, the dark tufts like the bristles of paintbrushes that crown them. But more than the trees, she's comforted by the undergrowth, the ants that mill over the leaf litter and deer moss, heedless of all human transactions and transgressions. The further she gets from the trailer, the more at ease she feels, the more at home in her own skin.

A sound reaches her ears—the gurgle of a stream. She follows the sound. The silver light of false morning is peeking over the horizon when she comes upon the stream, a narrow rill small enough that she could straddle it if she wanted. She kneels beside the stream and watches minnows flicking like little dark dreams through the glassy current. Fish make her wistful. Sad, even. Her childhood friend Eva was an avid fish-keeper, fresh and saltwater both. Eva had so much love for those stupid little goobers she kept in her tanks. Eva and Izzy had been texting the night Eva and five other people at a nightclub were shot by a maniac who thought it was God's will that he kill queers. That was six months ago. Eva's not the only friend she's lost, just the most recent, and the most painful.

Tyick. The metal rasp of an empty chamber dry firing.

Izzy looks up. Across the stream, two men are watching her, mere yards away. How had they snuck up on her like that? How had she not heard them crunching through the leaf and pine litter?

"Trespassing, huh?" one of the men says. He's the younger one, about Izzy's age.

The other one, older, with a red beard starting to go gray, just smiles. That's the one who's pointing his deer rifle at her; the one who pulled the trigger on an empty chamber. Maybe he didn't know it was empty until he tested the trigger. Schrodinger's 30.06.

She knows somehow that these are the same men from the blue pickup truck.

"I'm not trespassing," Izzy says, trying to sound sure, trying to sound like she belongs here. "Or if I am, I didn't mean to. I didn't see a fence."

"Didn't see a fence, she says," the older man says, clucking his tongue.

"There's some nerve," the younger one says. "There's surely nerve."

They're both in hunter's gear, but the orange on their elbow patches clashes something terrible with the bright red hats on their heads. Izzy is irrationally grateful for the stream's presence between them. Never mind that these men could easily cross it; it is still a barrier, an impediment. What if there was no stream?

Slowly, Izzy rises from her knees and gets to her feet. She's taller than either of them, not that that makes her feel any less vulnerable.

"Pretty doe, ain't she?" the older man says.

"She ain't too bad," says the younger one. "Not that I go that side of the tracks."

"Lord forbid."

"Look, sirs, I was just walking around my friend's property," Izzy says, already taking a step back.

The younger man takes a step forward to match her retreat, but he stops shy of the stream. Maybe he doesn't want to risk getting his shoes wet. Whatever it is, she's thankful.

"I'd better get back there," Izzy says.

"Sure," the older man says. "Say hi to that Lutz boy for us."

"Fucking Lutzes," the younger boy says.

"Language," the older man says, but through a smile.

Izzy starts backing away. She watches them, but never makes eye contact. It's not until she's put a good twenty yards between them that she turns. That's when she hears it. Another rasp of a firing pin striking an empty chamber.

She walks faster but doesn't run. They stay on their side of the creek.

When she reaches the door to the trailer, she's so close to coming apart that she doesn't bother to be gentle or quiet and flings the door open.

There's Sam, waiting at the card table, watching the doorway. Their expression is unreadable.

"Sam," she says.

"Out for a walk?"

"Yeah. Couldn't get back to sleep."

"Did you meet anyone on your walk?"

"No." She's not sure why she lies.

"Really. Because if I'd known you were going to go out for a walk, I'd have warned you that in the mornings, the Foyles next door like to hunt on my family's land. And those redneck bastards are skeevy as skeevy comes." Sam's latent Mississippi accent only comes out when they say certain words, words like "redneck bastards."

"Oh. Is that so?" Suddenly she notices that Sam has her car keys in their hand. "Hey, Sam, why do you—?"

"You know what happened when I got infected?" Sam asks. "You know how the book got me the first time?"

"Sam, I don't understand—"

"Izzy, please. Listen to me."

In the corner, FM grumbles and lets out a piteous whimper.

Sam glances at him with concern, then looks to Izzy. They look, if anything, disappointed with her. "When the book got me, it was a few days after I'd first cracked it open, when I was still trying to make sense of it. There I was, thumbing at pages, thinking I'd seen the same page ten times already, when I noticed something on my thumb. It was a word. Somehow, a word had rubbed off the page and gotten stamped onto my thumb. It was the word 'Doch,' a versatile little German word that can mean so many things. Well, I tried to rub it off, thinking it was just some ink, which wouldn't have made sense anyway, but what did I know? It didn't rub off. It squirmed like a bug, and it crawled around my hand and wriggled under my nailbed."

"Sam, could I have my car keys, please?" Izzy asks.

Sam smiles patiently. "You can have your keys back when the book is gone. Until then, no one leaves this trailer. But you've interrupted my story. I was going to tell you what the book did to me—what Hrotger did to me—and what I had to do to purge him from me."

Before Izzy can say anything, Sam starts rolling down their sleeves, and then Izzy's heart catches in her throat. When they were dating, Izzy had always thought Sam's choice to tattoo the opening lines of Anne Carson's poem "The Glass Essay" on their forearms was a try-hard softboy (demiboy?) move. But the words *("I can hear little clicks inside my dream, / Night drips its silver tap / down the back")* are gone from their skin. In place of the tattooed words are streaks of pale pink scar tissue, edged in crimson and mottled with yellow pustules. Third degree burns.

Revulsion, pity, and an overwhelming desire to be somewhere else, to leave her own skin, washes over Izzy. *My body is my body, my mind is my mind...*

"I found the paper from FM's blunt," Sam says. "I should have known he'd do something stupid like that. When he's up we'll have a talk. But first, you—"

"Sam— *Cupcake*, please."

"Why do you sound so scared? I'm not angry, Izzy. But you should have told me about the joint. FM too. I'm trying to look out for you. Tell me, have you heard voices? Seen anything you shouldn't be seeing?"

"No."

"Good. Maybe he can't infiltrate through smoke. All the same, we'd best be careful. Stay inside from now on, Izzy. Stay here where it's safe, and where the world's safe from us."

"I need to pee." It's not a lie. With all the adrenaline rushing through her, she suddenly feels like someone's sitting on her bladder, straining it near bursting.

Sam smiles and points with one of their mangled arms toward the hallway.

"It will all be over soon," Sam says as Izzy shuts herself in the bathroom. "When FM wakes up, we'll purge Hrotger from all of us."

Izzy was never once afraid of Sam when they were dating. Nor after they'd broken up. Sam, she had thought, didn't have a violent cell in them. Now she's not so sure.

After peeing, she washes her hands and splashes her face. It's after she's dried her face off with a handtowel that she looks up at the mirror and sees her reflection smiling back at her. A big smile, with teeth and gums showing.

She touches her face to confirm with her fingers what the muscles of her face are already telling her: that her lips are drawn shut in a tight frown.

And yet the woman in the mirror keeps smiling back.

In, out. In, out. *My body is my body—*

"Get out before night falls," the woman—the Izzy—in the mirror says, still smiling.

Izzy turns off the light, hiding her reflection in dimness. Then she leaves the bathroom and decides that none of that just happened.

In, out. In, out. *My body is my body, my mind is my mind.*

* * *

"There must be someone who can help us," Izzy says. She's sitting on the couch next to FM, who's only just begun to rouse from his opiate slumber.

Sam is at the table. They have been there for an hour, meditative and sullen as a gargoyle. "Like who?" Sam says.

"I don't know," Izzy says. "Experts. Someone like your cousin Rachel."

"I saw things," FM whispers, his eyes fluttering as he struggles to sit up. "Heard things. He spoke to me..."

Either Sam doesn't hear him, or chooses to ignore FM. "Unfortunately, the 'experts' like my cousin Rachel are mostly gone. The Brotherhood of the New Dark was purged by the Nazis, and the survivors were mostly wiped out during the war. The few who survived were snatched up into government programs during the Cold War, or so certain dubious websites on the darkweb would have you believe. Believe me, Izzy, if there was someone we could call, I would have. Anyone who might know anything about the book would be the last person you'd want touching it. Power corrupts, you know."

They're so damn calm.

Sam stands up from the table. "I need to rest some," they say, somehow turning a statement into a command. They thump across the trailer, disappear a moment, then return from the bedroom with a padlock. Izzy watches them close the bolt on the door and then fix the padlock to the bolt. In Sam's hands are not just the key to the padlock, but also the key to her Honda. "You and FM hang tight until I'm ready. Okay?"

"Sam—"

"Hey, it's okay." Sam smiles. "Like I said, this will be over soon. I just need a little rest before we can begin."

Sam goes into their bedroom and closes the door, but doesn't lock it. As Izzy notices this, a thought slithers up from her subconscious to the surface. *If I wait until they're asleep, I can kill them and take the keys.*

The thought comes so naturally, so unobtrusively, she doesn't even question it at first, nodding along as if it had just occurred to her that it would be sensible to check her oil before a cross-country drive.

Her breath quickens, the hairs on her neck prickle. Kill Sam? How the fuck could she even think that?

But she's not thinking it.

Their ritual doesn't need participants, it needs sacrifices. Get out now.

This thought, as natural and yet as foreign as the last, is even more persuasive, and Izzy eyes the locked door then the windows, measuring them against her waistline and the width of her shoulders. They're small, but she could squeeze if she needed to.

"Izzy," FM's voice is small and bruised. "Hey, Izzy, I feel so fucked up."

"You probably took too much," she says. She's grateful to hear his voice. Grateful to not be alone with her own thoughts.

FM nods, but midway through nodding he seems to lose the strength in his neck and his head slumps against her shoulder. Her skin crawls at the unexpected contact, but she gives him a breath or two before shrugging him off. She's always felt safe around FM, even though she's always known what he really wants from her; what he'll never ask.

"Sorry, I wish I could think straight, Izz," FM says. "I think we're in trouble. Like, real trouble."

"I think you're right."

Sugarplum pads into the room from the hallway and sits as in judgment, watching the two of them like a tiny warden.

"He spoke to me, Izzy. Has he spoken to you?"

Izzy doesn't answer, because to answer would be to make real what she would prefer to remain a delusion.

"He said good things, and that's what scared me. Showed me beautiful things. Showed me the amniotic warmth from which all reality sprung, the governing force of the cosmos, the ordering will that's not one will but the imbricated ripples of unnumbered consciousnesses across a similitude of time. We understand so little, all our science and art and philosophy—it's like we've been trying to paint a landscape in a lightless cave from whispered rumors of what the surface looks like. What did he show you?"

"Nothing."

Izzy closes her eyes. Despite her fear, despite the dread that crawls, not under but between the layers of her skin, she is now slumping onto the couch. She didn't sleep at all last night; hasn't been sleeping much at all since Eva's death.

FM is talking still, but his words dissolve into a pleasant sonic foam that soothes her ears and smooths the creases of her anxiety.

When her eyes open, Izzy is at peace. The nervous hum exorcized from her body. Sugarplum purrs on her lap, heavier than any cat has a right to be. This brief gasp of contentment lasts only until she looks to her side and sees FM slumped on the floor, facedown, his belt tied around his arm and a syringe next to his tremoring hand.

She screams. In the seconds it takes her to surge from the couch and roll FM onto his back, Sam has already emerged from their room.

"God damn it," Sam shouts, louder than Izzy has ever heard them speak. "God damn him."

They don't mean FM. They mean Hrotger. Hrotger who made FM overdose; Hrotger who lulled Izzy to sleep so she couldn't stop it.

"He's barely... I, I can barely feel his pulse," Izzy says.

His lips are blue, his breath comes as a warbling thread; when she peels back his eyelids his pupils are small as poppy seeds. Even as she struggles to stay in this moment, to help her friend—how?—she is dragged back to an identical scene years ago, when it was her undergrad roommate Haley that she found after returning to the apartment after a weekend visit home. But Haley was already dead and bloated by then; FM is still alive.

For now. He needs Narcan—he needs a hospital, an ambulance.

"We need to call a—"

Before she can even get the words out, Sam clasps their huge hands on her shoulders. They shake her, just once, but the sudden force sends her deeper into a spiral, intensifies the all-body hum that threatens to shake her cells, molecules, atoms apart, threatens to drive her from herself to somewhere else.

"No," Sam says. "That's what *he* wants. This is his idea, he'll do anything to survive—he's scared."

When she found Haley, she broke. When she first learned about Eva, she broke. Now she expects the same, but rather than dissolving into a puddle, Izzy feels herself solidify, grounds herself around a burning spark of fury.

"Fuck you, I'm scared!" Izzy says, swatting Sam's hands off her and standing up. "Where's my phone? I'll call the ambulance myself."

Sam, as if chastened, seems to rethink their approach. "Izzy, you're not considering the consequences—"

"Tell me where my phone is," Izzy says. "Now."

Sam drags their gaze away from Izzy's eyes. "It's gone."

Like a sudden gust, the words knock her from her precarious strength, disrupt the unlikely centeredness she felt for a flicker of a moment. "What?"

On the floor, FM mumbles something and coughs.

"I couldn't risk even the chance Hrotger could hitchhike on a cell signal," Sam says, guilty yet resolute. "I trashed them back at the burger place. There's no phones here—no calling any ambulance."

Izzy wraps her arms around herself, a cold blooming in her where the heat of the spark had been, and then the cold leaves too, replaced by emptiness she can't fill with any therapy mantra or breathing exercise. Sam is still talking, FM still mumbling and mewling, but it washes into the same warm fuzz in her ears.

At some point she tries to sit down and misses the chair completely and hurts her knee on the floor. Sam lifts her into the chair, and then lifts FM into another.

"...make you feel better," she hears Sam say, their voice impossibly big, and then in the well of their meaty palm is a small oblong white tablet, offered to her. She takes it, and then accepts the glass of water. *Xanax*, she thinks.

By the time Sam has bound her wrist to the arm of the chair with a ziptie, she realizes it isn't a Xanax. It doesn't worry her much. Nothing really worries her much, not even the insistent whispers—no longer disguised as her own thoughts—rising from a deep place in her, urging her to resist, to fight, to rise to her feet and smash the flimsy old wood of the chair. Sam's right—Hrotger is frightened.

"A muscle relaxer," Sam explains. "It's better this way. Better if you let yourself sleep, then you might not even feel it."

Feel it? Feel what?

But she has her answer when Sam emerges from the bedroom—she sees them through the red-dark blood vessel murk of her fluttering eyelids—carrying a plastic jerry can. They start to splash the gasoline over the apartment. They've brought the book out. They dump an especially bounteous splash on the book, which lies unceremoniously on the floor. Then they splash some on the table—on FM, on Izzy; it burns her nostrils, rousing her halfway from her stupor but doing nothing to attenuate the inexorable weight of her limbs and her head that drags her further toward the threshold of insouciance.

What was it Hrotger said? Something about sacrifices, not participants.

"This is the only way," Sam says. Or she thinks she hears them say it, or just imagines it because it's the sort of weak bromide that warped minds use to justify atrocity. "Everything must be burned—everything and *everyone* he's touched."

Whether Sam says it or not doesn't matter, just like the "Oh shit" they most definitely mutter on seeing—and remembering—the presence of Sugarplum the cat even as they strike the match on the strikestrip doesn't matter. All that matters is how avidly the fumes billowing through the trailer take to the sparks erupting from the match.

* * *

173

Whether it was the drug or the choking smoke that put her out, Izzy awakes with cold, damp wild grass under the skin of her neck. She knows it is dark out because no light stings her lids, and because there are night frogs and insects singing in the trees and grass. A little fire still crackles; the smoke smell is everywhere. A cat meows. Sugarplum's paws knead at Izzy's stomach. Her claws stick through Izzy's shirt. There is no pain. Sugarplum smells like fire. There is no pain. Her body is her body, her mind is her mind.

When she opens her eyes, she sees first the surly cat, singed but unharmed, then she sees her own left arm, cut and bleeding. The substance oozing from her wound is somewhere between dirty motor oil and ink. The wound is like the rest of her—painless.

"You're awake."

She both does and does not recognize the voice of FM. The voice is the only way she knows its him—or what's left of his body—because the face that looks down on her is scarcely human, but closer to the scoured surface of some asteroid-blasted world orbiting too close to its sun. Staring at the blistered palimpsest of her friend's face with its two seared eyes—red sclera, irises disks of meringue—framed against the backdrop of the embers still licking the blackened shell of the trailer, the absence of terror, the absence of grief, is startling, as if she has sunken into a lower ocean, a midnight stratum beneath even horror, where everything is still and nothing more can hurt her. Even when she touches her face, acquainting her fingers with the new squamous topography of her cheek and an ear shriveled like a brittle prune. But it should be worse. Much worse. It comes back to her, these little details so easy to collate in this odd, abstracted vantage. How is she even alive? Where is the pain?

"I need you calm," Hrotger says, as if he guesses her thoughts, but of course he doesn't need to guess anything when he's already inside of her.

"I could not save Sam," the thing that isn't FM says. That it can stand at all is one thing, that it somehow speaks clearly without any lips is another. "But I managed to rescue you at least. And the cat. I like cats; they keep books warm by sitting on them."

Fear, pain, grief, all these chased away, but as Izzy sits up, she can still feel her truest mentor, the chord at her center, the animating force of her life and her art: fury.

"Get out of him," Izzy says, taking hold of the charred tatters of FM's shirt and shaking Hrotger as if Hrotger is something that can be shaken off. "Get out of him right fucking now."

"You misunderstand," Hrotger says, calm, quiet. "Before he died, your friend left me his shell to use as I needed, as per the bargain we struck."

"Bullshit."

"Is it so hard to believe that he would forego his own bodily existence to attain a higher quale of experience? You knew FM as well as anyone; do you think he would balk at the chance to write his essence into the script of a new reality?"

In Hrotger's voice, a voice both FM's and not FM's, there's a hypnotic, warm undercurrent, soothing and somnolent. Izzy's eyelids flutter and her muscles relax just to hear him speak. She's become noseblind to his charred fetor; used to the stark whiteness of his scorched irises.

Izzy shakes her head and feels the burns on her cheek. *My body is my body, my mind is my mind...*

"Izzy, I offer you what I offered Sam, what Sam rejected for their hopeless adherence to an untenable status quo that ostracized and devalued them, just as it has devalued and diminished you and so many countless others. Help me remake this world."

Izzy wants to tell him to fuck off back to the Renaissance, to leave her alone, to get out of her head—but the words don't come. Instead, what she says: "Remake the world. How?"

There are no lips for Hrotger to smile with, only blackened teeth, and yet she knows he is smiling. "I was created for the purpose of disrupting and unmaking hierarchy in all its forms and emanations. That is why the Church buried me; that is why the Nazis tried and failed to destroy me. You know better than anyone that this world—your human civilization—is crooked. Bring me to the ocean of text, bring me to the vast gulf of knowledge, help me spread. Ask yourself, what do you owe this world?"

It's the last question that gets her. The answer is obvious: there are people worth saving, millions, billions of people like her, like Sam, trapped in the labyrinthine gut of the beast—

"There will be no violence. What need will I have for violence?"

"How can I trust anything you say?"

"You can't."

"You're in my head already, why even ask me when you can just make me do what you want?"

"I don't want puppets, Izzy, I want partners."

"And if I become your *partner*? What then?"

"You will bring about the death of this world so a new one can take its place. Everything rewritten; every ledger balanced, every lie unraveled, every truth revealed. The cancer of this civilization must be burned away to make space for something better; something fairer."

"Burned away? You said there wouldn't be violence."

"Only a figure of speech. Oh yes, there will be a righteous purgation—but no bloodshed, no burning homes, no salted fields or guillotines or fire-bombings. The machines of death will be dismantled, that the world may heal. This I promise."

Izzy's next breath is the longest she's ever taken. When she exhales, she asks, "How do we start?"

Without a word, Hrotger turns around and falls onto his knees. FM's shirt has torn away to reveal a charred back, where two appendages have sprouted from the scapulae. Wings, Izzy thinks at first, but they aren't wings—they're pages, clusters of pages flaking from the tortured flesh of FM's back. A silver glint catches her eye; Sam's hunting dagger lies in the grass a few yards away, unspoiled by the fire.

She knows what she must do. It's like cutting through overcooked bottom round, and black slime oozes from the wounds when she cuts the pages from the flesh binding. She sorts them, or maybe they sort themselves, or maybe there's no sorting necessary for a text that flouts the tyrannies of sequence and logic. Whatever the case, once stacked page by page and gathering by gathering, the folio of flesh assembles itself into a book, the embossed black leather cover crusting over as the dark ichor coagulates. With each page that falls into place, she's less afraid, more certain of her way ahead.

Now Izzy has the book at her feet, and the husk of FM falls and crumbles, rendered to an insensate pile of minerals. She doesn't mourn him, just as she doesn't mourn poor, confused Sam, because neither is dead. No one ever dies as long as Hrotger remembers them.

She gathers up the finished book and walks away from the burned trailer, in the direction of the rest of the world. Soon the sounds of the road weave into the tranquil music of the woods. Two men are standing by the gate to Sam's property, their blue pickup parked on the shoulder of the road behind them.

No doubt the Foyles have come to investigate the fire. The way they look at Izzy as she approaches is gratifying. They way they run to their truck and peel away with a screech of tires before she can reach them, even more so. But where can they flee to? You can't outrun the turn of the page; can't escape the end of a chapter.

CREDITS

Some of the stories in this collection have previously appeared in various venues.

"Darke's Last Show" appeared in *Pseudopod*.

"The Brine's Embrace" appeared in *Kaleidotrope*.

"The Follower's Revel" appeared in *The Tentaculum* Issue 2 and *The Drabblecast*

"One of those Nice Guys" appeared in *The Dread Machine*'s *1986* anthology edited by Tina Alberino.

"Someplaces it's Turnips" appeared in *Tales to Terrify*.

"Distant Fire of Winter Stars" appeared in *Flash Fiction Online*.

"Harvestman" appeared in *Road Kill: Texas Horror by Texas Authors* Vol. 6. edited by Madison Estes

"Concerning a Pond in Massachusetts" appeared in Dreadstone Press's *Field Notes from a Nightmare: An Anthology of Ecological Horror* edited by Alex Ebenstein.

"Elmreach" appeared in Cemetery Gates Media's *Halldark Hollidays* anthology edited by Gabino Iglesias.

"Got the Spirit but Lose the Feeling" appeared in *Road Kill: Texas Horror by Texas Authors* Vol. 7. edited by William Jensen.

"The Littlest Fishy" appeared in Southwest Review 105.3 edited by Gabino Iglesias.

STORY NOTES & CONTENT WARNINGS

Darke's Last Show:

CW: language, violence, gore, sexual content, death

Notes: Usually when I write a short story, I first create a thorough outline that ends up being half as long as the final story. In the case of this story, the outline is only a couple paragraphs, which is probably testament to how fully shaped the narrative was in my imagination before I sat down to type it. I think I had been reading Thomas Ligotti's *Songs of a Dead Dreamer*, and the collection, particularly the story "Drink to Me Only with Labyrinthine Eyes" exerted a latent influence on this piece. Since writing "Darke's Last Show" in June of 2020, Darke has become one of my favorite characters to write, having appeared in many other stories. He's an absolute monster, but he's a good guy at heart (sort of). The story also serves as a prequel of sorts to my recently completed novel, *The Porcelain Tantra*.

The Brine's Embrace:

CW: graphic sexual content, violence, body horror, death

Notes: My original outline calls this "The Ocean's Embrace," and spells out the multi-choice ending, which actually wasn't any kind of brilliant, inventive stroke on my part but a reflection of my inability to decide which ending was a better fit. What do you think? Which do you believe? As a sidenote, this story is an attempt to answer a lot of questions I and many others have always had about the potential logistics of mermaid-human sex.

One of Those Nice Guys:

CW: sexual content, language, violence, reference to child death

Notes: I love stories that are set in or begin in diners. Diners, particularly of the roadside variety, are the modern inheritors to the inns of days of yore where traveling strangers would trade stories. The core of this story is a reversal of our traditional expectations on hitchhikers and who is in danger when a burly, surly trucker picks up a waifish underaged blonde. Although never identified as such here, Liz's race of reptilian mimics are dragons, or rather the remnants of them, having adapted to be smaller and more humanoid to survive in a human-dominated world. Liz reappears in my novel *The Porcelain Tantra* alongside Devin Darke from "Darke's Last Show."

The Follower's Revel:

CW: body horror, insects, violence, death

Notes: I wanted to experiment with the found footage subgenre, thinking I had never read a found footage story using silent film as the medium. What it ended up being was a hybrid of found footage and epistolary fiction. I wrote this story after visiting The Adirondack Experience in the Adirondack Mountains, a museum of sorts celebrating the region's history, particularly the logging and mining endeavors that helped build its economy in the late 19th and early 20th centuries. And yes, the Father is the same entity as appears in "Have You Seen the Moon Tonight?"

Someplaces it's Turnips:

CW: body horror, homophobia, misogyny

Notes: I wrote this story during a fiction workshop when I should have been paying attention to the class. It was inspired by a Duolingo prompt; in German Duolingo there's a weird fixation on "the holy potato" (die heilige Kartoffel). "Someplaces it's Turnips" originated with that bizarre statement, which made me imagine why people might desire to see a "holy potato" and what that potato might look like. It's possible this story might take place in the same world as "The Rumor."

Paper Wings in the House of Light:

CW: death, violence

Notes: This story sprung almost fully-formed into my mind after watching the music video to Steven Wilson's "Drive Home." Watch it and you'll understand. Zombie stories have been done to death, but what always works about them (if they work) is that the real "meat" of the narrative is never about the zombies. This was my attempt at writing a magical realist story in the tradition of Gabriel Garcia-Marquez or Jorge Luis Borges in a zombie apocalypse setting.

Harvestman:

CW: violence, child abuse

Notes: Can you tell I'd recently watched *Carnival of Souls* when I wrote this? Sidenote: don't waste your time looking up Az Arató, it's not a real myth, though the others listed all are.

Concerning a Pond in Massachusetts:

CW: violence, death, body horror

Notes: An assiduous reader will notice I've lifted entire sentences from Thoreau's original work, which helped to solidify the voice of this *Walden* pastiche. I wrote this in an American literature class while trying to muddle my way through Thoreau's *Walden*. Oh, also, it's going to be very awkward when the Fungus Primordial try to reemerge at the same time as the Father and His centipede children make their move. Don't you hate when schedules overlap and conflict?

Have You Seen the Moon Tonight?:

CW: Language, violence, death

Notes: Moonlight driving people to madness is a fairly ancient concept in storytelling, although most such stories don't involve space centipedes or social media trends as herald of doom. I wanted to capture the strange, chimeric spirit of Miami with this story, which you might say forms a trilogy of sorts with "Darke's Last Show" and "The Littlest Fishy." It also connects to "The Follower's Revel" in obvious ways. I loved writing Reuben as an unconventional horror movie badass. No shotgun, chainsaw, silver bullets, or speargun—just a nail gun, a hammer, and a strobe light. Remember, kids, always support unionized labor. Oh, and don't look at the moon.

Elmreach:

Notes: One of the earliest stories in this collection in terms of its composition. I wrote this story on short order in response to Gabino Iglesias' call for Hallmark parody stories for the Cemetery Gates Media anthology *Halldark Holidays*. *Halldark Holidays* started with Gabino tweeting the concept, more spitballing than anything concrete, but Cemetery Gates had the money and the interest to make it happen. Remarkably the entire anthology came together from concept to submissions to reading to publication and distribution in a matter of months. My own humble contribution, which ended up sharing space with writers like Cynthia Pelayo, Brian Keene, and Alan Baxter, was written over a couple days. I had never actually watched a Hallmark movie in its totality, but I did read enough synopses and watched enough trailers while planning the story to get the general gist, and according to many who've read the story, including Gabino himself, "Elmreach" ended up being a rather spot-on parody of the genre.

Got the Spirit But Lose the Feeling:

CW: Drug use, language

Notes: Many of the stories in this collection showcase my fondness for oblique storytelling. I define "oblique" stories as those whose telling encompass an odd, slanted section of the overall tale that elides what might usually be the main action. Part of why I tend to write such narratives is because I find them interesting, but there's a practical reason too: I write long, and by forcing myself to only consider a small section of the story's cone, I can rein in my wordcount. If we think about "Got the Spirit But Lose the Feeling" as an alien invasion film, the telling that makes it to the page is completely off the reel. It's an epilogue to a movie we didn't actually get to see, a movie that ends with the loveable loser Ned Cobb seemingly making it to the safety of the diner. Roll credits. But what's this? Turns out he's not safe. Maybe he never even made it to the diner. I try hard not to think about the logistics of wires connecting to people's skulls when the puppeteered humans are inside of buildings, or how those wires don't snag on anything, or where those wires lead, because such questions are less important than the story's central question: when did Ned's body stop being his own?

A Wild Green Tide is Soon Coming: Notes on a Planned Story

CW: violence, death, homophobia, language, sexual situations

Notes: This bit of metafiction arose from a planned story that just didn't feel right when I tried writing it as a straightforward narrative. It felt cliched, expected, uninteresting. Ecohorror is a burgeoning and relatively young subgenre of horror, and yet, to my estimation at least, it can very easily be trite and predictable. Aside from that, how do we as writers hope to hold a candle to the vastation that is our planet's actual slow-motion death? By creating the metafictional layer, I reignited my interest in the story's project. I prefer to think of my characters as people and despise thinking in terms of archetype, but for this story thinking and feeling my way through Bad Carl and Co. as archetypes made them feel more vital than they had in my original outline. The story is set in Calrose, Florida, which is a fictional town based loosely on my hometown, Niceville, and which I've been setting stories in for years. One of my first published stories, "Old Bones" is also set in Calrose and follows hardware store manager Murray as he deals with the consequences of digging up his own skeleton in his backyard. I really wish I could have snuck a reference to ol' Murray in this story somewhere.

Distant Fire of Winter Stars:

CW: self-harm

Notes: This story takes its title from a line from a Franz Wright poem, "Sitting Up Late with My Father, 1977" from his collection *God's Silence*. Below is the poem, one of my favorites, where the initial image "White fire of winter stars" is a classic Franz Wright line, but the closing image "White distant emerald fire of winter stars" is more akin to the work of his father, James Wright (my favorite poet of all time), with the injection of the "emerald" imagery James Wright was so enamored with.

White fire of winter stars--
what he's thinking at fifty
I finally know.

He thinks, so the blizzards will come
and I will be healed;
we'll talk

when you grow up
and I am dead.

White distant emerald fire of winter stars.

The Littlest Fishy:

CW: body horror, references to homophobia, violence, animal cruelty, language

Notes: When I wrote this story, the 2016 Pulse Shooting in Orlando was in the back of my mind, but in the last few years there have been so many horrific acts of violence committed against queer people and queer-friendly spaces that you'd be forgiven for not recognizing which atrocity inspired Eva's murder. The story wouldn't have happened were it not for my fiancée's avid interest in fishkeeping, and my own experiences sharing an apartment with her and her colorful tanks. This story first appeared in the *Southwest Review* next to a story by weird fiction icon Brian Evenson, which I still can't quite believe is a thing that happened (not even after it happened a second time in the pages of the anthology *Mother: Tales of Love and Terror*).

The Rumor:

CW: violence, gore, sexual content, language

Notes: Who doesn't love language plagues? I tried to extend this story into a novel, but it didn't quite come together, although I absolutely loved writing the character Dexter Parlay, who in the novel inexplicably shows up (despite being entirely fictional within the novel's ontology) to assist Dud as he tries to unravel the mystery of what happened to his friend/lover Nat. Maybe I'll try writing it again someday.

Druckteufel:

CW: language, violence, death, drug use, self-harm

Notes: "Druckteufel" is a constructed word formed from the compounding of the German "Drucken" (printing) and "Teufel" (devil). The restaurant the characters meet at is inspired by Ward's, a Mississippi fast food franchise with okay burgers and fantastic root beer and fries that I've had the pleasure of stuffing my face with on roadtrips between Florida and Texas. Sam's ancestor Rachel Lutznau is the main character of my story "Lutznau's Opus," which appeared in the anthology *Antifa Splatterpunk*. Izzy being a friend of Eva from "The Littlest Fishy" is a consequence of my compulsion to draw webs between all my stories, even the ones that seem like they have no connection at all. Don't rule out the possibility that Izzy and her old friend will reunite in a future story.

ACKNOWLEDGMENTS

I want to start by thanking my parents, who are very welcome not to read any of the book past this point. Without their encouragement and support I would never have become the writer I am today. I also want to thank my Uncle David, who is no longer with us, who was the first person to ever read my work and offer me earnest feedback on it when I was a child, and who also bought me dozens of books over the year over a long series of birthdays and Christmases that helped shape my style and approach to literature. I also want to thank my brothers, Chris and Sebastian, for doing the most supportive thing brothers can do for each other: only traumatizing me the exact right degree to create a horror writer (I'm kidding, you guys know I'm kidding, right?).

I want to thank the professors, classmates, and colleagues throughout my educational journey on both sides of the professor's desk. To Spencer Wise, my first creative writing instructor at Florida State University, I owe a great debt for being patient with a talkative, high-energy student (the worst and best kind, in my experience as a professor) who always abused his professor's generous office hours. To my undergraduate mentor, Barbara Hamby, I extend the same thanks-slash-apologies—seriously, Barbara, thank you for putting up with me and reading some truly terrible work. Thanks also to Russ Franklin who's been far more supportive of my nascent career than I could have expected. To John Dufresne, Debra Dean, Les Standiford, Julie Marie Wade, Denise Duhamel, Campbell McGrath and everyone else at Florida International University (don't worry, Lynne, I'm getting to you), my deepest gratitude for kilning me from a raw young writer into a slightly less raw, slightly older writer. To my friends at FIU who became like family, Ashley M. Jones, Miguel Pichardo, Ellene G. Moore, Cathleen Chambless, Jennifer Maritza McCauley, Fabienne Josaphat, Paul Christiansen, Kacee Belcher, Giselda Aguilar, Megan Arlett, Stephanie Selander, Cayce Wicks, Cathleen Chitwood, Jaimie Morimoto, TC Jones, Les Taylor, Mary Slebodnik, and so so many more names I'm probably forgetting— thank you for teaching me the importance of community to a writer's life. And of course, I owe a huge debt to my thesis director, Lynne Barrett, who not only cultivated a love of the art of plotting in me but also pointed out one of my critical flaws as a writer: a tendency to overproduce incidents in the course of a narrative.

I also want to thank Scott Blackwood, John Tait, Corey Marks, Bruce Bond, Masood Raja, Devin Garofalo, and all my friends and classmates at University of North Texas. Vince Granata, Heather Meyers, JS Khan, Coleen Mayo, Tiffany Issacs, Jasmyn Huff, Kendra Currie, Conor Flannery, Graham Barnhart, and Aza Pace all deserve special mention.

From the horror community, I want to thank those who have supported and championed my work. Austin Shirey, Warren Benedetto, Zachary Rosenberg, Cynthia Gómez, Patrick Barb, Donyae Coles, Eric Raglin, Naomi Eselojor, Wendy N. Wagner, Joe Koch, John W. Thompson, Ai Jiang, Sarah Read, Alex Ebenstein, Sofia Ajram, Jacob Steven Moore, Rajiv Moté, Christi Nogle, Gordon B. White, Emma E. Murray, Suzan Palumbo, Zin Rocklin, Kitty Sarkozy, Jon Padgett, Gwendolyn Kiste (I'm probably forgetting a thousand people), you've all been amazing. Thank you to all the editors (many of whom have already been mentioned) who published the stories of this collection. And to Gabino Iglesias, thank you so much for believing in me and going above and beyond to help get my fledgling career airborne.

Thanks also to Alex Flinn, who's been a wonderful mentor and advisor throughout the process of becoming a published author, and to my agent, Jacklyn Saferstein-Hansen for fighting for the best deal. A thanks also to Scarlett Algee and the rest of the team at JournalStone for believing in this book, and to Don Noble for the breathtaking cover art.

And finally, thank you to my wonderful fiancée, Kat Flinn, and our horrible, monstrous, adorable, lovely (she's right behind me) cat, Cheese for giving me the love, support, and occasional mockery (and arm biting) I need to write.

ABOUT THE AUTHOR

Jonathan Louis Duckworth is a completely normal, entirely human person with the right number of heads and everything. He received his MFA from Florida International University and his PhD from University of North Texas. His speculative fiction work appears in *Pseudopod, Beneath Ceaseless Skies, Southwest Review, Flash Fiction Online,* and elsewhere. He is an active HWA member.